Who Killed MONA?

P. HANKIN TITLE

ISBN: 1466457023
ISBN 13: 9781466457027

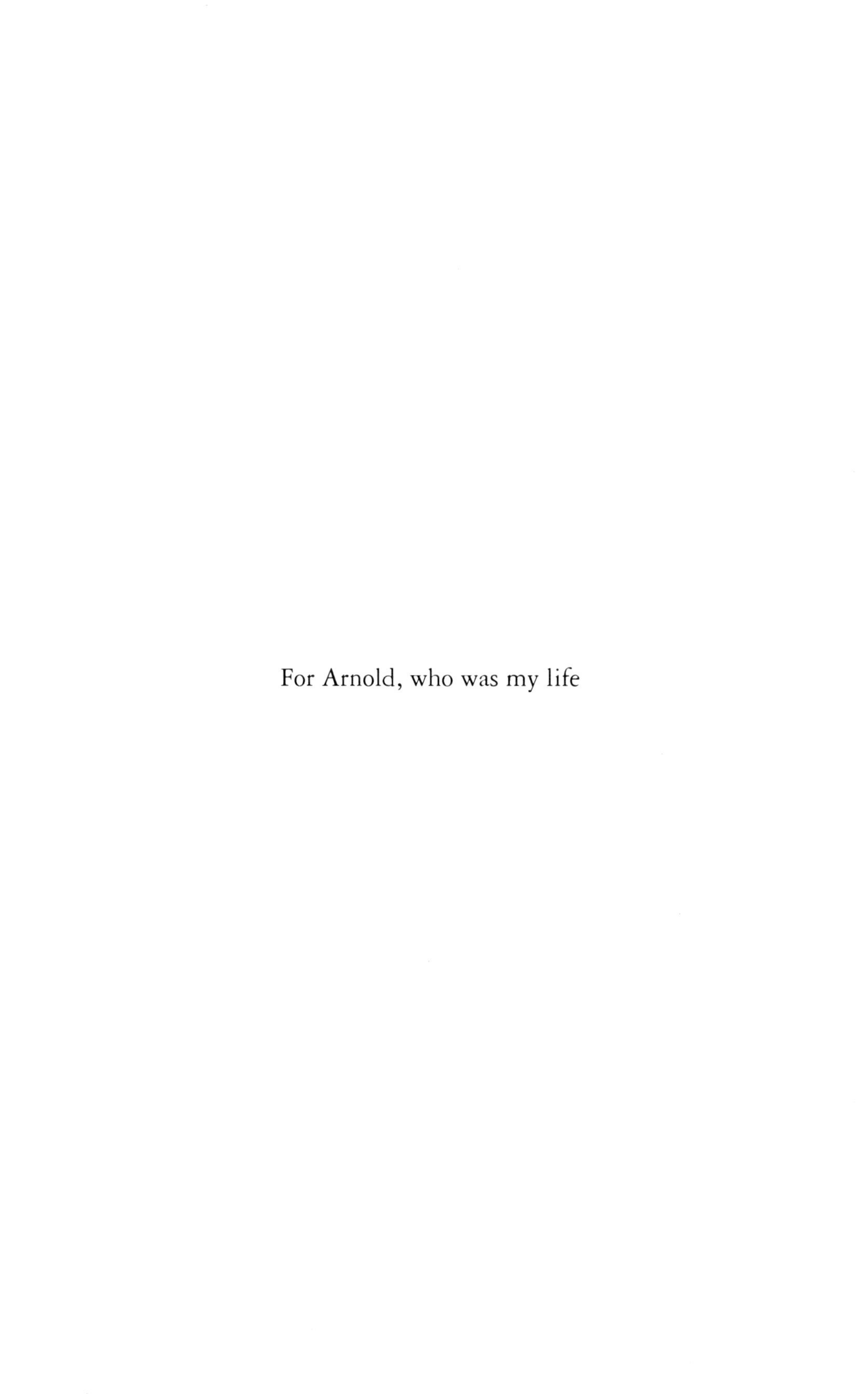

For Arnold, who was my life

I want to thank Daena and Jay, Charles Haas,
and my New York writers

Prologue

The audience was on its feet roaring applause, chanting: "Brava! Brava!"

Shrill and clear above the others, a single soprano voice sang, "Rae—burn!"

In her sleep, in her dream, Mona Raeburn threw open her arms to gather all her fans to her heart. She bowed deeply, first to the left, then to the right. Tears coursed down her face, ruining her makeup....

The theater vanished and she was running along a dank alley toward an iron door. It swung open before her, clanging shut as she stepped into blackness.

Now she teetered on a narrow ledge, gusts of wind churning her skirt into a parachute that dragged her perilously close to the edge. Her high heels skidded along the treacherous footing. She scrabbled to keep her balance. If she fell, she would spiral endlessly down....

Drifting half in, half out of the nightmare, her flailing hand found the bedside lamp, fumbled with the switch. Why didn't the light go on? Her eyes were open, but the room was as dark as if they were still closed.

The telephone rang, choked abruptly into silence. The dog growled.

"Oh...be quiet, Poochy." she mumbled and fell back into her dream.

In the darkness, slow as death, something dropped over her face, thick against her mouth. She raised her hand to tear it away, struggling to breathe, to suck in air. Her heart pulsed in her ears.

And stopped.

The dog whimpered.

CHAPTER ONE

Where were you on the evening of December 31, 1999?

I was gracing my stepfather Henry's ballroom in Old Westbury, New York, along with seventy-five of his best friends.

Why was I there working my way through the pate sandwiches when I am not Henry's friend? I am Jake Harmony, a thirty-three year old Homicide detective, divorced and between relationships. And Henry's stepson.

I was there because Laura, Henry's daughter and my sister-in-law was there. I wanted, I needed to see her.

A small combo hidden behind the potted palm trees scratched out golden oldies, heavy on the violins, to which Henry's guests, garmentos all, twirled, twinkle-toed, under the blazing chandeliers, their expensive perfumes mingling in the overheated air with tobacco smoke and the scent of Casablanca lilies.

At midnight, we toasted the New Year, the New Century and the New Millenium with Henry's excellent champagne. Feeling excellent myself, I hugged my brother Phil, slapped Henry on the back and kissed my mother who, that night, resembled a stuffed beefsteak tomato in her red Valentino gown - salted with the diamonds Henry had bought her. The diamonds with which he had bought her.

I kissed assorted ladies, working my way at last to Laura. My brother's wife. She kissed me back and promised me the first waltz of the New Year.

I waited until two a.m. for that waltz.

"Dancin'?" I said.

"Askin'?"

"Askin.'"

"Dancin'.

She waltzed into my arms and we were off.

Laura is five foot six and weighs in at about a hundred and ten pounds in her sequined Chanel and stilettos. I'm five six and a quarter in my cowboy boots, weigh in at a hundred and eighty-one, stark naked, before breakfast, on a thin day.

"You look great in that Kingsley tux. Don't tell me you bought it retail?"

"At Beau Brummel."

"Fool! What did it cost? Twelve hundred?"

"They give cops 25% off."

Her cheek touched mine and craving for her ratcheted through me. Yes, I covet my brother's wife.

She whispered into my ear. "I can't believe you bought it retail. You know Henry's the money man behind Kingsley."

"That's why I went to Beau Brummel. I don't want Henry's favors."

Buying retail is the first cardinal sin in Henry's litany.

She wound her arms around my neck. "That suit landed in the warehouse, costs $500."

I clasped the warm skin of her naked back drawing her closer.

"And in the factory in Vicenza, less duty, freight and clearance, it's $300."

"I don't want any of Henry's favors."

"Fool," she said.

We circled the floor faster and faster, the mirrored room swirling around us.

My beeper sounded.

When we stopped dancing Laura leaned against me for a delicious moment, catching her breath.

"I'm on call," I said, "I'm sorry." And I was. Life's pleasures are too fleeting.

"I'm sorry too." She trailed after me to the library telephone, listening while I called in.

"Possible homicide in Seaview," my supervisor rasped.

"Yeah?" I said, excitement stirring in the pit of my stomach.

"Go take a look. Four Wellington Road. Know where that is?"

"I'll find it."

I signaled Farley, Henry's butler, to bring my car. Laura helped me into my coat and went with me to the door of the million dollar hovel Henry calls home. She kissed me on both cheeks and watched me run down the ice-slick marble stairs.

In the curving driveway, dignified old Farley huddled under an umbrella alongside my gleaming '69 Corvette.

"Thanks for bringing the car around in this mess," I said. "Happy New Year, Farley."

"To you as well, Mr. Jake." His faded blue eyes were watering. Probably from the cold and not my sentiments.

He opened the door for me, stooping a little. "According to the midnight weather forecast," he said, "the snow plows have cleared the parkways, but the entrances and exits are blocked with stalled cars. I suggest that you avoid the Southern State. Sunrise Highway appears to be the better choice."

"Thanks, Farley. I'll do that." At midnight at the end of the century and on the brink of the Millenium, Farley was listening to the weather while I was kissing Laura. My own eyes watered a little. For him or for me?

He held the umbrella over my head as I ducked in.

"Drive carefully."

"I'm always careful."

I slammed the car door, waved goodbye and floored the accelerator, going to work. To do what I know how to do very well. I could say better than most. But I don't want to brag.

Seven minutes had passed since the Homicide Supervisor's call, and it took me another thirty-five to crawl the twenty miles from Henry Slater's estate to the village of Seaview, with the drone of the police band radio to keep me company.

Red and green reflections danced in front of my headlights, striping the wet pavement and the glazed snow-banks along the edges of the road. Thick flakes of snow clumped on the windshield.

Snow depresses me; ever since the day I stood with the tears frozen on my face, gripping my mother's hand while snow flakes piled up into a white shroud on my father's coffin. My mother, my brother Phil and I; stood mourning our dead hero.

We didn't want a hero. We wanted him alive.

At Seaview, I turned off Sunrise and drove south, keeping my eye peeled for Wellington Road. It turned out to be a cul-de-sac at the top of a hill. I skidded up the rise and rolled to a stop at a driveway blocked with police vehicles. Number four.

Crime Scene and Forensics were on the job before me, securing the scene. I pulled up behind a silver Jetta parked in the cul-de-sac. When I opened the car door, a small river eddied down the road. It'd ruin my boots.

I clambered across the leather bucket seats, hauling one leg at a time over the emergency brake, hunching my way out of the passenger door and ended up with a mean cramp in my leg.

While I was stretching it out, I noticed a curtain lift at an upstairs window at the house next door. Discreet. Usually they stand three deep outside a crime scene.

The wind bit at my face as I slogged up the path to the brick split-level already cordoned off with yellow police tape. Overhead, billows of snow clouded a string of blinking Christmas lights.

The officer stationed at the front door beat his hands across his jacket and stamped his canal-boat boots. I stamped the snow from my own silver-studded size nines.

"Jake Harmony. Homicide," I said.

The uniform lifted his chin out of his turned-up collar. "O'Neill," he said. He wrote my name on his time sheet with gloved hands, spelling aloud, "Detective H-A-R-M-O-N-Y. 2:45, A.M. Cold enough for you tonight?"

"Right," I said, and went inside. It was 2:48 on my watch. A Patek Philipe Henry'd given me for a birthday. Whatever it goes for retail, Henry didn't pay it.

In the entry hall, another uniform and Dr. Ritner, the Forensics Medical Investigator for Nassau County, stood in a holding pattern dripping melted snow on an antique Kilm runner. They had been busy looking at each other. Now they looked at me.

Ritner, the FMI, said, "Yo, Jake. Crime Scene's still working." He pointed to a room on the right. "Alberts is in there."

I looked around as I unbuttoned my coat. Directly ahead and up two stairs a formal living room was painted pale yellow and carpeted to match. Too fringed and tasseled for my taste.

I turned right, into the family room, and a fog of Shalimar.

A woman's naked body lay sprawled, face up, on a pillowed daybed; her matted red hair tangled across a mask of makeup and streaked black mascara. Maybe she'd been pretty. The body was middle-aged, big breasts sagging, heavy thighs dimpled.

One ringless hand hung stiffly over the edge of the bed, the other splayed palm up, almost touching a red plaid kilt.

My stomach heaved. After eleven years on the force, six in Homicide, I don't react to death with my gut. It was the Shalimar that got to me.

Charlie Alberts was studying the body. She popped a square of grape Bazooka gum into her mouth as I came in. I wish I could be as nerveless as Charlie; she's phlegmatic as a cud-chewing cow.

A big-bodied, fifty-five-year-old woman with a disillusioned stare and a flat nasal voice, Charlie's twenty-two years older than I am. And my mother's cousin.

"Hi-ya Jake. Cold enough..."

I gave her a quick peck on the cheek. "Happy New Year, Charlie."

"Oh, quit that," she said. Her bloodhound eyes traveled from my black tie to my boots. "Hoo-ha! Get a load of you. All dolled up."

I ignored the crack and pointed to the body. "What do we know?"

Charlie blew a violet bubble. "Name's Mona Raeburn. Divorced. Lived alone. Daughter was called to make the ID."

"And the daughter...."

"Is having hysterics in the kitchen."

"Odd," I said, "that kilt next to the body."

Charlie's hand disappeared into the inside pocket of her shapeless jacket and came out with a notebook. "It's a kilt? I called it a skirt." She worked a Bic pen out from under the rubber band and made a new entry.

I looked down at the corpse that had been Mona Raeburn. "Who found the body?"

Charlie shrugged. "Anonymous male called it in at one-thirty-five. The uniforms arrived at one-forty-five. By the time I got here they were all stomping around, busy destroying evidence. A goddam clusterfuck."

I walked to the glass door and looked out at the falling snow. "The murderer left through this sliding door. And didn't bother to close it behind him," I said.

"No," Charlie said, "The uniforms say they opened it to get rid of the perfume."

"Shalimar."

"Yeah? How do you know?"

"Paula wore Shalimar."

"Ah," Charlie said.

The room had been thoroughly tossed, desk drawers pulled out, their contents dumped on the blue rug. A silver picture frame had fallen or been thrown to the floor. Shards of glass littered the carpet but the picture was gone. What had been in that frame?

"Uniforms do this too?"

Charlie blew a king size purple bubble and sucked it in. "Bunch of fucking assholes. They say it was trashed before they arrived. God only knows what damage they did before they got around to radioing the station for a detective."

A red fox coat spilled from a blue armchair. Black high heels had been kicked half-under the chair and a black lace bra hung from a lampshade. A green satin dress and black panty hose were heaped on the rug to the right of the bed. A valuable gold bracelet and a pair of diamond earrings decorated the top of the TV.

There were two overturned wineglasses on the coffee table, and the remains of a candle.

I eased on a pair of disposable gloves and lifted the victim's eyelid.

Petechiae, tiny hemorrhages, dotted the skin of her face and the whites of the eyes. They indicate strangling or suffocation.

Charlie snapped her gum. "Looks like the victim was smothered with that there pillow. It's smeared with makeup gunk and it stinks of perfume."

I knelt on the rug to inspect the litter of papers. Dampness spread across my knee. When I touched it, the glove came away stained.

"Blood? Why is there blood on the floor if she was smothered?"

"Not the victim's, the poodle's. Look under there. It's head's bashed in."

I shifted the papers away from a little limp rag of a body with my boot toe.

"Peke," I said.

"I thought it was a poodle."

"It's a Peke. What's left of it."

"Peke, poodle," Charlie said. "What difference does it make now?"

Holding my pants by the satin stripe I swiped at the stain with my pocket handkerchief, drew off the bloodied gloves and dumped them, along with the handkerchief, into a collecting bag.

There was an outburst of muffled cursing in the front room and the assistant M.E. for Nassau County, `Dodo' Byrd, bustled in waggling all his chins.

"Who's catching?" he said.

"I'm up," I said. I'd be the lead detective on this case, Charlie would assist.

Byrd doled out latex gloves and the three of us pulled them on. He raised the dead woman's eyelid, pried open her lips. "Petechial hemorrhages."

Charlie and I exchanged glances.

Byrd scraped up a patch of caked rouge with a wooden stick. "Face is lousy with red specks under the makeup. Broken cartilage in the neck."

He rolled the body over. "Stains – could be semen – on the cushion under her. Lividity," he said, attaching a white tag to her bruised looking toe.

The toenails matched the scarlet of her long, unbroken fingernails.

Byrd peeled off his gloves.

"Crime Scene 'll collect everything. I'll call for a morgue wagon and I'm finished here. And don't you fart around too long either. Go home after they bag the victim."

"I want an immediate autopsy," I said.

"Ged-ouda-here! Do you realize how much taxpayer money goes into a case like this? They don't need to pay for unnecessary overtime." He strapped up his bag, said, "I'll be at the morgue tomorrow morning at ten," and waddled off.

Charlie pulled out her notebook. "There's a witness. He was hanging around giving the uniforms a hard time: 'What's going on; what are the police cars doing in the driveway; who's in charge here. Blah, blah, blah….' I got his story and sent him on his way."

"Who is he?"

"Name's Weston. Lives next door. Says the victim left his house just before midnight accompanied by the town library director. Name of Ashley Taylor. They were both at his New Year's party."

"Weston know she's dead?"

"I didn't tell him."

"We'll need the names and addresses of everyone at that party."

"Check."

Charlie scratched her dyed black hair. "Listen, Jake, one of us has to talk to the daughter. Name's Audrey."

I nodded, not volunteering.

"You'd handle it better'n me."

"Since when?"

She looked at her watch, a $10.95 Rolex knock-off she bought from a Senegalese street peddler. "Since three-fifteen A.M., January one, two thousand. I already did the walk through with her. She didn't find anything missing. If you talk to her, I'll finish here and write the report."

I shrugged out of my coat. "Deal. I'll go hold her hand."

CHAPTER TWO

The fake brick kitchen wallpaper almost matched the fake brick floor, and argued a little with the avocado refrigerator. I pulled a chair up to the kitchen table, my eyes lowering from Audrey Raeburn's wounded blue gaze to her ribbed black sweater. No bra. The undersized sweater outlined her small breasts and pointed nipples.

I went back to her unhappy face.

"Detective Harmony. Homicide. I'm sorry about your mother."

"Me too." She folded her arms on the table, rested her head on them and began to sob. She was eighteen, nineteen. Almost not a kid anymore.

I was fifteen when my father shoved his partner aside and got in front of a burst of Uzi fire that ripped his guts apart, leaving bits of him splattering a grungy hallway. I knew what she was going through.

Audrey stopped crying and pushed the mane of red hair from her face. "My mother's dead." She still didn't quite believe it.

I nodded.

"I loved her."

I nodded again.

"And she loved me. People are going to tell you we were always fighting." She hiccupped. "Well, we were! But it didn't mean anything."

"Sure," I said.

Audrey raised watery blue eyes, "I said, `I hate you! I hate you! I wish you were dead."

She put a hand to her stricken face. "I said... I said I'd kill her. But we always said things like that to each other. It didn't mean anything."

"Sure, families are like that," I said.

She brushed at her eyes with a sleeve. "I wish I could take it all back.... Oh, my God! Oh, my God! Oh, God!"

Fist to her mouth she began to sob again.

"Audrey."

Lost in her misery, she ignored me. I tilted my chair, folded my arms and waited. After a while, she quieted.

"Somebody killed Mama. Oh God!" She looked at me with wet eyes. "Did you hear what I said? Mama's killed? I...I can't believe it."

"I know. I know." I made my voice gentle. "Look...It's my job to try to piece together what happened tonight. Your mother came home with a man named Ashley Taylor."

"Taylor."

"Is...was he her boyfriend?"

She shook her head violently. "They...were friends." A plucked red eyebrow lifted. "My mother has...friends."

"We found two glasses on the coffee table. Her body was unclothed, I thought maybe...."

"With Taylor?" She tugged at her hair and wound a strand around her index finger. "No way, Jose."

The finger went into her mouth. More tears flowed as she chewed on the strand of hair.

"Audrey? Somebody was here with your mother and killed her. "

"You figured that out did you?"

I said, "Her kilt was beside the...."

"That's not her kilt! My mother wouldn't be caught dead in that color red. Oh God, did you hear what I said?"

The tears flowed again.

I righted my chair and fiddled with a wooden duck perched on the glass table top. Its bill was stuffed with scrawled memos and cards. I shuffled through them. A take-out menu from Lili's Deli, three car wash coupons, a floor wax service and a yellow business card: *Lloyd Gresham*, it read in raised blue script and there was a penciled number scrawled above the printed one. An unlisted number?

I got up and checked the wall telephone, Lloyd was on the speed dial.

Audrey pushed her hair back from her face wiping her leaky nose with the back of her hand.

"Who's Lloyd Gresham?" I said.

"Lloyd? What has Lloyd got to do with anything?" She dabbed at her eyes. "Lloyd? Taylor? You've got to be kidding! They didn't kill her."

Lloyd and Taylor. Henry sells his *Miss Chic* line to that store.

"Listen," she said, "where's your notebook? Why aren't you taking down everything I say? You know what I think? I think you're not a very good detective."

Her anger at her mother's death was surfacing, and she'd turned it on me. There are twenty-four hundred cops in Nassau County. Only twenty of them are Homicide. We're good or we're back in uniform.

"This Lloyd, is he another one of your mother's friends?"

"They know each other. For God's sake, everyone in Seaview knows him. He's Gresham Trucking–over on Merrick Road. Why don't you ask me when I saw my mother last? The way they do on TV."

I undid my bow tie and opened my collar button, settling in for the long haul the way they do on TV. "When did you see your mother last?"

"Yesterday afternoon. She was on the phone with her agent. She hung up on him, when I came in. She said...."

Audrey's voice broke and she gnawed at the bitten nail on her little finger while she fought for control. "Mama said... `I'm so tired of everyone trying to run my life.'"

"Your mother had an agent?"

"I told the other cop! She's Mona Raeburn."

When I didn't react to the name, surprise displaced grief. "Didn't you see Eternal Love on HBO?"

"No."

"It ran for two seasons. Mama was the second lead."

"I don't get HBO."

Her chin went up. "You wouldn't have liked it."

"Could be. I only watch sports and the news."

I folded my bow tie and stuck it in my back pocket. "Audrey, the killer left your mother dead and the room looking like a tornado hit it. Do you have any idea what he could have been searching for?"

Her face flushed to her hairline. She stood up, sauntered to the sink and filled a glass with water.

"No."

Turning slowly, she tossed her foxy red hair back and stood in profile to let me get a good look at her tight black sweater.

Maybe she wasn't so devastated by her mother's death, for all the tears in her blue eyes. She sure wasn't telling me the truth.

"I wonder if he found what he was looking for."

Sipping the water, she said, "How would I know? I told you... I wasn't here."

"Where were you?"

"Home. In my apartment until Tony called. He said there were police cars parked in Mama's driveway and I'd better come over quick."

"Where is home?"

"220 West Franklin."

"Anyone with you?"

"My Dad. My Dad was with me. He isn't invited to the parties Mama goes to."

"Your parents are divorced."

"Very."

"You were with your Dad when Tony called you. And you came straight here."

"Yes."

"Your Dad let you come here by yourself?"

Her eyes lowered and I waited for the lie.

"He doesn't know I'm here. He'd gone to bed like an hour before Tony called."

She gnawed at the fingernail, watching my face. "My Dad was asleep. He didn't hear me leave."

"This Tony, that's Tony Weston?"

She nodded.

"What time did he call?"

"I don't know. Around two, maybe."

"Weston....He's another friend?"

"The Westons live next door. They're neighbors not friends." Audrey flushed again. "Tony's cool."

"Where's your Dad now?"

"Still at my apartment, I guess." Her hand shook as she set the glass in the sink. "I told you, he was asleep when I left him."

She scraped a chair away from the table and sat down. "We were together...all night. Until I left to come here."

I stood up.

"Must you stand over me like that?"

"Like what?"

Her eyes widened and tears spilled out. "I don't know. Like a suspicious cop. Like I was doing crack and you caught me. I don't feel well."

I sat down. "That better?"

"No. I want to go home."

"Soon." I hooked my boot heels over the chair rung. "Would you like a cigarette, Audrey?"

Her tear-streaked face was offended. "I don't smoke."

"Your fingers are stained so yellow." I reached for her hand. "I thought from nicotine."

She snatched her hand away and looked at her fingers, stalling, deciding what to tell me.

"I broke a bottle of iodine."

She began to sniffle again, measuring me through drenched lashes. Trying to decide if I bought her story.

"I'm cold." She yawned without covering her mouth and stood up. "I'm cold and I want to go home. Now."

"All right." I was ready to end this interview. I'd get back to her when I had more information about this case and could separate her lies from the truth.

"You're tired," I said. "We'll talk again tomorrow. Just one more thing, before you go. The dog...."

"Oooh," she wailed, and her knees buckled. I caught her before she hit the floor and yelled for help.

The blond uniform I'd passed in the hall came to the doorway, his eyes behind horn rims looking a question at the girl in my arms.

I handed Audrey over to him. She fluttered her eyelids and mumbled, leaning her weight against his shoulder.

"Drive her home. Have someone follow in her car."

He rubbed at the flat nose spread across his wide face and looked doubtful.

"Do it," I said and walked out.

This case would attract publicity. Mona Raeburn was show biz. An actress. Not world famous, but not a nobody either. On December 31, she was enjoying life. She'd come home from a party with a man and walked with him through the snow, maybe clutching his arm, laughing, probably a little tipsy. A warm, voluptuous woman, judging from the body.

They'd had a few drinks and gone to bed. I hoped it had been good for her. The last time. On January 1, she was a stiffening corpse in a body bag, on her way to the morgue.

* * *

I sat on the edge of the daybed that still smelled of Shalimar. The stained pillow, the kilt and the body were gone.

Charlie's normally impassive face was disgusted. "All the forensic assholes left." She peeled the wrapper from a square of Bazooka bubble gum, glanced at the cartoon inside, crumpled it and popped the gum into her mouth.

"Everything's been vouchered and sent to the Mineola lab 'til we need it."

"And then it'll be lost," I said.

"Exactly." She chewed the wad of gum.

"So, let's see," I said. "We know the deceased returned home with this Taylor. What if they went to bed together and then quarreled. He kills her. The dog goes to protect her and he stomps it."

Charlie nodded. "I can see that."

"But what was he looking for, Charlie? He pulled the place apart and left all the jewelry. And who made the anonymous call to nine-one-one?"

Charlie took a comb from the inside pocket of her jacket and pulled it through her hair. It didn't do much for her.

"Maybe it was the ex-husband," I said. "Audrey was pretty anxious to protect him. And her reactions are stagy. Well, the mother was an actress and the apple...."

"Doesn't fall far from the tree," she chimed in with me.

"That kid knows something she's keeping to herself," I said.

"Don't they all." Charlie looked at her watch. "Almost four-thirty."

"Five and a half hours until the autopsy. I'll go next-door and talk to the Westons. What about you go to Audrey's apartment and get a statement from Raeburn. If he's still there. 220 West Franklin."

Charlie nodded. "That's north of Sunrise, between Balsam and Collins, I think."

"We'll meet up in about an hour, at the mobile crime lab. It should pull in any minute now."

CHAPTER THREE

Wellington Road was a cul-de-sac of five houses, fronted by five snow-crusted lawns edged with identical boxwood hedges. It was the kind of neighborhood where everyone votes Republican and forgets to pay the housekeeper's Social Security taxes.

I followed a set of half obscured footprints from the Raeburn's back door to the Weston's garage where a spattered Honda SUV was parked outside. Scraping the ice from the garage door window, I peered inside at three battered garbage cans, a wheelbarrow loaded with clay pots, stacks of twine wrapped newspapers and a clean white T' bird.

The house, flanked by a pair of yews tortured into spirals, was a two-story colonial with white horizontal siding and green shutters.

I rapped the antique-looking doorknocker, and watched the brass head of a man meet a woman's in a kiss.

Before I could rap again, a girl in pink flannel pajamas and matching bunny slippers opened the door.

"Is your mother home?" I asked. "Mrs. Weston?"

Her mouth curled up at the corners. "My mother's in 'lanta, Georgia. I reckon you want me. I'm Anne Weston."

Her eyes were pale gray, the silvery irises circled in black. She was about five foot four, and looking down into those eyes, lifted shyly to mine, I felt a little stir of excitement.

I held out my shield.

"Detective Harmony. Homicide."

Her straight black hair, flowing almost to her waist, brushed my hand as she bent over the shield. I was surprised at the shock of pleasure that light touch gave me.

"Come in, Detective," she said, moving aside. Her voice was softly drawling, the vowels drawn out.

I collected my wits and got down to business. "I'm sorry to wake you at this hour...."

"You didn't wake me. I never sleep," she said, proud of that distinction. "I'm insomniac."

"I'm afraid I have bad news about your neighbor, Mrs. Raeburn," I said.

"Mona?" Her pale eyes shadowed by thick black lashes widened. I could see now she was older than I'd thought at first. Twenty five, maybe even thirty.

There was no way to soften the statement. "She's dead."

"No! She was just here!"

Her right hand covered her lips; a small boned, delicate hand. "She can't be dead. She was here last night–this mornin'."

"Yes, I know. I'd like to ask you some questions about that if I may. You and your husband."

"Tony's upstairs." She looked down at her bunny slippers. "Of course we knew somethin' was goin' on...what with all the commotion and all. But, oh my goodness! Dead? Mona?"

She sat down on the love seat in the entryway.

"Dead! I can't–it just can't be. So that's why all the po-lice cars were there? We did wonder. But they wouldn't talk to Tony when he went out to ask. They were very rude to him! How on earth can Mona be dead? Unless...oh my sainted aunt! Was she...she wasn't... murdered?"

Detachment is the policeman's weapon but mine had deserted me at first sight of Anne Weston. I goggled at her.

"Well, I thought…." Her soft drawl was almost inaudible. I stepped closer. "You bein' from Hom-i-cide 'n all."

A sonorous voice called, "Who is it, Annie?"

"Come on down, Tony, darlin'. It's another po-liceman."

Weston, done up in a paisley silk robe, tramped noisily down the stairs and stopped short in front of me, searching my face with deep-set hazel eyes under a tangle of long lashes.

He was movie star handsome. Black wavy hair. High starved cheekbones. A thin mouth under a straight thin nose. A square cleft chin. Tall. I disliked him instantly.

"I'm Tony Weston," he said, displaying chiclet white teeth, capped and bleached to some dentist's dream of perfection.

"Tony! He's a detective from Homicide!"

"Detective Harmony," I said.

"Mona's dead! Murdered!"

Weston's olive skin paled. His hand went to his hair, stroking it in a nervous preening gesture. "How do you mean– murdered?"

"Lordy, lordy," Anne Weston said. "I can't believe it either."

The three of us faced each other, Weston and I at the foot of the stairs, Anne on the love seat. "Would you mind answering some questions?" I said.

"Oh, where are my manners? You come on along, Detective Harmony, and set yourself down. Can I fix you some coffee?"

"No thanks." I followed her into a living room filled with flowered sofas and deep chairs heaped with pillows.

Weston sprawled in a club chair, ostentatiously at ease, but his right hand plucked at a pillow's fringe. Although his wife perched on his chair-arm, I thought they seemed distanced from each other.

I took off my shearling coat, exposing my rumpled tux and felt their curious eyes on me. Sinking into the overstuffed sofa, I said, "I don't usually dress like this on the job. I was called to the Crime Scene from a party."

Anne Weston smiled into my eyes. She certainly knew how to look at a man.

Weston cleared his throat. "Humph."

I said, "I'll need the names and addresses of your guests."

Weston leaned gracefully towards me with a charming smile framed by deep dimples. "But most of them, my sisters and their husbands, didn't know Mona. They met her tonight for the first time."

"Even so, they may have noticed something during the evening that could be of help. What time did Ms. Raeburn leave the party?"

His nervous fingers loosened a strand on the pillow he was toying with and he looked at it without speaking.

Anne crossed the room and sat down beside me. I could smell her Jasmine perfume.

"Mona left right before the blackout," she said, "Ten, maybe fifteen minutes before midnight."

Weston's eyes locked with mine and then he looked away. "So somebody finally murdered the harlot," he muttered and threw the pillow across the room.

"Tony!" Anne said.

I looked down at her face. For just a second, the lovely silvery eyes had turned metallic. She caught me watching her, and licked at her lips.

"Did you think she was a harlot too, Mrs. Weston?"

She blushed, but I'd seen the steel behind her pink and white prettiness.

"Well…living next door to her an' all, we were virtually obliged to witness her slutty carryin's-on."

She left my side to retrieve the pillow and perched on the arm of Weston's chair again.

"I admit I was furious mad at Mona last night. My goodness, I declare I could have strangled her.

"Annie! " Weston said.

"Well it's the truth. Mona just ruined the en-tire party. Goin' off like that with Taylor? She deliberately upset Babe somethin' dreadful."

Weston's mouth thinned. "What are you talking about? It was all Babe's fault."

"Tony Weston, it was not. Why are you stickin' up for Mona? Anyone with one eye could see she was out to make Babe crazy."

"I know Taylor is the library Director," I said. "Who is Babe?"

"Babe Freeman. She an' Taylor are engaged." Anne Weston lowered her voice. "To be married?"

Weston frowned and stroked his eyebrows, hazel eyes brooding.

I said, "But Taylor left with the deceased... with Mona Raeburn."

"Yes, that's what I'm tellin' you," Anne leaned toward me. "Mona just strolled out of here with Taylor, leavin' poor Babe cryin' her eyes out. Boo-hooin' somethn' fierce. We were plumb embarrassed for her. Weren't we Tony?"

Weston's right knee began to jiggle up and down.

"Well, I declare, I was." She nodded twice to emphasize her point.

Weston's lids hooded his eyes as he finally spoke, "Babe has a murderous temper, and Mona sent her over the edge this time."

Anne Weston corrected him. "I wouldn't say 'murderous,' Tony, honey. Not to a detective from Hom-i-cide.

"Goodness knows, I did my best to maintain the gaiety of the occasion. But the lights went out an' the wind was wailin' outside, an' Babe was wailin' inside and everyone was stumblin' 'round in the dark huntin' up their coats. My head began to throb somethin' dreadful."

She massaged her forehead with delicate fingers for a moment and then looked earnestly at me. "I get these migraines? I could hardly hold my head up I was so tormented. But when Babe declared she was fixin' to go over an' break in on Mona and Taylor, I felt I had to speak up. `Sugar, I said, maybe you oughtn't to do that.'"

Anne shook her head. "She owned I was right and said she supposed she'd run over to the diner instead. The Seaview diner? I felt so bad by then, I crept upstairs an' into my bed an' lay my poor head down."

I said, "Why was Babe going to the diner? Does she work there?"

"She doesn't work there, darlin', she owns it. Her daddy left it to her when he passed on."

"What time did Babe Freeman leave here?" I asked Weston.

He shrugged wide shoulders. "After Annie went upstairs. I'd say about twelve-ten."

Anne said, "Our bedroom window looks directly out on Mona's front walk, an' I can tell you, Babe did not go to the diner! Not right away anyway. She marched over to Mona's door and started banging on it. That set Poochy to barkin'. Well, they didn't let her in, an' after a bit I saw her car lights go on. I closed my eyes an' it seemed like the very next second, course it wasn't—when I heard Poochy barkin' again. At Taylor."

"Poochy? Is that an expression for dog in Atlanta?"

Anne Weston smiled. "Aren't you a caution? That's his name. Poochy."

An image of the Peke's trampled little body flashed into my head.

"He was barkin' somethin' fierce when Taylor left."

"You saw Taylor leave?"

"No-o. It was too dark to see your hand in front of your face. The lights were still out."

"Then you don't know who it was."

"Who else would it be, darlin'? Taylor was with Mona and he left. My momma always says, 'if it quacks like a duck an' it walks like a duck, it's a duck'. The duck who went crashin' down that path? Trust me, it was Taylor."

Weston stood up, crossed to a bar cart set up between the white curtained windows and poured himself a drink.

"Where were you, Weston, while your wife was upstairs?"

He downed his drink, set the empty glass on the mirrored surface with a clink, and faced me.

"Here. Cleaning up. The housekeeper won't be in today and I didn't want to leave Annie alone with the mess. I got the emergency flashlight out and stacked the dishwasher and straightened up a little– put the empty bottles outside. Into the recycling bin."

"You didn't go to the Raeburn house?"

He turned back to the bar cart and poured another drink.

"No, of course not. Why would I do that?" His hand shook as he lifted the glass. "I got ready to go to bed. As a matter of fact, I was brushing my teeth when I heard the police cars drive up."

"And you went outside to find out what was happening."

"That's right. Much good it did me." His mouth had gone sullen. No more dimpled smiles.

"Then you came in and called Audrey Raeburn."

"Yes. It was a little after two in the morning, but I thought I ought to let her know what was going on, even if I woke her up."

"You knew her phone number."

"It's in our address book. Listen, I have a flight to L.A. " He looked at his watch. "My driver's picking me up in about ten minutes. I've got to get dressed."

"Tony, you're not goin'? After all this? You're not leavin' me when Mona was just murdered in her bed?"

He turned back to the bar cart and poured another drink.

I wondered if Weston was normally a drinker or if he was unnerved by the murder; or whatever part he'd played in that murder. He'd certainly lost his negligent self-confidence.

He said, "You can't possibly know where Mona was killed, Annie." And then to me, "Well where else would my wife assume she was killed? Mona was the town trollop."

Harlot...Trollop... I bit back the questions that sprang to mind. I couldn't ask them in front of his wife: Do you know how she was killed, Mr. Beautiful? Were those your footprints leading from the Raeburn house to your garage? Were you in that trollop's bed?

Anne pleaded, "Tony? Don't leave tonight."

Anger twisted Weston's handsome face. Regretfully, he was no less handsome. He said, "I bought you that little .22 just so you wouldn't whine like this when I go away. I have to go."

A muscle ticked in his cheek. "I'm a film distributor," he told me. "I travel a lot. There's no reason why I can't go, is there? I'll be back Tuesday night on the redeye." His eyes shifted from me to the bar cart and back to me again.

I waited a beat or two to rattle him, and shrugged. "Okay. Where are you staying?"

"The Beverly Hills Hotel." He walked toward the stairs. "Well then," he said, and left the room with an uneasy glance at me, his shoulders held high with tension.

I smiled at Anne Weston. "Did you offer me some coffee?"

"Indeed I did! I'll just scoot into the kitchen and make a fresh pot."

"I'll come with you, Mrs. Weston."

"My name's Anne."

CHAPTER FOUR

Cozying around, sharing coffee is a good way to collect information, but I followed Anne Weston into her bright kitchen with the disturbing feeling that this pretty woman with her gentle Southern manner could turn my brain to mush if I didn't watch myself. I couldn't stop looking at her.

I sat on a blue painted captain's chair and switched my mind-set to neutral. The homey kitchen smelled of fresh ground coffee and lemons and cinnamon. Polished copper pots hung from a wrought iron ceiling rack.

I watched Anne putter around, measuring coffee into the drip pot, opening a cupboard for two thin white cups and saucers.

Outside a horn blared and then Weston clattered down the stairs. "I'm off, Annie." His baritone could have carried to the balcony if there was a balcony. "Call you tonight."

The front door slammed. A car door slammed.

Anne stood motionless staring at nothing. "He's gone," she said.

Weston was a lucky man, I thought, and reached for a book lying on the scrubbed butcher-block table.

A Bible. Under my hand it opened to Ezekiel, Chapter 16. I glanced at it idly at first but the words jumped out at me, underlined by a thin green pen:

and you poured out your harlotry on every one passing by who would have it:

On the opposite page another sentence was underlined by the same green pen:

They shall also strip you of your clothes and take away your beautiful jewelry and leave you naked. Thus I will make you cease your lewdness and your harlotry.

I imagined Anne marking these pages in a frenzy over Mona's 'harlotry' and I felt my heart sink into my boots.

Those slender arms raised in a lovely arc as she reached into the cupboard, had they held the pillow over Mona Raeburn's face?

Anne turned from the cupboard, her face draining to parchment when she saw what I was reading. She whipped the Bible from my hands, shoving it into a bookcase above the Garland stove, between *The New York Times Cookbook* and *Mastering the Art of French Cooking*.

"Mrs. Weston, someone did strip Mona Raeburn of her clothes and make her cease her harlotry."

"Oh! Oh, my goodness gracious! Why are you looking at me like that? I didn't. Goodness! 'Thou shalt not kill' is the first commandment of our Lord."

I wanted to believe her. Her silvery eyes met mine so guilelessly.

It had to be Weston. And I'd let him go. Mistake.

She poured the coffee shakily, spilling some and sponging it up. "Do you believe in God?" she said.

"I don't know."

"I think you must. You may not be aware, but you believe."

She sat down beside me, looking grave and reached for my hand. My startled glance stopped her and she closed her fingers around the creamer instead. We looked at each other for a long moment.

"See, you are doin' God's work," she said. "Rootin' out evil and protectin' the innocent. It must be wonderful to be you and do such important work. It just thrills me to my very core."

I shifted in my chair.

"You said that Mona Raeburn was killed in her bed. How did you know that?"

"Oh goodness gracious, that was just a figure of speech! Trust me. I didn't know she was dead 'til you told me. I'll swear on the Bible if you like. This very moment!"

I stirred my coffee. "Did you mark those passages?"

The tip of her pink tongue explored the bow of her upper lip. "I... did," she said. "I did and I *was* thinking about that wretched Mona and feeling vengeful, but goodness, I know the difference between having a sinful fantasy and acting it out."

Maybe.

"Tell me about your party," I said.

"I know it's trivial, me puttin' so much store in an ol' party. I mean compared with what you do."

"I don't think it's trivial at all. I admire a woman who makes a welcoming home for her friends and family." Her hyperbolic style was catching.

"Do you really mean that?" She searched my face. "I will treasure that in my heart forever. What shall I tell you? I'm not sure what you want to hear."

"I want to hear the truth."

"I'm always truthful. You don't know me, of course, but I am." Anne circled her cup on the saucer. "Mona was the first to arrive. Dressed to kill! She came struttin' in while I was fixin' the hors d'oeuvres. But she didn't pay me any mind. She started right in flirtin' with Tony. He was flattered, of course. One thing about Mona, she was always right smart about gettin' what she wanted."

"You think she wanted Tony?"

Anne was still a moment, looking unnervingly lovely. She's a suspect in a murder case, I reminded myself.

"I'm not a jealous woman. I know Tony wants the lead in Mona's play and I know she wanted Tony...to be in it. What else she wanted, I couldn't say." Her voice dropped to a whisper. "Tony's the kind of man women fall in love with."

I remembered young Audrey Raeburn's enthusiastic, 'Tony's cool.' If Anne Weston was harnessed to a stud, did she resent it?

Anne said, "Tony was hangin' on Mona's every word until Taylor came in wearin' that fool kilt."

I set my cup down.

She went on, "He always wears his kilt to parties. I do believe that's what gave Mona the idea for her play, *Scottish Mists?*"

"I see. He's a Scotsman."

"Claims to be. Goodness, if you believe that, I'm Hillary Clinton!"

The waspishness was incongruous in her soft drawl.

"Floozie that she was, Mona dropped Tony an' went after Taylor, jigglin' her boobies so they nearly fell out'a her dress. She was all over him like dew on the mornin' grass. I just knew there'd be trouble. And sure enough, the very next thing, the two of them were in a corner together with glasses of Scotch in their hands. Now Taylor did promise Babe he'd quit drinkin'. I told you they're engaged…to be married?"

Her jasmine scent teased me as she leaned closer.

"Yes, you did."

"They've been engaged for months, on 'n off. On when he's sober, an' off when he's not. Well, there they sat together…Mona, the town tramp and Taylor, the town drunk.

Her lip curled with distaste. "It's not just that he's...a nig…a person of color–trust me. I'm not prejudiced against them. Why, I invite him to my home."

My heart sank again. I felt as if I'd found a worm in a beautiful peach.

"But a man in Taylor's position oughtn't to drink. Librarians, lord-sakes, they're the same as teachers, influencin' children 'n all. Don't you agree they should be…."

She hesitated.

"What should they be?"

"Well, I don't know what, but not fallin'-down drunks. And, that's not the worst of it.... Now, I wouldn't repeat this if it was mere gossip...."

I nodded.

"Well, it's common knowledge an' someone's bound to tell you! Taylor tried to kill himself. It was hushed up, but still an' all!"

She sipped her coffee.

Ashley Taylor, a kilted, black, suicidal, drunkard, had gone off with Mona Raeburn in a raging temper. And we'd found his kilt next to her dead body.

But if it was his, would he have left it there? More likely someone was trying to make us think he was the killer. I needed to interview Taylor, ASAP.

"You do want to hear what happened next?" Anne's voice drew my attention back.

"Sure."

She took a deep breath and leaned forward on her elbows. "Babe came in. Well! We all started talkin' real loud. To distract her? But when she saw those two gropin' in the corner, my goodness! She went up to Taylor and slapped him. And do you know what? That awful man slapped her back!"

Anne looked to me for a reaction.

"He did!" I said.

She nodded, and went on with her narrative. "Well, Babe took off her ring and threw it at him. It's just a bitty thing, not hardly worth callin' a diamond. Mona sashayed on over to him and said, `Come home with Mona, baby.' She always could talk out of both sides of her face. I've already told you the rest, about poor Babe cryin' and poundin' on Mona's door, an' Taylor leavin' an' Poochy barkin' his fool head off at him."

I held my cup out for more coffee and she refilled it without losing a beat:

"I fell asleep for a bit but then Poochy woke me with his barkin'. Or maybe it was the lights comin' back on. I pressed my head against the cool window, and that's when I saw Fred. Mona's ex? I saw him come barrelin' out of the house and run straight into a big fella on the porch. Plumb knocked him down."

"Whoa," I said, "Let me get this straight. Mona Raeburn left your party with Ashley Taylor. Babe Freeman followed them, banged on the door, and left. Then you think you heard Taylor leave, but you didn't actually see him."

"It was Taylor," she insisted.

"Later, when the lights came on, you saw this man Fred run out of the house, knocking down still another man."

"That's right. Fred Raeburn came scootin' out like Lucifer was chasing him and jumped into his van and drove off."

"You saw two men. Are you sure one of them was Fred Raeburn?"

"I should think I know Fred Raeburn when I see him."

"And the other man?"

"I don't know who he was." She frowned. "Fred left the door wide open, an' I saw this fella go into the house. Not a minute later, he came out again, got into his car an' drove off. He was wearing glasses. Yes, and he was tall."

Tall. Women say the word tall with such approval!

"Describe the car."

"A silver, foreign one."

Headache and all, she'd stood watching all this.

I said, "Why would Poochy bark at Fred? He must know him."

"He didn't know the other man."

"But you heard Poochy bark before you saw this man."

"Ye-es." Anne sighed. "I went back to bed but I didn't close my eyes. Then the police cars started arrivin'. Tony came upstairs an' phoned Audrey to tell her about the to-do at her mother's house. He suggested she might want to come see what it was all about. She never did call us back. Of course, now I understand why."

"Do you know what time it was when Fred Raeburn ran out of the house?"

She shook her head. "I don't. Wait! My goodness, yes, it must have been after one-thirty 'cause Tony called Audrey 'round two. "

I stood up. "You've been very helpful. I appreciate your cooperation."

"Thank you, Detective Harmony. Whatever I can do to help, you just have to ask."

We walked to the front door together. A sampler, worked in red and blue cross-stitch, hung next to the light switch: *Let me live in a house by the side of the road and be a friend to man.*

"Now listen," Anne blushed, and said, "Don't be a stranger, hear? Y'all come back any time."

CHAPTER FIVE

I walked down the cul-de-sac, thinking about Anne Weston. Clearly she'd been playing me, using her smiles and blushes and southern accent. I'm a cop. I've seen innocent faces mask guilt often enough.

Did she really like me? What an idiot I'd be if I fell for her tricks like a green rookie.

Those tracks I'd seen in the snow leading to the Raeburn house. I couldn't prove they were Weston's... but I had a strong hunch.

The mobile crime lab had arrived; a fully equipped, Winnebago type vehicle: our temporary office until the Raeburn case was solved. It was parked at the bottom of Wellington Road on a wooded lot with a good view of the entire cul-de-sac above. And a good view of us from the cul-de-sac.

I got my duffel bag from the 'Vette trunk and trudged down to the mobile lab.

Sergeant Wolfe, the crime lab computer tech assigned to us, was hunched over some papers, the fingers of her left hand raking her short brown curls, a coffee mug in the right one.

"Hi, Wolfie. How are you?"

She rolled her desk chair back. "I'm here, before dawn, at the crack of the new millennium, freezing my ass off and working with you guys. How do you think I am?"

"That's a rhetorical question right?" I said.

"Get out of here!"

"Yo, Jake," Charlie called.

I walked to the rear where she sat at a table littered with crumbs.

"What did Raeburn have to say?" I asked.

Charlie bit into a glazed donut. "He was with his daughter in her apartment all night."

"Yeah, well he wasn't. Anne Weston saw him running from the crime scene. Saw him get into his van and drive away."

Charlie set the donut down and looked at it for a while. "In the old days I'd go back there and ream him a new asshole."

I said, "I'll go back for you."

Digging into the Dunkin' Donuts sack, I helped myself to a jelly donut and poured a cup of coffee from the half-full pot.

"I'll give you one guess what the librarian wore to the party."

Charlie shrugged. "Reading glasses?"

"A kilt," I said.

"No shit." She lumbered to her feet. "How about I interrogate that fucker while you go back and drag the truth out of Raeburn?"

"You do that."

By then it was 5:30. I went into the bathroom and exchanged my tux for the jeans and sweater I keep in my kit bag. The bathroom's about four inches wider than the stalls on airplanes. When I emerged, strapping my gun holster to my belt, Charlie had left.

* * *

Two thirds of the way down the 200 block on West Franklin, I came to a screeching halt at an empty parking space, pulled in and walked back to 220, the Nassau Arms Gardens. The wind chill was minus four on this squally New Year's morning. I burrowed my chin into my coat collar and walked faster.

A group of two-story red brick buildings formed a U around a flat expanse of frozen snow. I walked up the cracked cement path. A few seagulls pecked at the litter of coffee grounds, dried-out orange rinds, damp cigarette butts, shriveled tea bags and some unidentifiable debris decomposing beside a row of overflowing trash cans.

I searched the tarnished brass directory, found Raeburn—2G, and pressed my thumb against the cracked yellow-ivory disk.

"Who is it?" a woman's voice squawked from the intercom.

"Detective Harmony."

A buzzer hummed and I dove for the doorknob. Too late.

I tried again.

"Yes?"

"Buzz me in again."

The buzzer sounded and continued to drone while I opened the inner door and climbed two dark flights of chipped marble stairs, choking on the nasty odor of stale cooking.

At the end of a hallway covered in dried-up wallpaper that had seen better days, Audrey Raeburn, wearing black tights and the same clingy sweater, lounged inside a half-opened walnut-grained door. Her bare feet were grimy, her red hair uncombed.

I said, "Hello again."

She straightened up and stood flat-footed inside the doorway, hands on her hips. "It's six in the morning. What do you want now?"

"How about letting me in?"

"Why should I?"

"For openers, to rehash the fairy tales you and your dad have been spinning. Bring them more in line with reality."

She eyed me sullenly, but decided to stand aside. I brushed past her into the apartment, overheated after the deep freeze outside. The air smelled sour. I tried taking shallow breaths.

In the living room, a sandy-haired, bearded man in jeans and a tattle tale gray T shirt had carved out a space in the clutter. He squatted on the floor eating corn flakes and milk and looked up as I came in.

"You Fred Raeburn?"

His Adam's apple waggled as he swallowed cereal. Opaque tobacco-colored eyes in a foolish, empty face tried to focus on me.

"Fred Raeburn?"

He nodded and tossed his head, sending his gray-streaked ponytail into pendulum arcs across his thin back.

Audrey stood in the doorway watching. I took off my coat and parked on one of two big hassocks.

"Hot in here," I said.

Raeburn nodded in my direction again with a vacant smile and some milk dribbled from the spoon in his unsteady hand onto the floor.

"I'm Detective Harmony, Homicide. About an hour ago, you made a statement to Detective Alberts to the effect that you and your daughter Audrey were here together all of last night. Is that correct?"

"Uh-huh." Raeburn shivered, barely holding himself in control.

Was he sick? Or just scared?

Audrey drew closer to us. "That's right," she said. "I told you that too."

I spoke to Raeburn. "Then how come you were seen running out of your wife's house? A little after one a.m."

"Jesus." Raeburn's mouth went slack in his pasty face.

"That's not true! Who saw him?" Audrey shrilled, her hand protective on Raeburn's shoulder. "Don't answer, Daddy. You don't have to say anything."

"You're in no position to give advice," I said. "I'm thinking of charging you with obstruction of an official investigation. I don't like being lied to."

"I..." Her defiance vanished and she burst into tears like a frightened kid. Like the bereaved and frightened kid she was, I reminded myself. The victim was her mother.

"I was afraid you'd think Daddy...my Dad killed Mama." Tears rained down her cheeks. "You do, don't you?"

"Until I find the killer, I suspect everyone."

She sank to her knees beside Raeburn. He looked at her with a calm that verged on stupor and shuffled to his feet.

"I didn' waste her, man," Raeburn said.

He shambled to a corner piled with odds and ends, picked a guitar out of the junk and strummed a chord. "I never expected Mona 'd be there."

I was sweating under my turtleneck. "Go on."

"She was partying at the Weston's. Isn't that what you told me, baby?" He played another chord, croaking tunelessly along with it. "The electricity-was-out. The e-ee-lectrcity waas...out. It was da-a-rk when we drove up...."

"We?"

Raeburn looked muddled. A pause stretched into silence.

Finally, Audrey said, "I drove him."

She wiped her reddened eyelids with the back of her hand. "But I didn't go inside. I waited outside in the van."

Raeburn laid the guitar down and began to crack his bony knuckles.

"If you didn't think your wife was home, how'd you expect to get in?" I asked him. "You have a key?"

"Hee-hee," Raeburn cackled. "No, man, I ain't got a key. Mona changed the locks when I moved out." His voice whined with self-pity. "I let myself in with the spare she keeps under the doormat."

"And then?"

"I thought I might pick up a few bucks, you know, while she was out. Mona stashes bread all over the place. Don't even know how much she has. Forgets where she put it half the time."

I looked at Audrey. Her nose was leaking. "You drove him to the house to rob your mother?"

"No. I mean...it wasn't like you're making it sound. Mama was mean about money if you asked her for it. But... but... she never missed it... if you just took it."

"I see. That makes it legal." I gave her a package of tissues to blow her nose.

She blew, and offered the rest back to me.

"Keep them."

"Mama was mean to Daddy," she said. "She didn't have to be so mean."

"Damn straight. Bitch wouldn't part with cent one. Said if she gave me any money, it'd go up my nose. Hey, I'm chilled out, man."

"Maybe you still have…a weekend habit?"

He smiled and his face took on a charm that dissipated as he lapsed into self-pity. "I was just going to take a couple of bucks she wouldn't have missed."

I said, "Do you mind if I open a window?"

"Yes," Audrey said. "Daddy has to keep warm."

"So you burgled the premises," I said to Raeburn.

His unfocused tobacco-colored eyes almost crossed. "Burgled? Hey man. It's my premises."

"A judge might not see it like that."

Raeburn's mouth hung open stupidly.

I sighed. "Tell me exactly what happened, and maybe I won't pull you in for B and E. Or Audrey, here, as an accessory. Understand?"

He looked at Audrey. She flung her arms around him, glaring at me.

"Don't you threaten my dad."

She loved him. This drugged out aging hippy. What could Fred Raeburn, have ever done but disappoint her? She loved him anyway.

"What time did you get to your mother's house?" I said. It was a sauna bath in here. Sweat ran down my armpits, dampened my back.

Audrey buried her face in Raeburn's shoulder.

"I asked you a question."

She turned her head to answer. "We left here about one."

"That right?" I looked at Raeburn.

He scratched at his straggly beard, silent for so long I thought I'd lost him. Then the slack mouth worked again and I bent forward, intent:

"Yeah, if Audrey says so. Yeah, that's copasetic."

"You let yourself in and...."

"I thought get in, and get out. Fast. So I'm going through the drawers and that friggin' Poochy! Dog's always been jealous of me. Used to piss on my side of the bed. Mona thought it was funny.

"I step on Poochy in the dark. The damn mutt sinks his teeth into my leg. I'm bleeding like a pig."

He blinked at Audrey, and cringed. "I only kicked him a couple of times. I didn't mean to off him. It just, you know, happened."

"What?" Audrey shrieked. "You killed Poochy? Oh, daddy!" Tears wet her cheeks. "Poochy was my friend."

Raeburn mumbled, "Wasn't my fault. I didn't mean it. It was like a reflex. He bit me, I kicked him." He patted her shoulder. "Don't cry, baby."

Ignoring her sobs, I asked Raeburn, "What did you do after you stomped the dog's head?"

"The lights came back on." He blinked. "All of a sudden, lights. Blinded me. Then I saw Mona. Naked on the daybed. Christ! I was scared shitless she'd wake up and put my ass in a sling. I figured she was, like crashing. But then I saw she was dead to the world. I mean...like you know...I didn't think she was dead, dead."

His Adam's apple waggled in his scrawny neck. "I was all set to split, man, when the doorbell rings and I look out the window and this frigging guy is standing outside on the porch. I think...if I streak past him with my hood up, he won't recognize me. So that's what I did."

He balled up a fist. "I gave him a shove. Hard, you know. I'm not so strong, but when I'm psyched up, the strongest man doesn't have a chance. And then I ran."

"Why didn't you go out the back door?"

"Oh. Yeah, man. Cool. Well, I didn't think of it."

"What time was it when you left?"

"Get off my back, man. I didn't look at no frigging time."

Audrey wiped at her nose with a disintegrating tissue. "It was Alan Berger, Mama's agent. In his Jaguar. I looked at my watch. It was one-twenty-five."

I got to my feet. The temperature had to be over a hundred in this room. I felt as if I'd melted off five pounds.

"You claim you didn't murder your wife?"

"Never touched her, man."

Audrey cried out, "Daddy 's telling the truth! Don't you know the truth when you hear it?

"When I hear it."

"My leg was bleeding bad where Poochy bit me." Raeburn whined. He hiked up his pant leg to display a wide swathe of yellow.

"When we got home, I tried to disinfect it with iodine," Audrey said. "But I dropped the bottle and it spilled. I was mopping it up," She held up her yellowed fingers. "when Tony called about the police cars in Mama's driveway."

She turned on Raeburn, her swollen eyes brimming, "Why didn't you tell me you killed Poochy?"

"Knew you'd be upset. Didn't want to upset you."

I said, "You might need a tetanus shot. Dog bites are serious."

Raeburn smiled, an unrepentant wolfish grimace. "If Mona'd bit me, maybe, but Poochy? Mr. Clean. The groomer brushes his teeth every week and Mona takes him to the dog dentist twice a year."

I didn't smile back at him. "Where's your phone?"

"In there." Audrey pointed to the kitchen.

The kitchen was a windowless hot box about six by six with all the basic equipment shoehorned in. I found the telephone under a pile of newspapers. The receiver was sticky. I wiped it with the only thing I could find, a damp mold-smelling sponge. Wolfie answered my call.

"Charlie there?"

"Left about ten minutes ago. Said to meet her at the Seaview diner."

"I need gas. Where can I find an open station today?"

"Wait a minute. I'll check." She came back on the line. "Jake? There's an ad in the yellow pages says Rube's Service 24/7. Where are you?"

"Franklin."

"O.K. I'm looking at a map. Here, I found Franklin. Just go east till you hit Park Place; then take a right. Rube's station's between Merrick Road and the Marina."

I replaced the telephone and went back to the living room.

They were sitting on the floor, eyes closed. An incense burner guttered fumes into the stifling air.

"Ohmmm," Fred chanted.

"Ohmmm," Audrey echoed.

I picked up my jacket.

Eyes closed, Audrey said, "We're going to have tea. Do you want a cup?"

"Hot tea? No thanks."

She vaulted neatly to her feet. "It's cranberry tea. Good for your uterus."

"I'll take a rain-check," I said. "I don't drink on duty."

Raeburn's narrow chest lifted in a deep breath, and collapsed as he exhaled. I looked into the vacant bearded face. Anybody could be a killer.

I said, "Don't leave Seaview." And then thought, what am I saying? This guy's already left town.

I walked to the car. The cold air felt good at first after the sweltering apartment. Then I began to shiver. I burrowed into my coat collar again but couldn't get warm. In the car, I switched on the motor and the heater.

Fred Raeburn. I laughed out loud. What a flake! He'd killed the Peke though. Nothing funny about that. And he'd had time enough to kill Mona before the agent, Berger, surprised him. I stopped laughing. Plenty of murders start out as burglaries.

I couldn't tie Audrey to the murder if she'd stayed in the van. But maybe she was lying again. Still, Anne hadn't seen her and Anne had kept Mona's parade of visitors under tight surveillance. Wait a minute. Anne couldn't have heard the dog bark when Fred left. He'd silenced it, for good.

If Anne was lying....It didn't add up. Nothing added up yet.

CHAPTER SIX

I turned into Rube's Full Service Station Open 24 Hours and pulled up at one of two gas pumps hung with pine wreaths and red satin ribbons.

"Fill it up, super." I gave the attendant my Amex card and headed for the whitewashed building marked OFFICE. The door closed with a cheerful ding-dong and a wide-shouldered man squinted up at me through a cloud of smoke. I eyed the red embroidery on the breast pocket of his coverall.

"Rube?"

From behind his battered metal desk, Rube nodded his thatch of graying hair. One of his weather-rough hands poised over a tire-shaped ashtray overflowing with cigarette stubs.

"Hi," I said. "Mind if I come inside to warm up? It's cold out there."

"Come in."

Above a display of oilcans behind him, Mona Raeburn smiled down at us from an eight by ten Lucite frame. I didn't smile back.

"You're open 7/24?"

"Yup, never close. I relieved my manager eleven o'clock. Been here ever since."

Not a likely candidate for the Raeburn murder. "Isn't that a picture of that actress...."

Rube grinned. "Mona Raeburn. You recognize her, huh? She gave me that personally. Lives here in Seaview. Comes into my station all the time."

"That so."

"Nice lady. Plain as you and me. Calls me Rubie. Gave me a real expensive fruit basket for Christmas."

"Was she in last night?"

"Nope. I filled her up the beginning of the week. Haven't seen her since."

I didn't tell him that the lady was no longer with us. He'd find out soon enough.

I said, "Where's the Seaview diner? "

"You going there?"

"Yes."

"I ain't allowed in. She banned me."

"Who did?"

Rube's eyes went flinty "Babe. Been six years now. Ever since her boyfriend, the foreigner one, died. Her name's really Babette, but she'd kill anyone called her that."

Babe seemed to be famed for her murderous temper.

A buzzer sounded and six feet of blue coverall unfolded as he stood up. "Come outside with me."

Coatless, he strode out into the cutting wind. I followed.

"Well, lookit that!" he said pointing to my 'Vette. "That yours? Don't see one of those every day. Some headache to find parts I bet. Your right tire's low. Needs air."

I kicked the tire. "Think you're right."

"Pull over to the air. I'll fill 'er for you."

I did, and got out of the car.

Rube squatted to set the gauge. "You can't miss the diner. "Go north. About a block before you hit Merrick Road you'll see the

Paradise Insurance sign. It's still called that even though old man Paradise retired five years ago."

He squinted up at me. "After Babe's boyfriend died, old man Paradise refused to pay the insurance. Supposed to be big bucks, in her name. Babe don't talk to him now and she don't talk to me neither, ever since that day she come in here yelling for me to keep my big mouth shut, or she'd shut it for me.

"It wasn't just me. The whole town, everybody was talking about it. How fishy it was that he passed away so sudden. Such a young guy. And why couldn't she collect the insurance?"

He bounded to his feet.

"There's smoke, there's fire, I say. My son's a lawyer. A Cornell graduate. He offered to try to collect for her. No charge. But she wasn't in'erested."

He wiped his hands on a piece of red flannel and stuck it in his back pocket. Then he reached down for a squeegee and wiped my windshield.

"You make a right at Merrick. It turns into Main Street. You go past the stores and the movie theater and the town Parking Lot. You can park there two hours for free. Best bargain in town. Then there's the Seaview Department Store, the Post Office, the bank and the diner. You can't miss it."

"Thanks."

Before I got back in the car, I offered him two-dollars. But he shoved his hands in his pockets, shaking his head in refusal.

CHAPTER SEVEN

The town of Seaview in Nassau County, Long Island, is forty-six miles east of Manhattan. Main Street, the main drag, is centered around five shop-lined blocks, its high curbs planted every twenty feet with potted blue spruce trees. It's the kind of town that before you realize you're there, you've passed through it.

The Seaview Diner was the last commercial building on Main Street. Behind it a chain link fence separated its blacktop parking lot from a willow bordered pond, with a pair of swans gliding along its surface. Flocks of wild ducks and Canadian geese mingled on the bank, pecking at crumbs in the snow. Beyond, the road wound eastward into wooded countryside.

I parked and locked up and stood in the cold sunlight for a quiet second or two.

A man in a yellow slicker and hip boots came plodding along the pond's edge, scattering the flock. He knelt in the snow and dumped out the contents of his fishing creel.

A pack of cats emerged from the willows. They slunk forward on their bellies toward the fish, their silent shadows creeping before them. The furry shapes slinking along the dead white snow gave me a jolt of horror.

I can't be near cats. Even one can send me into suffocating fits of wheezing. A grisly pack like this could....

Even though I knew they were too far away to kick off my allergies my throat closed up and I reached for my Ventolin inhaler.

When I could breathe normally again, I sprinted for the chrome-fronted diner, to the safety of its flashing red and blue neon sign, and leaned against the storm door sucking in the freezing air.

All the tables were empty but I recognized Charlie Alberts' big rear overflowing a counter stool. Sitting beside her, a skinny waitress in a thigh-high black skirt dangled a black patent flat from a narrow ankle. Her long black-stockinged legs were crossed at the knee and she was laughing with Charlie.

"Yo, Jake," Charlie said, "This 's Babe Freeman. Babe, meet my partner, Jake Harmony."

Babe slipped from her stool with a curt nod. She was about five-ten in her flats.

Dark eyes traveled over my shearling coat and lingered on my lizard boots. "You're a cop?" Her clear skinned face said she saw a short balding man and she didn't much like what she saw.

"Homicide Detective." I flashed my gold shield.

She gave it a glance. Still didn't like me.

I took the stool she'd been sitting on. "You know," I said, "this place reminds me of a restaurant that I hear NASA's planning to open on the moon."

"Why?" she said.

"No atmosphere."

"First thing on New Year's Day, I have to get a comedian cop in thousand-dollar boots."

Whatever else this woman might turn out to be, one thing was sure: she was a smart-ass.

"Coffee, regular," I said and watched her stride behind the counter. Goodish legs. The tiny skirt was half-covered with a black apron tied around a neat narrow waist. Her shiny brown hair was pulled back. It was clean silky hair, tied with a velvet ribbon. Prominent collarbones showed at the open neck of her white shirt. Skinny. Not my type. Skinny women are hostile women.

She plunked the coffee down in front of me and turned away.

"Sensational pancakes," Charlie said with her mouth full. The stack on her plate glistened with grape jam and a pool of melted butter. She doused the lot with maple syrup. "Have some?"

I stirred Sweet'n Low into my coffee. "I'm on a diet."

"Again?"

"Still." I gulped the coffee. Scalding.

Charlie belched softly. "It took a lot of will power, but I gave up dieting." She pointed to the display case. "Apple pie?"

"Homemade," Babe said.

"I'll have some."

Babe cut a wedge; added caramel sauce and a mound of whipped cream and set it in front of Charlie. My mouth watered.

"I haven't seen you two in here before," Babe said. "You just passing through?"

"Why?" I said.

"Just asking. It's odd, two strange cops in here, this early in the morning, on New Year's Day. Nothing ever happens in Seaview during the winter. It's soporific."

My mug clattered to the counter. Soporific? It was too early in the morning for `soporific'.

She wiped up the spill and gave me a cool stare. "More coffee?" Her attitude telling me to get lost.

"Not yet."

Babe said, "Seaview's a nice town. People are nice here."

"Well, last night one of you nice people killed another of you nice people."

"What? Who? Who was killed?"

"Mona Raeburn. Know her?"

She turned away to fuss over a tray of dishes. "Everyone in town comes in here. I know them all."

"Mona Raeburn was just another customer?"

"Umm."

All right. You want to play tough, lady, I can be tough. "You're lying."

She whirled to face me. "I? Lying?"

"Mona Raeburn was not just another customer. You knew her somewhat better than that. Maybe you mean you didn't want to know her, since she walked off with your fiancée last night. I hear you were more than a little upset about that."

Her eyes, full of distrust, met mine and her narrow face went hard. "A farrago of half truths."

I was beginning to admire this woman.

She spoke to Charlie, "I was upset. I didn't know what I was saying." Then to me with a sneer, "Couldn't you see that?"

"No, actually, I thought you seemed pretty cool."

The look she gave me was supposed to wither me away. Only it didn't.

Charlie snapped a toothpick in half. "Good pie, Jake." Through a mouthful of apples, she said, "Nine on a ten point scale."

"I'll have a piece," I said.

"You're not dieting anymore?"

"Right. I forgot." I swallowed the last of my coffee and held up the empty mug. Babe wasn't so skinny. I glimpsed the tops of very nice breasts as she leaned over to refill the mug.

"Did you see Mona Raeburn again after she left?" I said.

"I did not. I came here."

I could almost taste the pie with Charlie as she shoveled it in.

"I came back to check the freezers," Babe said.

"You left the Weston's about 12:10. What time did you get here?"

She looked up at the ceiling, lips pressed firmly together.

"What time?"

She inspected the counter in front of her, rubbed at a spot with her index finger and finally decided to acknowledge my question. "I didn't look at my watch. Perhaps about twelve-forty."

She turned to Charlie. "The roads were treacherous. I guess it took me over half an hour to drive here. I'd almost finished my work when a man came in. Scared me at first."

"Was he threatening?"

Her dark eyes were scornful beneath lashes lightly coated with mascara. "Not at all. But I was alone, I didn't recognize him. And it was late."

"How late?" I was watching Charlie work on that pie. A little taste couldn't hurt.

"Why are you so concerned about the time?" Babe's fingers drummed on the counter. I watched the short unpolished nails tap tapping. Then she said, "It was about two."

"You checked the refrigeration for an hour and a half. What have you got down there? A freezing plant?"

"Before I went down to the basement, I made a pot of coffee and had a cup. A circuit had blown and I reset it. Then I took inventory to see if anything had spoiled. I came back upstairs and had some more coffee. That's what I did for an hour and fifteen minutes."

I shrugged. Maybe. Maybe not. "You were telling us about a man who came in."

"Yes. He stood at the door. I thought he was going to turn and leave, but he took off his raincoat and said, `If you're open, I need some coffee. Black and very hot.' He was tall. About six-four. I have a predilection towards tall men."

Was that a dig at me? A sneer at my height? "A predilection?" I said.

"It means I like tall men."

"I'm conversant with the term. Describe him."

"Chalk-striped gray suit. Double breasted with double back vents and pleated trousers with cuffs. A white shirt with a spread collar and a gray satin tie. And a pocket handkerchief - yellow dots on gray silk, with a red border and a red carnation in his buttonhole."

I'm trained to observe. Most people are not. I cocked an eyebrow at Charlie. *Did you hear that?*

Her barely perceptible nod said, *sure did.*

"That's what he was wearing," I said. "What did he look like?"

Babe closed her eyes. "Tall. Thin. A gray mustache and gold framed aviator glasses. Brown eyes. About fifty. A mole on his left cheek."

She opened her eyes again. "I couldn't see his hair. He was wearing a hat. He sat at the counter two seats to the left of where you're sitting.

"When I brought his coffee, his hand shook and he spilled it all over the counter. I stared to wipe it up and he burst into tears. He threw down a five dollar bill and ran out. I heard his car start up. Vroom, vroom, you know? I looked out to see what he was driving."

"And?"

"A silver Jaguar. XK8."

I said, "We don't need to know the color of the upholstery, but did you notice his license plates?"

"A-L-A-N."

"Good girl."

She frowned. "Is that all? Boy?"

What was she so touchy about? She didn't have to bite my head off. I grabbed the last of the pie from Charlie's plate before she could polish it off and chewed slowly, savoring the taste. I'd diet tomorrow.

"What do we owe you?" I said.

"It's on the house."

I stood up, digging in my pocket to pull out some bills. I don't take handouts. Babe shrugged and rang up the sale, the register clanging angrily. She slapped a coin on the counter.

I dropped it, and had to bend to pick it up. I felt her eyes riveted on my bald spot and a self-conscious rush of blood heated my scalp.

"He left his raincoat," she said. "There's nothing in it, no I.D. I looked. It's there, on the coat rack, if you want it."

I straightened up, got into my coat, grabbed the raincoat and threw it over my arm. "Thanks a bunch," I said. "You comin', Charlie?"

CHAPTER EIGHT

Charlie tossed a splintered toothpick and said, "I got a flash for you kid: Babe don't like you."

"I'm way ahead of you," I said. "I figured that out for myself. So I won't ask her for a date."

"Hardy-har-har," she said and rummaged through her pockets.

I said, "There are people in this town who suspect Babe did her last boyfriend in."

"Fucking small towns. Go on. You got my undivided attention."

We race-walked to her car, out of the cold. "He left a big life insurance policy in her name when he died. But the insurance company wouldn't pay."

"Hm." She took a package of gum from her pocket, frowned, replaced it and brought out another. "Easy enough to check that out."

I stretched my hands toward the warmth of the car heater. "Did you question the library director or were you here eating pancakes the whole time?"

"Ashley Taylor? I did. Name like that and the son of a bitch turns out to be a black man."

"I know."

"You didn't bother to let me in on that?"

"Didn't think it was important."

Charlie unwrapped her gum and threw the wrapper on the floor. "He's not very black. What we called high yaller in the old days."

"Bottom line, Charlie."

"He has real attitude. Sticks his head out the window. Says, "You know what time it is?' and slams it shut. Wouldn't come downstairs. Spoke to me over the fucking intercom. I say, `Can I have a word with you?' He says, `No you can't.' Know what, Jake? I'll bet you that Taylor is our nigger in the woodpile."

"'Nigger in the woodpile'? Someone's going to call you racist one day."

"When I have the time, I'll worry about it. You know that statistically most murderers are men. More than half of them are alcoholics or on drugs and they murder their relatives or their neighbors. And mainly they're black."

"Taylor drinks and he's black, so he's our killer?"

"I got a feeling here," she punched her stomach. "When you've been around thirty-four years you'll know what I'm talking about. This guy's a bad ass. There was no way I could persuade the fucker it was in his best interests to talk to me. He says, `Mona was alive when I left her', and shuts off the intercom."

"What did you expect him to say?"

"I did it. I'm guilty."

"Ha! Not in this world."

"I tell ya he's a shifty fucker. Didn't you tell me he tried to off himself?"

"I told you Anne Weston said that."

"Whatever. Listen, he's black, right? Waddaya say we call headquarters and ask Foster to interrogate him."

"Because Foster is black too?"

"Yeah, one brother to another."

"I think I'll take a crack at him first myself."

She shrugged her shoulders. "Be my guest. I bet you don't get anywhere."

"Where will you be?" I said.

"Mineola. Catch up on the paper work. Meet you at the autopsy at ten."

"It's 7:55 now," I said

"Two hours to go. You wanna give me that raincoat? I'll drop it off at forensics."

* * *

I parked the 'Vette on Main Street, retrieved a scarf and knitted cap from the car trunk, wound the scarf up to my nose, and tugged the woolen cap on, fastening the flaps over my ears.

I walked past the Post Office and Flowers by Blossom to the Seaview Department Store, a three-storied gray concrete rectangle. Two big windows displayed an assembly of snow shovels, earmuffs, gloves, yellow slickers and wildly patterned sweaters, all crowding each other on a bed of Styrofoam snowflakes.

The library was above the store, one floor up. A plate glass door at the far end of the building, stenciled in gold with the library hours, was locked. I thumbed the buzzer to the left of the door. After a long minute in the biting wind, I buzzed again.

Upstairs a window wrenched open.

"Jake Harmony, Homicide, down here. Appreciate it if you'd please let me in. I'm freezing to death."

A disembodied voice said, "Wait a minute," and the window closed. I stamped my feet, blew on my gloved hands, watching the clouds my breath made.

It took forever, but the door opened.

An unsmiling honey-skinned man stood in the entry. The red button pinned to the bib of his denim overalls declared *I READ BANNED BOOKS* in white script. He hitched his thumbs through the shoulder straps, and glared at me from startlingly pale blue eyes.

"You Ashley Taylor?"

"I'm Taylor."

Son of a bitch looks like a young Harry Belafonte, I thought. I showed him my gold shield.

He looked briefly down his knife-edged nose at it. "I've already spoken with one detective."

"You haven't spoken to me," I said through teeth beginning to chatter. "If you offered me some hot tea, you'd save me from hypothermia."

Taylor gave me a searching inspection and unexpectedly, smiled. "All right. I live two flights up. One flight up from the library."

He vaulted the steep stairs two at a time. I kept up with him and was only slightly winded when we reached the landing. Square brass plaques were nailed to two of the three doors that opened onto the wide hallway at the right of the stairs. One read TRUTH, the other, BEAUTY.

"The truth is there's not much beauty in this world," I said.

He raised one eyebrow, wrinkling his high forehead. "And not much beauty in truth," he answered. "If truth is beauty and beauty truth, there's a shortage of both these days."

The eyebrow returned to its natural arch but faint lines remained across his forehead. "My apartment is over here." He pointed to the left. "This is the conference room and these two are storerooms. Adult Education keeps their stuff in TRUTH and the Seaview Players use BEAUTY. They rehearse in the conference room."

He added, "And the walls aren't soundproof."

I followed him into a good-sized room stacked with books, and caught a whiff of sweat as he snatched some clothing from a lumpy looking sofa and pitched it into a corner. "Wait here," he said. "I'll get your tea."

I heard water running and the clatter of dishes. He came to the doorway.

"Lemon?"

"Yes, and Sweet'nLow if you've got it."

A few minutes later he came back with a steaming mug and straddled a straight-back chair next to a table heavily scarred with burns.

"Take off that wonky hat, man, and sit down."

I sat opposite him and tried the tea. "Good."

"Sorry I can't offer you a real drink, I got rid of all the booze last night. New Year's resolution."

"I'm good."

"So what do you want from me, Detective Harmony?"

"Answers to one or two questions."

He nodded.

"After you left the Weston's party...."

"I didn't want to go to that damned party." He dug in his overall pockets, found a crushed pack of Camels. "I detest stupidity and Anne Weston is stupid and pretentious to boot. You know what she said the first time we met? To impress me I suppose, she said she reads a lot. What does she read? Biographies."

He tapped out a cigarette. "Whose biographies? You know whose biographies she reads?"

I shook my head.

He lit the cigarette and took a long drag. "Donald Trump. Princess Diana. Why are the people who already know too much the only people who keep trying to learn more?"

"Beats me," I said.

He let a plume of smoke trickle from his nostrils.

"Tony Weston's an all right guy–did the library a big favor. Donated a load of educational films. So when he asked me to give Anne some basic computer lessons...well, I owed him. Mistake!"

"Why?"

"She's a pure white Southern flower and I'm a lowly black. Hated me to be in her parlor."

I said, "I'm sure she didn't..."

Taylor's mirthless laugh mocked my words. "Yes. She did. She thinks my kind should wash floors and sweep the sidewalks and keep their place. Can't figure out how I got to be director here."

I looked into the amber depths of my tea for a while, letting its warmth thaw my hands.

Taylor's words hung in the air. The silence dragged out and then he said, "Poor Tony. Married to that clinging vine. Shee-it. He's fed up to his eyeballs. That's why he was shagging Mona."

"Tony Weston and Mona Raeburn?" I said, thinking about the half buried footprints in the snow I'd seen, leading from the Raeburn's house to the Weston's.

"You heard me." His startling eyes, so unexpectedly light in his honey-skinned face, drilled me.

"How do you know?" I said.

He blew a perfect smoke ring. "He talks. I listen."

The gray smoke flattened out and hung in the air.

"I understand you were the last person to see Mona Raeburn alive," I said.

"You understand wrong. Someone was there, inside, waiting for her."

"Who?"

"Don't know. Mona unlocked the door and a man's voice said, 'Mona? You back already?' She jumped a foot and steered me away. 'Go home, baby,' she said. `I'll call you later.' Slammed the door in my face."

Anger flared in the pale blue eyes and hardened his mouth.

He obviously had a hair-trigger sensitivity to slights. No wonder he'd refused to talk to Charlie. "You didn't recognize the voice?" I said.

"It was a man's."

"Why didn't you tell any of this to Detective Alberts."

"The fat racist bonehead? I wouldn't tell her she had spinach on her teeth. I've been up against her kind before. And I'm not easily intimidated." His proud face said he'd had practice. "She accused me of killing Mona."

"And you deny it?"

"Categorically."

I set the mug on the scarred table "Did the dog bark at you?"

"Why would he bark? I was with Mona."

I tried to jolt him. "I have an eye witness, saw you entering her house."

"Saw me enter?" Taylor mimicked me. "I never got past the door."

I watched the long ash build up on his cigarette, waiting for it to fall.

He shook his head. "You're a detective. You know eye witness identification is unreliable. And how could anybody see me in the dark? Your witness is lying."

"As you said, there's a shortage of truth these days."

"Ha, ha," he said, not amused.

I changed direction. "You slapped Babe Freeman at the Weston party."

He shifted his feet but made no attempt to dislodge the growing ash. Any second now it would fall.

"Someone enjoyed dishing you that story. I'd had a few drinks and I had an arm around Mona. Babe blew up and slapped me. I slapped her back."

"That's what I heard."

"I was sorry I hit her. I would have apologized, but she turned on Mona. Said, `I'm going to kill you, you bitch, if you go near him again.'"

"Unfortunate choice of words, considering," I said.

"Just talk." The cigarette ash spilled down the front of his overall. He made no move to brush it off.

"You say Mona was alive when you left. You didn't go inside with her."

"No."

"You went home, wearing your kilt."

"That's right."

"Will you show it to me, please."

He stood up sending his chair hurtling. "You want to see kilts? Come on. I'll show you kilts!"

He strode into the hallway and unlocked the door marked BEAUTY.

A row of tartans hung on a rack.

"The Seaview Players are rehearsing a play Mona wrote, *Scottish Mists*. As you can see, mine's not the only plaid in town. Take your pick of the cast wardrobe."

"Mona Raeburn wrote the play."

"That's what I said." He tossed his cigarette to the floor and ground it out with his toe. "It opens in two weeks. The world premiere, on the thirteenth."

Friday the thirteenth. I pointed to the blue plaid under Taylor's hand. "That one yours?"

"No, this is the Colquhoun kilt. According to legend, Sir Humphrey Colquhoun had an unlucky affair with a MacFarlane chief's wife. He was captured, butchered and served up to her for dinner. That tartan next to it is the MacFarlane kilt, the scarlet...."

"Yours?"

"No. My clan's the Camerons. Our tartan's the icon of the conqueror. Old Sir Ewen Cameron killed the last wolf in Scotland."

"But your name's Taylor," I said, wondering how this black man could claim to belong to the Cameron clan.

"My father's grandfather was a Cameron of Loch ell. They're descended from the Camerons of Erracht. We trace our family back to the seventeenth century."

Taylor dressed up in a skirt and presto he was a conqueror. And maybe fuddled with enough booze, a murderer.

I said, "I'm not here for a lecture on your family tree or the clans of Scotland. Where's your kilt?"

He slammed the closet door shut. "Did you know that *c-l-a-n-n is Gaelic for family*? Or that the word Scotti is Latin for speaker of Gaelic?"

"Where's your kilt?"

He locked the closet. "Why?"

"Police procedure."

"If you must know, I don't have it."

"Is the Cameron plaid scarlet and green?"

He pulled out his crumpled pack of Camels. "Yes."

"That plaid turned up next to Mona Raeburn's dead body."

He dropped the cigarettes and knelt down to retrieve them, taking longer to do it than necessary.

I turned away and marched back to his apartment, forcing him to follow behind.

"You think it's my tartan you found?" He said when we were inside his apartment. He righted his fallen chair and straddled it again. "I never went into the house."

He lit another cigarette and threw the match on the floor. "So how could it be mine?"

"Maybe one of the wee people who play tricks on the Camerons of Erracht planted it."

"Tony wears the Cameron plaid in *Scottish Mists*." he said.

"You're implying it was Weston who left the kilt we found at the murder scene."

"If the kilt fits.... When Babe hit me, my drink spilled all over mine. I took it off in the car and when I got home I threw it in the car trunk before I went upstairs."

"Let's go down and get it."

"My car was stolen."

I said, "You want to run that by me again?"

"My car was stolen."

"Neat coincidence."

"I reported the theft. Check it out."

"I will."

He dragged on the cigarette he'd been fingering and his pale eyes squinted at me through smoke. Apt, I thought. He'd been putting up a figurative smoke screen.

"What time did you get home?"

"A few minutes past midnight. I know because the church bells were ringing when I got out of the car. And a couple of kids on the parking lot were blowing noisemakers."

"Describe them. Maybe they stole your car."

The ash was building up again, still unnoticed. "I didn't pay attention. No idea what they looked like."

"You got home after midnight, took off your kilt, left it in the car. Then what did you do?"

"I went to bed. Usually, I read for a while but the electricity was out. I fell asleep. When I woke up and looked at my watch, it was five to one. Mona had said she'd call me. I decided to call her."

"And?"

"She picked up the phone and hung it up again."

"This was at five of one?"

"Is it important?"

I nodded.

"Give or take a minute or two. I thought we'd been disconnected and I called back. She kind of mumbled, `I'm sleeping. Call me tomorrow.'"

"You recognized her voice?"

He dragged deeply on the cigarette.

"You'd have recognized Mona's voice?"

"Well, it was hoarse. I'd wakened her."

"She died about one o'clock. You may have been speaking to her murderer. You heard a woman's voice?"

"I'm not sure. I thought it was Mona at first. But then...I expected it to be Mona, you see. At the time, I did think it sounded more like...."

"Like whom?"

He shrugged and more ash spilled down his front. "I don't know. I guess it was Mona."

"Listen," I reached for my coat. "If you should want to talk to me again, here's my pager number."

Taylor ground out his cigarette. "Thanks."

"One thing more. With Mona Raeburn dead, the Seaview Players will cancel the play, right?"

"No, I expect Audrey will do it."

"Audrey Raeburn?"

"She was Mona's understudy. I used to hear her rehearsing with Tony. I told you, these walls aren't soundproof. Maybe they were acting." Taylor's pale eyes flickered. "It sounded to me like they were... talking business."

The expression was unfamiliar to me, but his meaning was clear.

"O.K. I'm off." I bundled up to face the cold and walked downstairs. If Taylor was speaking the truth, who was the man waiting for Mona? Not Weston, he was at home with Anne and Babe before midnight.

I opened the outer door to a blast of cold air. The stolen car story could be confirmed.

Taylor had thrown me a few zingers. For one, he'd accused Tony Weston of having an affair with the victim and at the same time, making love to her daughter; for another he'd implied that the kilt we found at the crime scene was Weston's. I would ask Anne if she knew where Weston's kilt was. And get to see her again.

My windshield was iced up. I started the 'Vette, turned on the defroster and waited for the ice to melt. If Taylor thought that the voice answering the phone wasn't Mona's, did he know whose it was?

I pulled out and headed west on Main Street.

CHAPTER NINE

In front of the mobile crime lab, I turned off the motor, slumped against the upholstery and sat shifting my car keys from one hand to the other, ruminating. Anne had said Poochy woke her up `barkin' his fool head off at Taylor.' But Taylor drove home at least an hour before she fell asleep. So who had the dog barked at? If he'd barked.

And she said she'd heard Poochy bark at Fred Raeburn. An impossibility. Raeburn had already killed the dog.

Witnesses often misremember what they've seen. Anne had been sleepy. She had a migraine headache. She....

Even if I didn't want to believe it, Anne Weston was very much a murder suspect. What if she'd discovered Mona and Weston together....

I nudged myself into action. Too cold to sit out here.

Inside, Sergeant Wolfe was sifting through a box of Mona Raeburn's effects.

I pulled up a chair next to her. "What have you got for me, Wolfie?"

"Want to see Raeburn's checkbook?"

"Not now. What else have you got?"

She held up a black crocodile Filofax. It had been cleaned out of last year's appointments and refilled with six month's worth of blank violet pages. There was only one entry for this year: Friday, January 13. One notation on that page was heavily underscored by a black felt tip pen: Scottish Mists.

Thanks to Taylor, I knew what that meant. "Do we have her address book?"

"In the box."

I dug through the papers, found a small book that matched the Filofax and flipped to the listings under `B.`

Alan Berger had a whole chapter.

He had a home number, an office number, an 800 number, a beach house number, a beeper and a cell phone. There was an E-mail address and a fax number. Extension numbers and beeper numbers for two assistants were listed as well.

Evelyn Blackmon, the name after Berger had almost as many listings. I called her home and office numbers and left messages on the answering machines asking her to call me. She wasn't available on her beeper or cell phone. I sent an Email with the same message.

I ran both names through the computer. No Evelyn Blackmon. But Berger had been arrested in 1995 for non-payment of alimony and I had him.

He was an agent with Original Artists on West Fifty-fifth Street in Manhattan. He was forty-seven years old, divorced, and had earned two hundred thou a year for the last four years. The Jag was leased but he owned a condo on Riverside Drive and a house in Bridgehampton.

I looked at my watch. It was 9:10. Time to rev up with some coffee and drive to headquarters for the autopsy.

My father had taken me to my first autopsy when I was eleven years old. Me and my brother, Phil. It wasn't so much different than watching him eviscerate the deer he killed on our hunting trips. Phil and I still drive up to our cabin in the Adirondacks every year on the third Saturday of October, the first day of the hunting season.

My father, like his cop father before him, had wanted us to see the procedures and not be afraid. Afterwards he drove us into the city to the Second Avenue Deli where I enjoyed the first of many meals there: split pea soup and an extra greasy salami and egg sandwich.

After this autopsy was completed, Charlie and I drove to the Seaview Diner to go over the results.

"Lunchtime," Charlie'd said. "Good burgers at the Seaview Diner."

"Trust you to know where the food is."

"First things first, kid."

* * *

Tantalizing smells of fried onions, fresh baked bread and brewing coffee greeted me as I parked beside Charlie's dark blue Ford and locked the 'Vette. I cast a nervous eye at the pond for signs of the pack of wild cats. Not one in sight.

Inside, I said, "Hi," to a frizzy-haired woman behind the cash register, but her cheery smile and fluttering false eyelashes were for a lanky man outfitted in a gray warm-up suit, not for me.

At the end of the crowded diner, Charlie's big butt hung over the edge of a counter-stool, exactly as it had six hours ago. Her strident voice rang out clearly over the lunchtime din: "Over easy. I don't like 'em runny but I won't eat 'em petrified either. I'm fussy about my eggs. I'll send them back if they're not just right. I'm telling you up front. Pay attention and you'll get a good tip."

I sat down next to her.

This waitress was a small neat woman with neat blonde hair scraped back into a snood trimmed with sequined red bows. She wore a white shirt with 'Josie' embroidered in red script across the breast pocket. It was the same style white shirt Babe had worn. Josie filled it out better.

"We make eggs here the way we make them," she said. "You eat them the way you get them or you can eat somewhere else. Got it?"

Charlie swiveled around to face me, her bloodhound face split with a smile. "The customer is never right."

"I'll have an egg white omelet and a toasted English, no butter," I said.

Josie's ballpoint pen hovered above her order pad. "That's one dollar extra for the omelet."

"Okay."

"What?" Charlie said. "Why charge more to leave something out?"

Josie said, "It's one dollar extra."

"Let it go, Charlie," I said, and ordered a diet Dr. Pepper, lemon, no ice.

"Diet Coke, Diet Pepsi or Sprite. No Dr. Pepper."

"Coke."

Josie pushed through the swinging doors into the kitchen.

"I thought you wanted a cheeseburger," I said.

"I didn't have breakfast. I like to start my day with eggs no matter what time it is. I'll have the burger too, if I'm still hungry."

The man on the stool next to me stopped slurping his soup and stared at us.

I said, "Let's move to a booth."

We settled in on clean white banquettes at a clean white table. From a basket of assorted breads, Charlie reached for a corn muffin. Under her shapeless tweed jacket, her rumpled shirt gaped open at the buttonholes and crept out of her waistband.

She doused the muffin with maple syrup and stuffed it in her mouth. "In a place like this, never order scrambled eggs," she said. "They beat up a batch in the morning and let them stand all day. You always gotta order either sunny side up or poached."

I hate when Charlie pontificates, especially when her mouth is full.

We spread our autopsy notes on the table. Charlie looked at them shaking her head.

"What?" I said.

"The deceased was a very friendly woman."

"You draw that conclusion because of the semen found in her body cavity?"

"Fuckin' right," she said, "I mean, petechiae in the conjunctuva: expected. Time of death, approximately 12:30 to 2:00a.m. also, expected. Death by asphyxiation, we knew that too. But there was a fuckin' parade at the Raeburn's before she got murdered."

"Everybody and his brother," I said.

"Fuckin' Grand Central Station. One after the other, in and out of that house." She ticked them off on her stubby fingers. "Ashley Taylor, the librarian, and Fred Raeburn the victim's ex- husband, and then her agent, Alan Berger. Three guys."

"Fred wasn't invited," I said. "But there's another man. According to Taylor, he called out to Mona from inside, before midnight."

"So that's four. One of them had sex with her before she was killed. Who?"

Charlie's hand hovered over the bread basket and nabbed a sticky bun. "And little Mrs. Weston, so eager to help you. Doesn't she seem a little too cooperative–looking out her window taking notes like she was paid to do it."

I felt my face flush. "I think she's attracted to me."

"Kiddo, this is a m-u-r-d-e-r case."

"You don't have to remind me." I felt unexpectedly defensive. I was keeping what I'd seen in the Weston Bible to myself for the moment.

She bit into the bun and licked her fingers.. "I don't think you've got the right attitude here, kid, if you get my drift."

"I'm thirty-three years old, Charlie. Stop calling me kid."

"Okay. I'll call you dumb fuck."

Josie served our eggs.

Charlie sprinkled hers with about an inch of salt

My egg whites had been cooked in so much grease I might as well have ordered them intact. A half pound of home fries accompanied them. Hungry, I blotted up some of the grease with my napkin and dug in. Charlie dumped what was left of the ketchup bottle over her plate. We ate in silence.

Josie approached us softly in her white Reeboks, wiped her small neat hands on her black apron and stood in front of our booth watching as Charlie mopped up the last crumbs with buttered toast. "Everything all right, here?"

Charlie held up her right hand, making a circle with her thumb and forefinger. "A gourmet like myself, Charlie Alberts, wants to tell you, those eggs were perfect."

Josie's eyes flicked a question at my plate.

"They're fine," I said. "I eat slow."

"Our special tonight is lobster ravioli with jalapeno pesto sauce."

"That so," Charlie said, "Save a double order for me."

I said, "You just finished lunch."

"That's when I start to think about what I'll have for dinner."

Waitresses and bus boys scurried between the tables, adding their clatter to the sounds of chatter and laughter and the intermittent clang of the cash register. No sign of Babe.

Josie began to clear away our dishes. "Babe around?" I asked.

"She's in the kitchen."

"Tell her Detective Harmony wants to talk to her."

"She's busy."

"Tell her."

"She won't like that." Josie slapped our bill down and turned on her heel.

Charlie took out a small mirror and picked at her front teeth as I checked the addition.

The double stainless steel doors to the kitchen flew open and Babe Freeman emerged in a drift of soap-smelling steam. She stood tensed for a moment, her eyes sweeping the occupied tables. Then she strode toward us, rolling down her white shirt sleeves. "How can you be so inconsiderate?" she said. "Can't you see that I'm harried at the moment?"

I reached over and fastened her cuff button, beckoning for the other arm. She allowed herself to be helped with restrained distrust. "I suppose you have more questions."

"That's right," I said.

Her eyebrows drew together in annoyance. "What are you waiting for, then?"

She slid into the booth beside Charlie.

"You are, or you were, engaged to Ashley Taylor," I began.

"What business is that of yours?" she said. "Oh, I see...the fight we had over that scheming bitch, Mona. That was a valuable learning experience."

I cut to the chase. "You followed Taylor and the victim and knocked on the door but they didn't let you in."

"Aren't you well informed," Babe said.

"A little after midnight this was?"

She raised her shoulders and lowered them again. Couldn't care less.

"Then you drove here, to the diner."

"I told you that!"

I didn't believe she'd spent an hour and a quarter alone here. I said, "I don't think so. I think you went back to the Raeburn house."

"No." Her tongue flicked across her lips. "Well, not exactly."

"Either you did or you didn't," Charlie said quietly.

Babe focused on a stack of paper napkins, aligning them. "I did start to come here to check on the generator. As I told you. But I changed my mind—on an impulse I turned around and drove back to see if Taylor was still with Mona."

She stopped fussing with the napkins and looked past me to Charlie. "I was so furious. If I had seen that miserable–if I had seen Taylor leaving at that moment, instead of...." She dropped her eyes. "If I had seen Taylor then, I think I would have run him down."

"Instead of whom?" I said.

Babe buried her face in her hands.

"Who'd you see?" Charlie said.

Her hands fell to her side and she shook her head.

"Come on!" I pressed, "You saw–"

Her lips barely moved. "Tony."

I flashed a look at Charlie and she took it from there.

"You saw Tony Weston leaving the Raeburn house?"

She nodded.

"It was dark. How can you be sure?"

"I saw him in my headlights before I turned them off. He ran across Mona's lawn and back into his own house."

I said, "He didn't see you?"

"No, I don't think so. He was in a hurry to get home."

"Did you hear the dog bark?"

She took some time to think about that. "I was in my car with the doors and windows closed."

"But you didn't see Taylor," I said.

"His car was gone."

"What time was this?"

"You're always asking what time it was."

"So answer me."

"If you must have a time, say 12:45."

"The time you originally said you arrived at the diner and checked the generator and took inventory etc. etc."

"Yes."

"Why didn't you tell us this before?" Charlie said. "Why protect Weston?"

She lifted her pointed chin, "Because I was afraid you would think Tony killed Mona. He could never...."

Behind us dishes clattered, and a woman's laugh joined a man's baritone.

Babe lowered her voice. "You don't know him. Tony's not capable of murder."

"But you are," I said.

"I don't know." With a tight smile, she added, "Isn't there a law against it?"

She picked up a napkin and tore it to shreds. "I'll tell you one thing, though, if you ever find Taylor murdered, you can come looking for me."

"When you returned to the Raeburn house, how did you feel?" I said.

"What do you mean? How should I have felt?"

I realized suddenly that her dark eyes were blue. Very dark blue.

"Were you angry? Angry enough to go inside and kill Mona Raeburn?"

"You cretin," she said and stood up.

Maybe she killed Mona Raeburn and maybe she didn't, but she sure wanted to kill me at that moment.

I said, "I'm not finished questioning you."

"Yes, you are. Until you come back with a warrant. Good afternoon, gentlemen."

We watched her go through the swinging doors into the kitchen.

"I knew it was Weston's footprints I saw in the snow!" I said.

Charlie stood up and brushed the crumbs from her slacks. "Just 'cause you think Mrs. Weston's got the hots for you, kid– that don't make her husband a murderer. You don't know whose fucking footprints you saw."

"Why don't you go take a flying leap in the toilet, Charlie?"

I glanced out the window. "Charlie!"

She bent down to peer out the window with me.

Outside, Ashley Taylor staggered across the parking lot to the diner's rear entrance behind the kitchen. He turned his back to the wind, and crouched down. Then he tossed aside a bottle and covered his ears with gloved hands.

"He's had a few," Charlie said.

Babe came out, enveloped in a mink coat, and wrestled the wind to close the back door. She headed for the parking lot, walking past Taylor as if he were invisible. He ran after her, running unsteadily and caught up to her just as she got to her car, grabbing her arm. Babe wrenched it away, climbed into a Lincoln Navigator and locked the doors. Taylor banged on the windows with both hands.

"Jake?"

We sprinted for the door without our coats, but we were still about forty paces away when Babe slid the car window open and raised her face to Taylor.

We stopped short and watched. He was obviously pleading. She gave him a curt nod, motioned him into the car, and they drove off.

Charlie shivered beside me in the wind. She turned up her jacket collar.

"Think she's taking him to some deserted place to murder him?"

"I'm going home to bed," I said.

CHAPTER TEN

I was so tired, I felt drunk as I drove home to the guest cottage on Henry's estate where I'd been living since my divorce. Henry built the cottage after Laura and Phil were married but Laura likes to stay in the main house when they visit, so the place was unoccupied until I'd come to stay for a few days after I left my now ex-wife, Paula. I was still here three years later.

Henry and I are no romance, but we get along.

I went in the main entrance where the gardeners, Bennett and Willard, had cleared and sanded the drive. My remote opened the wrought-iron gates. It was an easy drive along the curving road to Henry's Garage Mahal.

I pushed the remote again to raise the garage door, and docked the 'Vettte next to Henry's Mercedes SUV, my mother's Mercedes, Henry's Bentley and the little Miata I use when the 'Vette's in the body shop in Ozone Park.

My 1969 'Vette is a dream car. I was born in 1969. Henry gave it to me for my twenty-first birthday. Before I told him I was going to be a cop like my Dad, and his Dad before him, instead of going to Law School.

The garage doors rolled down behind me and I jogged the few bitter cold yards to the guest house, carrying my duffle bag. The wind lifted the snow and hurled it at me in gusts. If the path had been shoveled here, new snowfall had buried it again.

I went in the back door that's always left open. The gardeners keep stuff in my fridge so they don't have to go all the way back to the gate house when they're working at this end.

I was sixteen, my brother Phil nineteen and Laura, twenty, when her father, Henry Slater, married my mother. I fell in love with Laura with all my sixteen year old heart, trailing after her like a pet puppy, trembling for attention. She was kind to me and to my dazzled eyes she seemed not only beautiful but wise. She was the only brightness in my life during that period of grief for my father.

I went away to college after she married my brother, Phil. To Berkeley, which was as far away as I could get and met Paula in my senior year.

I set my 9mm Glock on the night table next to the bed, pulled off my boots, wiped the boots down, treed them, shelved them in the shoe closet, fell on the bed and went unconscious.

When I woke up, it was dark. My watch read 11:30. I stretched, got out of bed and went to the kitchen. There was a tray of chicken sandwiches from the party on the counter. I unwrapped two and wolfed them down.

I bundled the sweater I was wearing and the bloodstained tux into a bag for the dry cleaner to pick up. The blood stains evoked a vivid memory of the Peke's crushed head. Fred had said he killed the dog and tore the room apart looking for cash.

He had means, opportunity and motive. The pillow was at hand; he was at the crime scene, and he wanted Mona's money. He wouldn't inherit directly, but he would gain control of it as Audrey's guardian.

I stripped off my jeans and jockey shorts and dumped them with my tuxedo shirt and black silk socks into the clothes hamper. I took a long hot shower and brushed my teeth, looking at myself in the bathroom mirror. At the rate I was losing my hair, I'd be bald in a couple of years. Rogaine, supposedly helps, but I already take TheoDur and Clortrimitron for allergies. How much medication is too much?

I tapped the bathroom scale. "Enter your memory number," it said. "Please step on the scale."

In a cartoon I'd taped to the scale, a husband is telling his tearful wife not to weigh herself after she eats. Wise advice.

But I needed to know just how bad the news was.

"Your weight is one hundred eighty-three pounds. You have gained two pounds. Have a nice day."

The outer limits.

I repacked the duffle with a change of clothes, laid out a pair of jeans and a N.Y. Giants sweatshirt for the morning, set the alarm, and flopped on the bed, my laptop on my knees.

I started to write up my report making sure to state all the facts as far as I knew them to date, omitting my speculation:

Had Mona Raeburn's murderer found what he'd been looking for? What did the kilt mean? Maybe nothing, maybe everything.

Henry belongs to the Book of the Month Club and never refuses a selection. But in among his unread best sellers in their bright dust jackets, he's assembled a definitive collection on fashion.

I'd go to the main house and look up kilts. Right now.

Outside, a deep blanket of snow glistened, untracked to the edge of the evergreens. Cold air whistled through the windowpane. Tomorrow would do. I went back to sleep.

* * *

Sunlight streaming through the window woke me at seven-thirty before the alarm went off. I switched off the alarm, got out of bed, had a quick shower, shaved, and entered my memory number on the scale. It was eight hours since I'd last weighed in.

"Your weight is one hundred eighty-two pounds. You have lost one pound. Have a good day."

If I watched what I ate today, I could maybe lose another pound. I dressed and pulled on black lizard boots. In my boots, I'm five foot seven and a half. As tall as Robert Redford.

I made a stab at straightening the quilt and looked out at the morning. The clouds had blown away and sun flooded the ice-crusted snow, dazzling my eyes.

I opened the fridge, flipped open a can of Diet Dr. Pepper, switched on WLIW while I drank it, wound a scarf around my neck, slapped the knit cap on my head and shrugged into the shearling coat. I tossed the empty container into the recycling bin, turned off the radio and headed for the main house.

Not a creature was stirring this early. I punched in the alarm code, made my way to the library and searched through the bookshelves with my pocket flash. I found a paperback, *The Highland Clans*, tucked it into my pocket, opened the door to slip out again and almost crashed into Henry, toting a 12 gauge Browning in unsteady hands.

"Jesus, Henry," I said, "You scared the daylights out of me."

"How do you think I feel?" Anger mottled his face. "Shit, Jake!" He lowered the shotgun. "I could have killed you. What the hell are you doing creeping around at this hour?"

Recovering from the shock of gunmetal blue steel pointed at my heart, I said, "I came to borrow a book."

"I could have killed you," he said.

"This book," I said "I'm off to work. See you later."

He stood there splay footed, wrapped in a purple silk robe that only half covered his hairy bowed legs, and watched me head out, scowling speechlessly after me.

Henry had a gun. I never knew that.

CHAPTER ELEVEN

My car phone rang.

"Mornin, Jake," Charlie said. "Did you want me to check out the houses in the Raeburn's cul-de-sac before I report in?"

"Good idea. I'm on my way to Gresham Trucking. We'll meet up about 10:00 and drive into the city to check out Berger."

"The agent."

"Right."

"The MBU at 10. O.K."

I smiled to myself. She meant our mobile bus unit. Charlie loves to use initials. I almost said,' Roger and out'.

On Merrick Road, I overshot the Gresham Trucking lot, backed up, made a U turn and drove along the chain link fence to the entrance. The lot was full of bright yellow trucks sporting a blue Gresham Trucking logo.

I parked in a visitor's slot and crunched my way across cinder strewn ice to the warehouse. It was painted a vivid blue and flanked by flagpoles waving American flags. I shoved the entrance door open onto a dimly lit hallway.

A woman in a stretched out purple cardigan, and a yellow baseball cap waddled out of a door on the right. Her suspicious blue eyes peered out of folds of fat. "Who're you and wadda ya want?"

I flashed my smile and my badge. "Detective Harmony to see Mr. Gresham."

Her flat voice leached from her wide flat nose. "I'll ask."

She turned and waddled down to the far end of the hall. Ten seconds later, a door was yanked open and a man's head bobbed out.

"In here."

I negotiated the length of the crate-piled hall, the sound of my boot heels muffled by the shouts and curses and crashings, and the grinding of gears on the other side of the wall.

A mean-looking geezer, in a cut off sweat shirt that bared his ropy arms, gestured me into a cubby-hole of an office. Blue-white fluorescents strobed the windowless space.

"Jake Harmony. Homicide."

"Lloyd Gresham, trucking. Take a pew."

His voice was gravelly. It could even be described as hoarse - like the voice Taylor described on Mona Raeburn's telephone the night she was killed.

Gresham shuffled the chaos of papers on his desk, his shrewd eyes watching me settle into the cracked leather chair facing him.

I went into a spasm of sneezing.

"Water," I gasped.

He disappeared into a tiny closet. The tap ran, and then his liver spotted hands offered me a plastic cup.

"Sorry," I said when I could speak again, "It's the dust.

"What dust?" he said.

His pink scalp, mottled with brown scaly patches, had a tuft or two of white hair left on it. His eyes were underlined by dark gray circles. Bad casting for the role of Mona's lover, I thought.

I said, "I'm investigating Mona Raeburn's death."

"Yeah. I read about it in Newsday. Terrible thing. Ya want more water?"

"I'm good. That's an impressive fleet of trucks on your lot."

"Gresham Trucking's primo on the South Shore." He rifled the papers on his desk. "Up to my neck. Is this gonna take long?"

"Thing is, your name turned up among Mona Raeburn's effects."

"So? Everyone in Seaview has my name."

"Tell me about your relationship with her."

Gresham had powerful shoulder and arm muscles, and they rippled. "Wadda ya mean relationship? I knew her. There ain't no 'relationship'. I'm a respectable citizen of this community. Married to the same woman for forty-eight years."

I sneezed. And sneezed again and again.

Gresham retreated behind his desk, lowering himself into his chair. "I better not catch whatever it is you got."

I gasped. "I'm allergic to dust."

"Then maybe you should get outta here. Jeez. Nobody but you ever complained about dust."

When the sneezing fit subsided, I said, "About Mrs. Raeburn… if you read about it in Newsday, you know she was murdered."

"Yeah, and that's all I know. What I read." He half-rose from his chair, his instinct to pick me up and throw me out.

I was smaller than he was and I was sticking my nose in his privates. But I was the law so he wasn't about to do anything but ripple those thick muscles.

We sat and stared at each other for a while.

"Listen, I knew the lady," he said. "Period. No 'relationship'."

"You were friends."

"Business associates. She wanted me to invest in her play."

"You're interested in theater?"

"I'm interested in trucking. But these days it's good to diversify. Mona heard how I'm a venture capitalist. That's how come she came to me."

The office door flew open and a sweating giant in a Gresham Trucking shirt stood in the doorway. "What ya want we should do with the shipment for 38th Street? Customs just called in the release."

"Who's at Kennedy?"

"No one." The giant tugged at the diamond stud in his left ear. "Artie's in Richmond Hill."

"So get him to Kennedy."

The door slammed.

I said, "Did you invest?"

"We were discussing. Nothing definite. Mona had eyes for Broadway. Well, Off-Broadway. Her idea was the Seaview Players should give it a try-out, here in Seaview. I said after the preview, I'd decide. Yes. No."

The door flew open again. "That's C.O.D., right?"

"Damn frigging right. Be sure Artie gets the cash before he unloads."

I waited for the door to close. "Is it a good play?"

"How do I know?" He crumpled a paper and smoothed it out. "Mona acted out some of it for me, private. A reading, she called it. I guess it was O.K."

"You didn't read it?"

"I was gonna see it, wasn't I? I don't read no plays. You read plays?"

"Occasionally. You and Mrs. Raeburn were business associates."

"I told ya."

"And you were friends."

"Friends? Yeah, you could say that."

"There was an autopsy," I said. "In the police lab we can test any nucleated cells - saliva, skin, hair. A strand of hair, pubic hair for instance, can be matched up exactly to a sample of the semen we found in her body. Like fingerprints."

He picked up one of his invoices, studied it for a while, threw it back on his desk. "Yeah," he said. "I see all that on TV all the time. Last week on Law and Order that's how they nailed a rapist. His DNA"

"And that's how we'll identify the man who was with Mrs. Raeburn the night she died."

"What are you inferring here? That it was me?"

"Was it?"

"Fuck you."

"How friendly were you and Mrs. Raeburn?"

He sat back in his chair and scratched his lower lip with his ring finger, measuring me. "O.K. O.K. So we went to bed together a couple of times. It was no big deal. Strictly sex."

The semen in Mona Raeburn's body cavity was Gresham's? I looked at his mottled pink scalp, the tufts of white hair, the liver spots. The guy was seventy at least. I was impressed.

"If you were with her on New Year's Eve it is a big deal."

"Yeah? How's that?"

"If you were the last person to see her alive."

"For the record, I was with her. But the last guy to see her alive was the creep that murdered her. And that wasn't me."

He hunkered over the oak desk and pulled open a drawer, straightening up with a bottle of Jack Daniels in his hand.

"Give me your cup."

I shook my head. "I'm on duty."

He tipped the bottle into his mouth, took a long swallow, and set it on the desk in front of him.

"It was just sex with me and Mona. She didn't want more than that and I didn't neither. Just sex. She made me feel young, you know? No. You wouldn't know, you are young." He wiped his mouth with the back of his hand.

I said, "I'm trying to put together the sequence of events before Mrs. Raeburn died. I'd like to hear the true version for once."

"Nothing I say here gets back to my wife. Understood?"

"That depends on what you tell me."

"I don't want my wife should find out I was with Mona. She'd go nuts."

"I won't tell her if I don't have to."

He lifted the powerful shoulders in a shrug. "My wife is with her family in Florida for the holidays. New Year's Eve I'm feeling lonely. So I visit Mona, we have some friendly drinks together. She's going to a party, but I come over early and we bounce around in the sack. After, I watched her get dressed, pour herself into a tight green dress. She said, `You look too fucked out to move. Stay a while. Lock the door behind you when you go.'

"I had a snooze. When I woke up the electricity was out. I'm getting dressed in the dark when I hear Mona's key in the door. And she's talking to some guy. "

The office door opened again, pushed in by the fat woman's rump. She dumped an armful of papers on his desk.

"For Chrissake, Judy! What's all this?"

"Invoices. They can't go out if you don't sign 'em. I got people out there, waiting on you."

"I'll sign, I'll sign. Gimme another minute here."

Gresham waited until she left and then he said, "Where was I? Yeah, Mona was opening the door and she wasn't alone. I called out to her and when she realized I was there, she shooed him off."

"You're sure it was a man with her."

"I'm sure."

"Was Mrs. Raeburn upset that you hadn't left?"

"Hell no. Mona was always glad to see me. We went into the TV room. Had a midnight drink to the New Year. And to the future. She lit candles. One thing led to another...you know and there she was stark naked in my lap. Except she had on her necklace."

"Describe the necklace."

"Gold, with a shitload of diamonds that spells Mona. She liked to wear it when she did it. After, we're laying on the couch together and she was dead to the world. I figured to let her sleep it off and got dressed. Just pulling my galoshes on when that pansy waltzed through the front door."

"Who?"

"Tony Weston. Too much at home, if you want to know. Had a key. I grabbed my coat and faded out the back door. Didn't want him to see me."

Two witnesses now placed Weston at the crime scene. Babe Freeman and Gresham.

"You could see Weston in the candlelight?"

"Saw him and heard him calling to Mona."

"When Weston came in, did the dog bark?"

His face turned an unattractive purple. "Yeah, but see, Mona always locked him up when we...did it."

"When you left, the dog was locked up?"

"I didn't let him out."

"Weston came in and you went out the back door. Mrs. Raeburn was asleep."

"Right."

"Where did you go?"

"Home. I went home and called my wife and wished her and her whole frigging Florida family a Happy New Year and then I had a couple more drinks and went to bed."

I stood up and shrugged into my jacket. "I'll get out of your way now. Be at Mineola headquarters tomorrow morning at 9:30 to sign a statement."

"I ain't signin' nuttin'."

"Your wife doesn't know about you and Mona. I wouldn't want to have to ask her questions that...."

"Who in hell do you think you are? Get your ass out of here before I burn it. I got influential friends. Politicians. Judges. They won't like it, me being harassed."

"You've been lying to your wife for forty-eight years, so just in case you're lying to me too, I need your signed statement."

"Get this straight. When I left Mona she was alive and happy and satisfied. You know what I mean? Satisfied? Ya wanna know who killed her? Talk to Weston."

He went to the door and threw it open. "You're outta here, cop. We got no more to say."

"See you tomorrow. 9:30. Be on time."

CHAPTER TWELVE

I took a short cut to the mobile bus unit, the wrong way down a one way street that brought me out on Wellington Road. I took the turn on two wheels and skidded into a parking space.

It was 9:45 and Charlie was waiting for me.

"Ready to move out?"

"Feel my head, Charlie. I think I've got a fever."

She swiped her hand across my forehead. "Nah, you're cool. Let's go. Where we going?"

"Original Artists Inc. 56 West 55th Street."

"I'm driving," she said, holding up a finger. "One, we can't park that hot-rod of yours on a city street and two, I don't like the way you drive."

"Pack up your bubble gum, Charlie, and let's go."

On the Long Island Expressway going west toward the city she cut off a semi trailer belching clouds of black smoke. The driver honked his road rage. A milk truck's horn joined the serenade as Charlie cut across him into the fast lane. My right foot moved in a futile braking motion.

"Relax," Charlie said. "There's only one brake."

I decided that if this was my day to die, so be it.

She peeled away from the car in front, passed it and cut back into the fast lane.

"I checked out the five houses on the cul-de-sac," she said. The two couples living in numbers one and two went to Las Vegas together and won't be back until the end of the week. The Weston house is number three; the Raeburn house is number four. Mr. and Mrs. Fletcher in number five are in their eighties. Very sweet old couple. They went to bed at nine o'clock."

She popped watermelon gum into her mouth and stuck the wrapper in the ashtray.

"Let's talk, Charlie. What do we know about this case?"

"You talk. I'm driving."

"All right." I told her about Gresham's testimony.... "So we know that Taylor never got a toe in the door when he brought Mrs. Raeburn home. Gresham was already in the house and he confirms Taylor's story. Remember Taylor said that when he heard a man's voice call out from the house, he left without going inside.

"She had sex with Gresham. He admitted it. Says he was with her until he heard Weston come in."

"Bull!" Charlie said. "I know that fucking kilt we found next to the body is Taylor's and the forensics report is gonna prove it. He must have come back later."

"Why would he leave his kilt next to the body?"

"Compulsion to confess?"

"His kilt is in his car somewhere," I said.

"He says."

"He also says Weston has a kilt identical to his. Listen to me, Mona Raeburn was alive when Gresham left and Weston arrived. My question is, was she still alive when Weston left?"

"Why do you think she was alive when Gresham left?"

"Because I believe his story and because I think Weston killed her."

"But," Charlie said, "we gotta look at all the angles. What if Weston tells us he found the victim dead, when we question him?"

"Then we're back to Gresham."

"I say Taylor came back."

"His car was stolen."

The bubble gum snapped. "He's got legs."

I wrinkled my nose at the sugary fruit odor. "If Taylor walked to the Raeburn house in that storm, he wouldn't have made it back within the time frame unless he flew. He lives ten, fifteen minutes away by car."

"Next."

"Babe Freeman," I said.

"No way. She rapped on the door, got no answer, drove to the diner, changed her mind and drove back in time to see Weston leaving the crime scene."

Charlie was tooling along, her right hand playing through her hair and two fingers of her left hand resting lightly on the steering wheel.

I said, "She has no alibi from the time she saw Weston leave at 12:45 until Alan Berger came into her diner at 1:50. An hour."

"I don't know. She went from the Raeburns' to the diner, checked the refrigerators, took inventory, made coffee..."

"Charlie! That's what she told us. We don't know what she did in the diner. Or when she got there."

"The coffee was ready when Berger came in. Shit! She didn't know ahead of time she'd have to account for every minute. Plenty of innocent people don't remember what they did night before last. And can't prove it if they do. Weak alibis don't mean guilty. Talk about alibis! How do we know Mrs. Weston didn't pop in next door and do the job when nobody was looking?"

"We don't know," I said. "She could have. What we know is Mrs. Raeburn was dead when Fred Raeburn left. He either found her dead or ... left her dead."

Charlie maneuvered across two lanes without signaling. I closed my eyes and tried to rub the tension out of my neck.

She said, "We don't have enough of the pieces yet. Tell you what I'm gonna do. I'm gonna take the Grand Central and get out at Northern Boulevard. Stop at White Castle."

"It's not even eleven o'clock. You want lunch already?"

"Who said anything about lunch? Couple of White Castle hamburgers isn't lunch. I hardly had any breakfast."

"I bet. What did you have? A short stack of pancakes?"

"Don't be a smartass. I had two egg McMuffins. What did you?"

"Diet Dr. Pepper."

"No wonder you're so jumpy."

We picked up a sack of hamburgers with extra pickles and backed out onto Northern Boulevard headed west.

The Empire State Building came into view.

"Almost there, Charlie. Traffic's light."

Near the 59th Street Bridge, construction workers waved us into a single lane and stalled traffic clogged the approach.

"Shit!" Charlie said. "Why'd you open your mouth? You jinxed us."

"We made good time until now. Take the upper level."

We sat on the bridge for twenty minutes and I watched the four Con Ed chimneys discharging their fat clouds of pollution while I ate six of the little hamburgers.

The skyline loomed up, New York's great wall of glass pasted against the dull gray sky. The buildings fronting the East River from the southern tip of Manhattan northward were as recognizable as celebrated stars. I gave them a friendly nod.

The Twin Towers, the green rectangle of the UN, the Empire State spire, the Chrysler building, and the white slice of the Citicorp scraped the wintry sky, their thousands of windows blankly unlit at this hour.

"New York, New York," I said, feeling the thrill I always get seeing the skyline. "I love this city."

"There's nothin' here we don't have just as good on the Island. Without the hassle."

"We don't have this," I said, pointing to the view.

"Who needs it?"

Traffic in our lane began to move. Charlie was about to make the turn to exit the bridge, when a taxi driver yelled, 'Move it lady,' gave her the finger and cut us off.

"That son of a bitch! Did you see him?"

We were stuck behind a back-firing bus at a red light. When it turned green, Charlie zoomed down Second Avenue weaving in and out until she caught up to the cabbie. She leaned on the horn, cut in front of the taxi, and turned west on 55th street.

We crawled behind a clanking garbage truck all the way past Third, Lexington and Park. Even with our windows closed, it reeked. The truck turned off on Fifth and we found a parking spot near the corner of Sixth, in front of a space created by a roped-off open manhole.

At the entrance to number 56, a bundle of rags held up a hand lettered sign: *I HAVEN'T EATEN IN THREE DAYS.* I threw a fiver into the cup beside him and looked away. I'd help him but I couldn't look at him. Three days with no food?

"God bless you. Have a good day." The cracked voice trailed after us as I circled through the revolving doors with Charlie behind me, and walked down a cavernous lobby to the bank of elevators.

Charlie ran a finger down the glass encased directory.

"Original Artists. On thirty -four."

CHAPTER THIRTEEN

I leaned against the marble wall stabbing the up button until the elevator doors glided open in front of us. On the way up to Original Artists, we had to listen to the speakers pipe out 'Jingle Bell Rock'. Real original artists would have had a better sound track.

At the fourteenth floor, the doors opened onto a glass wall with a breathtaking view of the city up Sixth Avenue to the north. The rest of the reception room was covered in walnut, all sixty feet of it. From behind a curved desk facing the elevators, a snooty blonde wearing New York black said, "Can I help you?"

"We're here to see Alan Berger."

"Do you have an appointment?" Not too much disdain in the voice in case we turned out to be Somebodies.

"No appointment." I flashed my badge.

She worked the console and gestured, "Have a seat in reception. Someone will be out to take you in."

Nobody was being received but Charlie and me. We had our choice of a brown leather day bed with a leather pillow roll at one end, or two matching chairs. Charlie strolled around, inspecting the framed movie posters on the paneled walls. I sat on the day bed and picked all the cashews out of a silver bowl of nuts.

I'd started to work on the Brazil nuts when a new blonde showed up. This one wore gray slacks, a man's shirt and tie and wing tip oxfords. Her yellow hair was gelled into spikes and her mouth was thickly, glossy red.

She led us into an office with tasteful pale apricot walls and coordinating rugs scattered here and there on the polished wood floor. A pile of boxes in Christmas wrappings, shared a window sill with a life-sized stuffed gorilla that leaned against a white poinsettia and looked glassily down at Central Park.

The fiftyish man behind the empty expanse of lacquered desk had to be Berger. He matched Babe's description – neat gray mustache, mole on his left cheekbone, brown eyes behind gold framed glasses. But no longer wearing a hat. Without it, his hair turned out to be salt and pepper, thick and springy.

"Good afternoon, officers," he said.

I tried the trusty 'Cold enough for you?' on him, and sat down on the suede couch flanking his desk.

"Coldest winter in my recollection," he said.

Not a bad comeback. I'd have to remember that one.

"Can I get you a nosh?" Berger offered. "Coffee? Bagel?"

"No thanks," Charlie said sitting down next to me. "This isn't a social call. We're investigating the murder of a client of yours. Mona Raeburn."

He raised an eyebrow, frowning slightly. Trying to remember if he knew a Mona Raeburn.

I said, "You were identified at the scene of the crime."

"I?" Light glinted off his tinted lenses as he turned to me. "I was? How was I identified?"

"Your car. Your vanity plates."

"Ah, yes." Berger turned the palms of his long bony hands up. "I suppose I knew you'd find me."

"Why didn't you come forward?" I said.

"I called 911."

Charlie fixed him with a weary stare. "Anonymously. Nine times out of ten the one reporting the body is the killer."

"What are you talking about? I saw the killer. He attacked me! Left me for dead!"

He stood up behind the bare desk. A very tall man in a yellow and white striped shirt. Red bow tie. Sweating now.

"Do you hear me? I was attacked," he shrilled. "Some lunatic ran out of the house, and tried to kill me."

"What did he look like, this lunatic?" I said.

Berger shook his head. "I don't know. It happened so fast. I didn't see his face. He ran at me and struck me down. I think he had a knife. It was so fast I don't know what happened. When I managed to stand up again, he was gone.

"I went into the house, calling out to Mona. All the lights were on, but it was quiet. Too quiet. I had this creepy feeling. And then when I saw her…I almost had a heart attack."

He came around to us and dropped into a leather chair. The skin tautened around his nostrils and his nasal voice rose an octave.

"My God. I've never seen a dead body, but something about the way she was lying there…. I said, 'Mona? Mona?' and then I…I broke out in a cold sweat and I just had to get out of there. I was completely unnerved. I don't know what I was thinking. Maybe I was afraid he'd come back. I ran."

"You didn't try to get help." I said.

He looked a little sheepish. "It wasn't my finest hour. I admit it. I got into the car and drove off but I had the shakes so bad I couldn't drive. I pulled over. I don't know how long I sat there. And then I called 911. That's the emmis."

"Emmis?" Charlie said.

"Yiddish for the truth. Rock bottom true truth."

"Want to give us the emmis on what you were doing at Mona's house," I said, "one-thirty in the morning?"

Berger fingered his mustache. "I had a business meeting with clients in the city that night, at nine o'clock. A conference about a movie deal for Mona. I wanted her there. Maybe she'd be alive today," his voice broke, "if she'd listened to me. But no, she said I didn't need her. She wanted to go to this suburban party instead. Headstrong. Mona is headstrong. I agreed to drive out after the meet."

"Audrey Raeburn says you quarreled with her mother on the telephone."

"Audrey! You listen to her? Quarrel? No, no. It was a matter of options." His hand agitated the moustache. "I wanted Mona to come to the city and make the deal and all she had on her mind was that lousy play she wrote, *Scottish Mists*."

Now the nervous hand swiped across his forehead. "I was looking out for her interests, but can you reason with an artist? She was obsessed. Her play let me tell you, it's not just from hunger, officers, but from starvation."

He picked up a pencil, snapped off the point.

"She wanted me to invest in it. Who would invest in that turkey? Not I. My mother didn't have any dopey children. If I threw the money out that window there it would be a better investment."

Berger's rat-a-tat voice rattled on. "So if it turned out to be a smasheroo when she previewed it in Seaview? What would that mean? Seaview! In Seaview the audience pays two dollars admission and the seniors go freebie. The Seaview Players. I ask you!"

I said, "An actor named Tony Weston had the starring role."

"The starring role? In a production of Mona's, Mona is the star. Weston was the male lead." Berger's face tightened with vexation. "Tony Weston, a local yokel from Seaview. Get out!"

"Do you know him?"

"I never had that pleasure. I was supposed to meet him at the New Year's party."

I said, "Why would a professional actress bring an amateur to Broadway?"

"Off Broadway. Why do you think? They were shtupping." He looked at Charlie. "Shtupping is Yiddish for fucking. Mona was all passion. Never had any discretion."

He shook his head. "She saw him once in some local piece of crapola. Thought he had something. He had something." Berger slapped his fly. "A big shlong is what he had. This guy is a nobody. A nothing. As soon as she signs the movie deal he's todt-dead-finito! Believe me. "

He walked to the window, a lanky 6'3", gazing down with his back to us. "Mona had agreed to sign for the movie if they met her terms. And I saw to it that they did. I was bringing her the contracts. Excuse me gentlemen. I am beside myself. I had the greatest respect for that woman."

Behind Berger's back, I held my hand, palm up in a hold everything gesture, to Charlie. "She agreed to do a movie? What about the play?" I said.

Berger whirled around. "Play, shmay! Mona was no dummy. This movie is a great career move and she knew it. A shoe-in for an Oscar. Listen, did you ever see `Imitation of Life'?"

Charlie shook her head.

I said, "Yeah, on AMC. A black woman with a daughter who passes for white?"

"That's it." Berger rubbed his hands together. "Only in our version, Mona marries a light-skinned black man and she has his baby. It's coal black. A boy. The father's ashamed of him, and walks out. The kid grows up fixated on his father and rejects Mona because she's white. Then Mona is dying. Heart attack. The kid comes to the hospital. Mona forgives him before she goes. A dynamite part. Not a dry eye in the theater."

Berger gestured with his outstretched hands and a diamond on his pinkie finger caught the light. "Offer an actress a part like that - I'm talking Academy Award here – She couldn't grab it fast enough. So she had a twinge of conscience, maybe a mini-second. She said, `Tony will be devastated if I drop the play.'....

'He'll get over it,' I said." Berger's eyes blinked behind the gold rimmed glasses. "So that's who attacked me!"

Charlie and I exchanged glances.

"What makes you think it was Weston?" Charlie said.

"Who else? He was counting on her. When she told him she was dropping him to do a movie, he killed her.

"Mona didn't have an enemy in the world. Everyone loved her. Well, maybe not that leech of a husband. If I had a nickel for every tear Mona shed on my shoulder over that dead beat I could retire."

Charlie unwrapped a square of bubble gum, her face expressionless. I watched her blunt fingers extract the gum. Orange flavor.

Berger said, "And Audrey... when it comes to her father she hasn't got the sense God gave a chicken."

Charlie snapped her gum. "You know Fred Raeburn?"

"No, they were divorced years before Mona came to me. Must you chew a mile a minute like that? You make me nervous."

Charlie blew a bubble and gave the gum an extra loud snap. "You drove to Seaview after your 9:00 meeting. But didn't get there until 1:25. Why?"

"I had a flat. In the middle of the night, in the middle of the boonies, on New Year's Eve no less, I had to have a flat. The AAA didn't come and didn't come. Finally, I had to fix it myself."

He spread his hands, looking at his manicured nails, "Can you believe I did that? Then when I finally get to Mona's....

"What a night! After I made the call to 911, I drove to a diner. For coffee. But my stomach was turning inside out. I couldn't drink it. I walked out. Left my raincoat."

The girl in the shirt and tie opened the door mouthing soundlessly at Berger. He stood up. "It was a Burberry. Maybe you could do me a favor? Get it back for me? If I never go back to Seaview again in my lifetime, it would be too soon."

Charlie said, "We can try."

Berger nodded and walked to a closet. He removed a handsome gray jacket and shrugged into it, eyeing himself in the full length mirror on the inside of the door.

"'I would appreciate it." He turned to us, smiling. "I'm always here if you want to talk again but I have to take a meeting now."

CHAPTER FOURTEEN

Outside, we ducked our chins into our coats and headed for the car, bucking the wind. On the corner, a blind black man sat on a camp stool caroling "Silent Night"

Charlie tossed him a quarter.

"Big spender," I said, fell back and emptied all the coins from my pocket.

Charlie said, "You trying to show me up? I don't have a rich stepfather."

I vented by slamming the car door closed.

It was colder in the car than outside.

"Heat, please, Charlie."

"You got it." The engine turned over on the second try. She turned the heater to high and freezing air gusted out along with the monotone of the police radio band.

I was miffed at her, for the crack about my stepfather but she didn't notice, or pretended not to, sitting beside me like a lump, chewing and staring out the window.

She broke our silence. "There's a good pizzeria on 60th and First, on the way to the bridge. Wanna get a pie?"

"Tell you what, Charlie, go to Papaya King; 86th and Third and I'll buy you the best hot dog you ever ate."

"That's way out of our way."

"It's the best hot dog in New York."

"Yeah?"

"If not the best on the planet."

That got her. She headed cross-town to Third Avenue, made a left, went north to 86th Street and parked in a bus stop, pulling into the front of the space, not totally blocking it. She flipped the sun visor down, exposing the `Nassau County Police Department, Official Business' card attached to the inside and we walked across the street.I ordered four dogs with relish and two Papaya drinks. At the counter facing the news stand on 86th Street, we slathered the dogs with mustard and ate them standing up. When we finished, I bought four more.

Charlie slapped me on the back, washing her last bite down with the Papaya drink. "Great idea, kid."

Back in the car, the heater was still breathing cold air, the police band droning on. She took 2nd Avenue to the 59th Street bridge, fiddling with the AM/FM radio, pushing one button after another. Most cops have no problem listening to the police band with one ear with another program on at the same time.

"I'm lookin' for 660. WFAN. Hear what Mad Dog has to say about the Philadelphia game."

She turned up the volume and we drove across the bridge listening to Mike and the Mad Dog. The Mad Dog picked Buffalo, minus four points. We stopped at a light in Long Island City and I clicked the AM/FM off.

"Weston's our killer. I know it. He was there and he had a motive."

We waited for the light to change. The longest light in history. Maybe it was broken.

A blue Audi ran the red light.

"Watch out," I yelled.

"I saw him."

"Do you know how close that car was to us?"

"What's eating you today?" Charlie said.

"Go," I said, "The light's green."

Charlie turned the radio on again and I closed my eyes and dozed off. When I woke, we'd left the expressway and were driving along the service road toward Wellington.

"You with me again?" Charlie said. "We should go to the morgue. Talk to the ME. He won't have sent in the protocol yet but we can go over his hand written notes with him."

"He won't have the total tox screen yet. I thought I'd get the party guest list from Anne Weston."

"You wanna talk about Anne Weston?"

"What about her?" My neck tightened up.

"She's as much a suspect as her husband. Mona Raeburn was breaking up her marriage. So maybe she got rid of her."

"Come on, Charlie! She wasn't at the scene. She was out on her feet with a headache. She and Weston both said she went to bed."

"Trouble with you, kiddo? You meet a good looking woman, you can't see straight."

I said, "That's not true, Charlie."

"No? Everyone but you knew that ex-wife of yours was two hands full of gimme and a mouth full of much obliged."

"Leave Paula out of this."

"That still hurts, huh?"

"I don't want to talk about it."

"O.K. I hear ya. So maybe I'll come with you to pick up the guest list." She cackled and pointed a finger at me. "Boy, did your face just fall a mile."

We pulled in next to the parking space where I'd left my 'Vette.

"Go yourself. Just remember you're a cop, she's a suspect."

"Fuck you, Charlie. What about you? Babe gives you a good meal and you believe every dumb alibi she feeds you."

"The pot's calling the fry pan black," she said.

"The expression is the pot calls the kettle black."

We glared at each other for a couple of seconds and then began to laugh.

"Where will you be?" I said.

"The morgue." She clasped her arms behind her head, and leaned back, hooded eyes half-closed. "And then the diner. The special's garlic shrimp in apple cider and ginger. Wanna meet me for dinner?"

"I'll pass."

I got out of the car and she waved as she drove off. I used my cell phone to call the Beverly Hilton.

'Mr. Weston is not in his room,' the operator said. 'Would you like to leave a message?'

I hung up. He was at the Hilton. Just checking.

I decided to walk to the Weston house from the parking lot and locked up the 'Vette.

A lone star twinkling in the darkening sky was obscured by a thin drift of clouds as I rapped the door knocker and watched the pair of brass lovers kiss.

"I'm a cop on a murder case about to interrogate a suspect," I told them.

CHAPTER FIFTEEN

Anne Weston opened the door with a cry of surprise. A waif in faded pink tights and a blue striped shirt, so oversized it hung to her knees.

"Oh," she said, "My goodness I'm glad to see you, Detective Harmony."

I caught a glimpse of myself in the hall mirror as I took off my coat and cap. That cap always flattens my hair down. Makes it look thinner than it is. I tried to fluff it up with my fingers inconspicuously.

"I truly am glad to see you." She led the way into the living room, and perched on the flowered sofa smiling up at me.

I smiled back and stood looking down at her, liking what I saw. A lot.

"You can't imagine how I was dreadin' spendin' this evenin' all by my lonesome."

Oh, yes. I felt the tug of attraction. She was small and fragile and she smelled like a garden after a rain.

I said, "I came by for the list of guests that were at your party. I can't stay long."

"Oh?" Her disappointment was flattering. "Well, of course, I understand how busy you must be." Her black lashes lowered. "Still, I'm right pleased you found a minute to look in on me."

She plumped the pillow beside her invitingly.

I almost sat down next to her, changed my mind and took the club chair.

She ducked her head and her long black hair swung across her face covering her eyes. "Imagine you arrivin' at my door just the minute I finished printin' up the lesson for the course I teach at the library."

"What do you teach?"

"Needlepoint. For beginners? It's an adult education class, on Wednesday nights."

"Do you use a computer?"

She nodded. "We have a li'l Mac. Bought it to keep Tony's files and things…."

Her voice trailed off. She looked up, and looked away and looked at me again. Her body was still but her eyes didn't know where to settle.

"Taylor got it for us through the library–usin' his discount. And then he...." Her voice faltered. I had to bend closer. "He most obligin'ly taught me how to use it. But…." She blushed and twisted her fingers. "But...he…wanted me to be...obligin', too. Imagine! The gall of that ni… man!"

Her face went fleetingly hard. "Goodness, gracious, I don't know why I told you that."

She twisted a strand of hair around her right index finger.

"Anything you can tell me will be useful. I'm investigating a murder case."

"He insisted I choose a secret password. Somethin' personal and easy to remember for security. Am I the CIA for goodness sake? I don't have any secrets to hide."

Her eyes lowered and then sought mine again. "Maybe Taylor has! But why on earth do I need a secret password? Just 'cause he has one? What secrets does he have, I wonder. An' how secret is it anyway, if he tole it to me?"

"What is his password?"

"I don't rightly remember. His name in Latin, he said. That man's so full of himself, he'd gag a maggot."

She smiled disparagingly at herself. "I didn't appreciate bein' told how stupid I am by Taylor. Oh, well, it wasn't worth the arguin', so I made up a password. A.E. Sayre. For Anne Elizabeth Sayre. My maiden name that was."

Anne got to her feet, smoothed her shirt collar, smoothed her hair. "I was fixin' to have dinner when you came by. Won't you join me? Just some cold turkey."

"Uh, no thank you. I had dinner."

"Will you keep me company while I eat?"

I forgot that I wasn't going to stay.

The polished dark wood dining table had been set with a pink linen place mat, a matching lace-edged napkin, silver flatware and a crystal wineglass. A rose-patterned dinner plate held her sandwich.

I was impressed. When I eat alone, I stand in front of the refrigerator and empty it. Or watch television, eating with my fingers.

She brought out a platter of potato salad, another wine glass and a bottle of Pinot Grigio and motioned to the chair beside her.

I opened the wine, poured it, lifted my empty glass to her and thought, `Here's looking at you, kid.' But I didn't say it. What I said was that I don't drink on duty.

"At least taste my home made potato salad," she said, holding out a forkful. "It's the Sayre family's secret recipe."

It was wonderful.

"It's great," I said. "A family recipe? I'll have to marry you for it." And was immediately sorry I'd said it.

"Unfortunately, I'm already married, Detective Harmony," she said. "Unfortunately." She ran a finger around the rim of the glass and overturned it. "I... Oh dear!"

We fumbled with napkins, mopping the spreading pool together.

"I declare I don't know how that happened. I am never clumsy."

She stacked the dishes and I carried them into the kitchen.

"Before I came here tonight," I said, watching her spoon leftovers into a plastic container, "I had a talk with Taylor."

The spoon rattled sharply on the counter. "Oh, please let's not discuss that man. If it was up to me, we'd have nothin' to do with him, but Tony likes him."

"He says your husband owns a kilt. Would you know where it is?"

"My goodness, no. It's prob'ly at the library with the other costumes."

"Anne, every minute that goes by in a murder investigation makes it harder to figure out what happened. Who was there. What they were doing. I need to ask questions that you may think are too personal."

"You can ask me anything."

I said as gently as I could, "What did your husband and Mona Raeburn...."

Her fluting laugh was thin. "Did Taylor make up some filthy story about them? That man's mind is a sewer. Tony thought Mona was common as dirt. And she was. You mustn't believe Taylor. He's a snake."

She tried for a smile. "You can't believe a word he says, and that's God's truth!"

She leaned in closer to me, her small hand on my arm. "I guess you can tell when people are sincere."

Her jasmine scent was in my nostrils, scrambling my thought processes. A warning sounded in my head. Leave. Now.

"It's late," I said, glancing at my watch. "I shouldn't have stayed this long. I have to go."

Anne held out the container she'd been filling. "This is for you. You liked it so much." She tucked the container of potato salad into a plastic *Big Dan's* grocery bag. "An' here's the list of guests who were at the party." A pale blue envelope went into the bag.

"Now you just take this li'l doggy-bag on home with you and think of me kindly."

I followed her out of the kitchen and stood in the front hallway, my coat in my arms. I said, "Taylor told me that when he brought

Mona home, a man was waiting for her inside the Raeburn house. Did you see him?"

"There was always a man in the Raeburn house. Oh, that harlot deserved to be murdered!"

She clapped her hand over her mouth. "My goodness, listen to me! You mustn't think that I…."

The color drained from her face and she swayed a little. I put out a steadying hand, felt her trembling.

"I'm investigating a murder."

"An' I so want to help," she said. "I sincerely do."

I dumped my coat and helped her into the living room. She half fell into the club chair, seeming to shrink into herself. I said, "You told me Poochy woke you just before you saw Fred Raeburn run out of the house."

"Yes."

I squatted on the ottoman in front of her chair.

"Are you sure?"

Something in my tone made her evasive. "Ye-es. I think so but, my goodness, well I plumb don't know what woke me. But I did see Fred. And…."

Anne stretched out a small hand that didn't quite touch me.

"I'm sorry…. I didn't tell you everything."

"Tell me now."

"I reckon it was wrong of me not to tell you before…oh, maybe it's not important."

A black line drawn under her bottom lids emphasized the circle of black that rimmed her pale irises.

I looked away. "Let me decide what's important and what's not."

"I truly hate to say this, but...I saw Babe come back. You see, I felt it was her place to tell you. It just didn't feel right to tell on her."

She leaned closer to me. "It was after I heard Taylor come crashin' down Mona's path in the dark…It was Taylor! I'm sure it was!"

I nodded.

She returned the nod, lifting her adorable chin. "Well, I looked out the window and there was a parked car. The driver's door opened, the light inside went on - an' I could see Babe. Sittin' there. After a second or two she closed the door without gettin' out. But she didn't drive away, she just sat there."

"Did you see her go into the Raeburn house?"

"No-o, but I went back to bed before she drove away so she might have."

"What kind of car was it?"

"Babe drives a big SUV." Anne shook her head. "She never did want Tony and I to marry. Maybe she was right."

Sighing, she looked at the floor and spoke to it in a whisper. "Tony and I, we have our ups and downs an'.... we've been down for a while now."

She brushed at tear-glistened eyes. "He never even kissed me goodbye when he left. I've always been too sensitive. The fact is, I'm a spiritual person and Tony is not. Oh, I mustn't burden you with my troubles."

This time her hand touched mine. The prettiest fine-boned trusting little hand. She leaned toward me. Our shoulders brushed.

The door knocker rapped.

Anne looked startled. "Who could that be?" she whispered.

The knocker rapped again.

"Why don't you see who it is?"

She went to the door and I heard her say, "Why, Audrey honey! I was just thinkin' about you. Come in darlin'."

I crossed to the hallway, picked up the doggy-bag and my coat.

Audrey Raeburn was sobbing in Anne's arms.

"Now, now, darlin'," Anne soothed.

"They called me," Audrey blubbered, "they said I could...said it was all right to...go to the house tomorrow. But I...I just can't go through Mamma's things alone. Oh, Anne, can I stay here with you and Tony tonight? Please?"

"Bless your heart, darlin'. Tony's not home, but you're welcome to stay if you like."

"Hello, Audrey," I said.

"Oh!" Audrey stopped crying abruptly and wiped her nose. A look of malice flitted across her face as she looked from Anne to me.

"Don't let me chase you away, Detective Harmony."

You're not. I'm late for another appointment."

CHAPTER SIXTEEN

I walked back to the parking lot, unlocked my car, buckled up and turned the ignition key. It was not my imagination. Anne Weston had definitely come on to me.

I searched my reflection in the rear view mirror. I'm no movie star. I certainly didn't measure up to Mr. Beautiful. But on the other hand, I'm neat and reasonably all right looking.

I drove back to the Seaview diner, hoping Charlie would still be there.

The few people in the diner were dawdling over their after-dinner coffees, reluctant to brave the cold night.

Charlie sat at the counter talking to the waitress, Josie. Like two old cronies, they mirrored each other on opposite sides of the Formica counter. Their respective chins, Josie's sharp and thin, Charlie's jowly and drooping, rested in their cupped hands propped up by their elbows. Engrossed in conversation, they barely acknowledged me as I dropped onto the stool next to Charlie.

I twirled on the stool and gazed idly out the frosted window, at the black branches of the trees shimmering in their casings of ice under the yellow street light. Beautiful to look at if you didn't have to be out in it.

Josie was saying, "Butter wouldn't melt, but what a bitter pill she is under that honey. Well, if I had her looks, what a bitch I'd be."

I wondered who she was talking about in that strident voice....

"But, listen, I wouldn't be her. Not for anything. She's not a happy woman."

"You don't know that," Charlie said.

"Everyone in town knew about Mona Raeburn and him. And it just so happens, I saw them with my own eyes, leaving the Holiday Inn motel on Sunrise Highway. Hanging onto each other. That's how I know Anne Weston's not a happy woman."

I felt a muscle twitch in my jaw. "Keep it down, can't you? You don't have to tell the whole diner."

"Well! The rudeness of some people, eavesdropping. I was not speaking to you!"

Josie untied her apron, elaborately smoothed it and folded it with her small neat hands. She gave me a withering look, marched out from behind the counter and swept past us, the effect spoiled a little by the white Reeboks.

"Hey, what's with you, kid, yelling at Josie? I was in the middle of an interrogation."

I said, "Eat another piece of pie, Charlie." Then I regretted my temper. "Sorry. I just saw red for a minute."

"People talk," Charlie said. "Mona Raeburn was the town celebrity. It seems to be common knowledge that she and Weston were a twosome."

"He's our prime suspect," I said. "What if he'd decided to leave Anne for Mona? But Mona kisses him off; tells him, so long it's been nice to know you, he goes into a rage and kills her."

"Maybe," Charlie said. "And maybe his wife got fed up with sharing her husband. Maybe she knew he was planning to leave her for Raeburn. We'll know more after we meet his plane Wednesday."

Babe came out of the kitchen and acknowledged us with an unsmiling nod. Charlie yawned and scratched her rump. "I'm thirsty," she said.

"Yo!" she beckoned with a forefinger to the stocky bus boy, washing glasses at the end of the counter. "Give us an egg cream, here."

The boy nodded and began to pump chocolate syrup into a tall glass.

"What are you doing?" Charlie yelped. "That's not how you make an egg cream."

She left her stool and went behind the counter. "Out of my way, I'll show you how to make a real egg cream."

The boy stepped back, squeezing himself as far from Charlie as he could.

"You pour in your milk. This much, see," She held up her thumb. "Measure to the first joint. That's an inch. Rule of thumb. Tilt the glass and spray your seltzer, slow, like this. About three quarters full. Not to the top of the glass. You want to leave room for the head. Push the nozzle the other way and give one fast shot. Chocolate syrup goes in last. Two short pumps, or one long one - either/or."

She glanced over to where Babe stood watching. "You should use Fox's U-Bet."

I expected Babe to lash out with the sharp side of her tongue but she looked at Charlie with all her toughness discarded.

"We make our own chocolate syrup," she said.

"Nothing works but U-Bet," Charlie said. "Now mix it up, add more seltzer till the head rises to the top of the glass and...." she sniffed and sipped.

"Aah."

She held the glass out to Babe. "That's an egg cream."

Babe unwrapped a straw and stabbed it into the glass. I might have been in Canarsie instead of four stools down.

I said, "It tastes better if you use two straws instead of one."

"Really. I am having a very instructive evening tonight." She sipped cautiously and then, setting the glass down, she leaned across the counter, cradled Charlie's head between her hands, said, "Thank you," and disappeared into the kitchen.

What was going on here?

"What was that about, Charlie?"

She sat down at a table with the egg cream. I pulled up a chair.

"Nuthin," she said. "Fuggedaboutit." And blushed. Charlie blushing!

"I talked to Dodo Byrd," Charlie said. "You don't light a match under his ass, he don't move it. Tells me our victim's not his top priority.

'Well, she's mine,' I say. And then he tells me that semen from two different secretors was found in her body cavity! Two guys fucked her before she died. Have we got a fuckin' problem here, kid?"

"Literally," I said. "Well, Gresham admitted he had sex with her. The other secretor may be Weston."

"We don't have blood samples from Weston or Gresham. Or Taylor. Or Raeburn for that matter."

I said, "The blood samples the techs scraped off the carpet come from a type O human, and a dog. The type O is probably Raeburn's. He was bleeding from the dog bite. We could ask the serologist to do a PCR test. In just a couple of days we'd know if we had a match."

"PCR's not conclusive."

"But it's fast," I said. "And it'd give us something to work with while we wait for the DNA analysis."

Josie appeared at our table with a pencil poised over her order pad.

"Tea," I said, "with honey and lemon."

She nodded and flounced off.

"I think I'm coming down with a cold. Feel my head Charlie."

"You're a little warm."

Charlie cracked the knuckles on her right hand. "Five sets of clear fingerprints dusted up," she said.

I ticked them off on my fingers, "One set's the victim's. Gresham's is two, and Fred Raeburn's, three. Raeburn's are probably all over the place – he ransacked it. And if Weston left prints - that's four sets."

"The fifth could be Taylor's," Charlie said, "If the skin and hair particles we find embedded in that kilt match one of the semen samples found in the body, it don't look good for Taylor."

"Weston has a kilt too. He wears one in the play they're rehearsing."

"But we know Taylor wore his at the party," Charlie said.

"I think the kilt was planted. Weston had sex with the victim, killed her and put it there to incriminate Taylor."

"Jake! Taylor was wearing a kilt. Not Weston. You wanna tell me why Weston 'd bring a kilt with him if he ran next door for a quickie?"

"When we pick him up Wednesday morning, I'll ask him."

I drained my cup.

Charlie said, "He and Babe are cousins."

"Weston is Babe's cousin?"

"Right."

"Where'd that info come from?"

She pointed toward the counter. "Josie."

"The local *National Enquirer*?"

"Josie's O.K." Charlie said. "Told me the whole story. Their mothers were sisters. Weston's father died when he was five and his mother married again. Two years later she died, leaving him with the stepfather. Only it turns out, the guy was a sociopath."

"We don't use that term any more, Charlie. We say anti-social personality now."

"He was bad news, whatever you call him. There was a court battle and Babe's parents got custody of Weston."

I signaled a bus boy for more hot water for my tea bag.

"The two of them, Babe and Weston, were brought up together. She was big sister, always watching out for his ass. She's four years – five years older than him."

I poured hot water over the old tea bag and added a Sweet-n-Low. I stirred the tea. "What else did Josie have to say?"

She said, `Tony runs to Babe if he has a hang nail. Doesn't cross the street without conferring with Babe first. And maybe Mrs. Weston resents that. I would.' "

I blew my nose. "Good work, Charlie"

She looked pleased. "You know, the killer doesn't have to be one of the guys that screwed Mona. Mrs. Weston could have done it."

"So could Babe."

"Go home and take care of your cold, kid," Charlie said,

CHAPTER SEVENTEEN

I turned into the unmarked road on the side of Henry's estate instead of driving in through the big gates. Here, you entered through a fence overgrown with rugosa roses, their heavy thorns menacing as barbed wire. The gardener's gatehouse was built up against the fence, latched with a simple hasp. In theory, the grounds were patrolled by the gardeners' schnauzer; a terrorizing growling bundle of nerves during the day. But at night once Toots retired to their bed with Bennett and Willard, she was off duty.

They'd been kind to me, after my mother married Henry; kind to an unhappy, unattractive adolescent.

* * *

I stowed Anne's potato salad in the fridge, put a kettle of water up to boil and changed into a sweat suit. I made a pot of tea, dumped in honey with a couple of shots of whiskey, swallowed two aspirins and carried the tea pot and the whiskey bottle to my bed. I crawled in, wrapped up in a quilt, and downed the tea.

When I woke, drenched in sweat, the bedside clock read 12:30. I changed into another sweat suit, swallowed two more aspirins, washed them down with the whiskey and fell asleep again....

Anne Weston's jasmine scented body yielded to mine. I pulled her down with me and she was laughing; laughing with all her velvety weight pressed warm against my naked skin. We lay together on white satin sheets, leg curved to leg, belly touching belly, breast against breast. I kissed her smooth shoulder, unloosed her beautiful hair.

She put her mouth to my ear and whispered, "Tony killed Mona. Don't let him kill me."

It was two a.m. when I bolted awake.

I got out of bed, padded into the kitchen and opened the fridge door. By the light of its fifteen watt bulb, I folded the potato salad into a slice of white bread, drank half a can of Diet Dr. Pepper, noticed that sleety rain was falling outside and shuffled back to bed.

I put my head on the pillow, drew the warm quilt close around me and listened to the rain until I fell asleep.

The telephone woke me at 8:30.

"Detective Harmony? Evelyn Blackmon, Mona Weston's personal assistant. I got back from Vermont last night. I listened to your messages this morning."

We arranged to meet at 12:00 at the mobile crime unit. She knew where Wellington Road was.

I must have sweated out my cold because I felt pretty good when I stepped out of the shower and onto the scale.

It said: You have lost two pounds. Have a nice day.

Outside, the rhododendron leaves were folded in on themselves, the lawn silvered with frost. It was still dark and bitterly cold. The sleet needled my face as I ran for the 'Vette.

* * *

Charlie was in court, giving testimony on a drug homicide case from last summer so I saw Gresham myself. He was punctual, arriving at 9:25. Subdued by the official atmosphere, he was cooperative and almost polite. We were done in twenty minutes.

After I showed him out, I headed for the squad room. Declining to sit in on the poker game, I poured a cup of burnt coffee and wrote up my paper work, checking and double checking the wording, getting the facts correct.

At 10:15, I went upstairs to my supervisor's office. Cynthia Martinez, the ADA was with my Lou, Lieutenant Faber. After I'd brought them up to date, I checked in with Sergeant Barton, the press liaison.

On Monday, a vegan postal worker had gone berserk at the Burger King on Sunrise Highway and shot everybody in sight including himself, leaving three dead and six hurt. Even the local free paper, *Viewpoint*, was showing little interest in the Raeburn murder case today.

After the session with Barton, I had time for some real coffee. I drove to the Starbucks on Old Country Road for a latte and chocolate biscotti. The rain stopped.

* * *

I usually arrive fifteen minutes early for an appointment, so I'd been waiting for forty-five minutes when Evelyn Blackmon's black Boxster (rental plates) pulled up to the crime lab at 12:30.

From the window, I watched long legs in black leather pants and black high heeled boots swing around to the pavement. A white turtle neck sweater under a short black leather jacket swaddled her chin. Black hair threaded with gray was cut chin length. She pushed a pair of granny sunglasses up her nose with one hand, reached behind her for a black leather briefcase with the other and stood up. Easily six feet tall.

Smiled when she saw me watching her, flashing straight white teeth in a narrow face. She climbed the two steps into the crime lab and removed the sunglasses.

I made her fiftyish from the gray in her hair and the lines around her brown eyes and scarlet mouth.

"Evelyn Blackmon," she said. "Detective Harmony?"

No apology for being thirty minutes late.

We shook hands. Hers were smooth, the nails well manicured, palely polished.

I led her to the back of the crime lab.

"Coffee?"

"Decaf?"

"No."

She frowned. "Where does it come from?"

"Shop Rite."

"I mean what country?"

I looked at the bag. "It's Columbian."

"Is it organic?"

"Probably not."

"Then it's been chemically sprayed."

"Could be."

She looked at the coffeepot. "Is it a fresh pot?"

"Made it while I was waiting for you."

"Do you have skim milk?"

"Half and half."

"Are you having some?"

"Yeah."

She sat down and took off her jacket. Drummed her fingers on the briefcase, considering. "I'll have a small cup."

I poured. A full cup for me, half a cup for her.

"All the pertinent documents are here," she said. "There are copies of Mona's will, her insurance policies, tax reports and canceled checks and diaries for the last four years." She piled a stack of folders on the desk in front of us.

"Is that how long you've worked for Ms. Raeburn? Four years?"

"Four very long years."

"You didn't like her."

"Not much. Sometimes not at all. But I'm extremely well paid."

"Were well paid."

"Still am. I'm executor of the estate."

"How did you feel about her murder?"

"I was shocked, of course. Did I shed any tears for her? I'm afraid not."

"How did she and her daughter get along?"

"Pretty well. Better than most."

"What does a personal assistant do?"

She sipped once and put the cup aside. "For Mona, everything but wipe her behind."

She meant for me to laugh so I did and then got down to business. "Let's begin with Saturday, December 31."

"I had already left for Vermont the day before, on Friday."

She leafed through a black bound diary, held it close to her eyes, squinted at it.

"On Saturday, Mona had appointments for a facial, manicure and pedicure. She was going to the Weston's party that evening."

"When did you see her last?"

"Friday morning. I brought the checks she had to sign and the stuff from the dry cleaner."

"What was that?"

"A pair of slacks, two sweaters and Tony's kilt. I put Mona's things in her closet and left the kilt on the hall table for Tony to try on."

"Why was Weston's kilt with Ms. Raeburn's dry cleaning?"

"Mona had sent it to her tailor to shorten it. She wanted to show off his legs."

I almost paged Charlie that instant, but reined myself in. "You left the kilt on the hall table."

"Yes. Can we start going through the papers, please."

* * *

We were Eve and Jake by three o'clock and Charlie still hadn't responded to her pager. Eve stood up and stretched. "I need lunch. How about you?"

I pulled takeout menus from the desk drawer.

Eve shook her head. "Mona had all her meals delivered to her by 'Mama David'. His food is entirely organic and very good. Shall I call him?"

"O.K. What are you having?"

"The baby field greens salad with spaghetti squash and tomatoes is very nice."

My ex-wife Paula used to tell me that if I wanted to be thin I should eat like a thin person. But field greens isn't eating it's grazing. I asked for a steak sandwich, medium rare, with onions, ketchup and mayo.

Eve pushed a button on her cell phone and placed our order. "Anything to drink?"

"I'm good."

She ordered a decaf with steamed soy milk, charged everything to Mona and we went back to work.

At six o'clock, Eve reached for her jacket.

"I've got a dinner date," she said, "and you don't need me any more. The rest is all very straightforward."

I had a dinner date too. Tuesday night is family night. We assemble around Henry's 18th century mahogany table at eight o'clock for an interminable hour and a half of roast beef, green peas, potatoes and Henry's opinions.

I walked Eve to her car, thanked her for her help and went inside to page Charlie again, still no response.

Mona Raeburn's estate wasn't complicated. She'd left everything to Audrey who would now have much more than the three thousand a month allowance she'd been receiving. But the death certificate would say homicide and that would hold up the probate procedure.

Driving home to change for dinner, cruising along at seventy I started to think about Henry and the speedometer jumped to eighty.

He never knew that I'd overheard him with my mother eighteen years ago....

CHAPTER EIGHTEEN

I'd come home from high school, gone into the kitchen, poured a glass of milk and heard a voice I'd never heard before. I stood behind the kitchen door, listening.

"He had a fine funeral," my mother said.

"Sure," a man answered, "A hero cop's funeral. Only he should've let somebody else be the hero, Meggie. If it had been me, I would have thought about my family first."

My mother murmured something indistinct and Henry said, "You know I've always loved you. That's never been a secret. For Christ sake we grew up together. We have the same memories. That counts for something. You can't deny there's always been something between us."

I'd spilt the milk then, bent to wipe it up, couldn't make out what my mother answered.

Henry's voice: "Marry me and you'll want for nothing. I can make life easy for you. Your boys will go to the best schools. You'll never have to lift a finger again. And think of my Laura. It's five years since her mother passed on. Five years without a mother's love."

"Henry...."

"It was always you for me, Meggie. Don't say no this time. Let me help you. You need me. Why should you nickel and dime it when

I'm loaded? You know what they say; if you're broke, you're a joke. You owe it to your boys to do what's best for them. Steve's gone. You should have a man ...."

I pushed open the kitchen door then and my mother had said, "This is Henry Slater, Jake. Henry, this is my youngest."

* * *

My father was a great cop. Older cops still speak of Steve Harmony with respect. His name is inscribed on the Honor Roll of members of the Nassau County Police Department who made the supreme sacrifice: Officers killed in the line of duty.

In front of Mineola headquarters, cobblestones of local stone pave the approach to a memorial set inside a circle of flag pole staffs. On holidays they fly eight different historical American flags. In season, geraniums flower.

I always enter headquarters from the rear parking lot to avoid looking at it.

After their marriage, Henry set up trust funds for his two new 'sons'. I'm grateful, but I can't like him.

'I have nothing against cops,' he says. 'I just don't want one in my family. Deal with stink, you begin to stink too. I can't understand why you want to be a cop.'

When Phil and Laura married, Henry manipulated Phil into law school. I guess Laura was worth the strings attached to her. Over the years my jealous ache faded. Not completely. I'm thirty-three now and she's still the only woman besides my ex-wife Paula who....

But she's family now.

* * *

My chalk-striped navy suit makes me look thinner. I chose a white on white shirt to wear with it. So much about me infuriates Henry, I didn't want to goad him by appearing at his dinner table casually dressed. And I like to look nice for Laura.

I held two ties up to my chin in the mirror. It'd be a cold day in Hell before Henry heard me call him Dad. I wince every time Phil says it.

Lucky for him stealing ideas from other designers is legal or he'd be doing ten to twenty in Attica instead of living in luxury on his Westbury estate.

Henry and I tip-toe around each other, keeping our antagonism in check because it upsets my mother. No, I, Jake, tippy-toe. But we're due for a knock-down drag-out one day.

I decided on the mini-dotted bow tie, and tied and retied it until I got it right. Just a shade crooked.

* * *

My mother sat on Henry's left, her diamonds glittering in the candlelight. She piles them on thinking that they distract from her bulk. Her clothes are as Parisian as Laura's, but she never gets them right.

Laura sat between my brother Phil and me, wearing one of the original models Henry buys in Paris to knock off in his sample rooms.

His Seventh Avenue dress house, *Miss Chic*, copies couture originals and sells them for $99.95 at retail. 'Sell to the masses and eat with the classes,' is his favorite witticism.

I watched Laura pick at her roast beef. In her sleek expensive clothing and careful makeup, she suddenly looked hard to me. Her chic almost vulgar compared to... Anne Weston.

If Laura's New York accent sounded harsh in my ears after Anne's drawling Southern vowels, at least Laura hadn't murdered anybody.

I hoped Anne hadn't either.

"Jake," my mother said, "Where are you tonight? Henry has asked your opinion twice."

"Kingsley's life is insured for $5,000,000," Henry was saying. "And I own his name. Wouldn't I be better off if he had a fatal accident?

I said, "Only if you had an unbreakable alibi."

I stole a glance at my watch and saw Henry's little piggy eyes catch me at it. He'd given it to me for Christmas and I love that watch.

That's the rotten thing about Henry. He always knows what you can't resist. That's why his business is so successful. He has a knack for knowing exactly whose designs to steal.

My mother was eating with ivory chopsticks, her ringed hands so weighted it was a wonder she could lift them. "You might try this, Jake. It's a wonderful diet tool. I can only lift one pea at a time."

"I can just picture Charlie's face if I pulled out chopsticks at the Seaview Diner."

"Is that where you dine these days?" Henry said. He has an insinuating fatty voice that drives me up the wall.

"Charlie loves it."

"That's because Charlie's crass. A crass, ugly, dyke."

"Henry," my mother said. "Please, she's my cousin. And she's had a hard life."

"You always say that, Meggie. But you never go into details."

"Her story isn't mine to tell," my mother said.

Henry lifted his shoulders. "Who doesn't have a hard life?"

I imagined Henry in a sudden paroxysm, flung across the table. Choking to death. No. The Heimlich maneuver could save him. A heart attack....

A maid edged into the room, nervously scuttled past Henry and bent to whisper in my ear. I don't wear my beeper in this house, because Henry has a fit of sulks if it goes off during dinner.

I got to my feet. "Excuse me. Phone call."

Henry scowled at me. "Sit down, Jake. It can wait until we finish eating."

"If it could wait, they wouldn't be calling me here."

"Bring the portable phone, Rose," he ordered.

I sat down.

The maid came back and handed me the cellular. It was Wolfie, in a state that rendered her almost unintelligible.

"What's wrong, Jake?" my mother asked.

"Charlie's been in an accident."

Henry sneered. "What happened? Did she get her foot caught in her mouth?"

I put the phone down and started for him, fists clenched, feeling like a charge of gun powder ready to blow.

My mother's hand fluttered at me. "Jake!"

I ached to push Henry's face in, knock those false teeth down his wattled throat. But not under my mother's pleading eyes.

I kissed her cheek quickly and ran.

CHAPTER NINETEEN

I drove to Mid-Island Hospital on automatic pilot, made a breakneck turnoff from the Meadow brook Parkway and shot into the Hempstead Turnpike traffic against the light.

Wolfie hadn't been coherent on the phone. Or maybe I'd been the incoherent one. A car explosion, she'd said. My vision blurred. Charlie, you cud-chewing, irritating bitch. Don't be dead.

God, don't let Charlie be dead. And not crippled either, please.

I pulled up in front of the emergency entrance, brakes screeching and abandoned the car.

"Alberts. Charlie Alberts. What room?" I rasped at the information clerk, wanting to wrench the People magazine out of her hands and stamp it to death.

She blinked at me.

"Alberts," I said again, ready to throttle her.

"Just a minute." She thumbed maddeningly through a file. "I don't see.... Oh, yes. Room 219. But you can't go up. Visiting hours are over."

I badged my way past the guards and took the stairs up, heart knocking against my ribs, dreading to see what I knew I'd see.

The figure in the bed, a dead ringer for the Invisible Man, lifted a bandage-wrapped head from a pillow and said, "Yo, Jake."

I felt my leg muscles sag, rubbery with relief.

She held up a bandaged mitt. "Looks worse than it is. The docs got carried away with the bandages."

Her bandaged head fell back on the pillow so that her eyes slitted at me eerily from the center of the gauze wrappings.

"You're okay?" I said. She didn't look okay.

"What doesn't kill you...hurts."

"What happened?"

"I skidded on some ice, hit a tree, got knocked out for a minute. Came to and the car was on fire. I jumped out and I remember thinking, `Put your head between your legs and say goodbye to your ass,' just before the whole damn thing went up. No sweat. I'll be outta here in two, three days tops. Superficial burns on my hands and face. Looks like you have to meet Weston on your own tomorrow."

"No problem."

"Jake, there's something.... I have to tell you something."

There was a knock on the door.

"May I come in?" The nurse entered, carrying a tray of pills. Obviously her question was a rhetorical one.

"You have to leave," she commanded me. "Visiting hours are over." She handed a paper cup to Charlie. "Here's your nightcap."

I said goodnight but I waited in the corridor for the nurse to come out.

"You shouldn't be here," she said, tapping her wrist watch.

"I'm going. Just tell me. Is Charlie really all right?"

"There's always the danger of complications - of pneumonia. The next twenty-four hours are crucial."

I left the hospital feeling too depressed to go home. The cold steady rain was an added affliction.

Food always cheers me up. I hadn't eaten much dinner. The 'Mamma David' delivery boy had left a menu. But maybe they wouldn't be open this late– 9:40. I decided to chance it.

'Mamma David' was in Old Harbor, a pretty town about three miles away. I turned north onto an unlit two lane road edged with reflector lights so drivers would stay on the road instead of landing in the trees the way Charlie did.

The slick road twisted and turned and twisted some more. Usually I enjoy handling snaky turns, but not tonight. At 9:45, I spotted Mamma David's neon sign in a small shopping center and pulled in, parking well away from the only other car on the lot, a battered Dodge.

A hand-lettered help-wanted sign was taped to the steamed-up window. I went inside and the aroma of fresh baked breads and brewing coffee made my stomach rumble.

Three announcements were tacked to a cork bulletin board inside the entrance. Under a picture of Mona Raeburn and Tony Weston the largest one said: *The Seaview Players Present Scottish Mists, starring Mona Raeburn, at the John Adams High School auditorium, in Seaview on January 13, 14 and 15 at 8 p.m..*

"What time do you close?" I asked the counterman. He was natty in a white jacket, a white paper cap perched over his left eyebrow.

"Ten, weekdays. But we're open later tonight. Doing a big wedding tomorrow. Take your time."

I didn't know if he was being sarcastic or magnanimous but I did that, casing the prepared dishes on display, the pricey markups on the vinegars and olive oils, imported mustards, English biscuits and Swiss chocolates. Overhead, baskets trailing gangrene-green plastic ivy hung from the ceiling. A cheapo note in this up-scale establishment.

A framed review from the *Harbor News* awarded 'Mamma David' four stars for his meat loaf. I ordered it with a side of potato salad, a side of good-looking baked macaroni and a diet Dr. Pepper and carried it all on a stainless tray to a table for four.

Someone had left a copy of today's *Newsday*. I caught up on the news while I ate.

The counterman brought me a glass of water.

"A bad week for New York," he said when I looked up. A nice guy, bored on this slow, rainy evening.

I said, "The Jets lost, the Rangers lost and the Islanders are a disaster. That what you mean?"

"And the Giants are favored to lose the Super Bowl."

"Always next year," I said.

As he turned to go, I said, "Can I get tickets here for that play in Seaview?"

"No. You can buy them at the door." He came back to my table and squatted beside me, lowering his voice. "The star, Mona Raeburn, is dead. Murdered on New Year's Eve. I guess you didn't hear about it."

"Did you know her?"

Solemn with self importance, he said, "I always delivered her dinners personally."

He pushed his cap further back on his head. "We delivered all her meals. Every morning we sent over breakfast and lunch. But I did the dinners.

"She usually answered the door herself. Real glamorous. Very good tipper. Some nights the guy in that picture up there came to the door. He never tipped."

He went back behind the counter and ran a spotless cloth over the stainless steel counter.

He was talking about Tony Weston. Which reminded me - I'd never told Charlie that Evelyn Blackmon had brought Tony's kilt into the Raeburn house.

When I started on the potato salad, I got a shock. It was the same as the one Anne Weston claimed as her family's recipe. She had to have bought it here. Why had she lied to me? Was it just one little white lie, or had she lied about other things? "I always tell the truth," she'd said.

I left the rest of it untouched, threw down a two dollar tip and replaced the newspaper on the magazine stand. Standing at the door, I watched the sleety rain washing down in silvery sheets.

"Rotten weather," the counterman said, "but at least it ain't snowing no more."

"No, it ain't," I said, and went outside.

I strolled the length of the covered arcade aimlessly and ended up at the Super X where I moseyed up and down the bright deserted aisles, in time with the Muzak, throwing items into a wire basket: razor blades, toothpaste, Kleenex, a six pack of Milky Ways, Diet Dr. Pepper.

In the soda aisle, I passed a young couple. She was looking up at him with all her loving heart in her eyes. The way Paula used to look at me when we were wildly in love. I went down a different aisle. I couldn't deal with my ghosts on a night like this.

I stowed my packages on the passenger seat feeling as mean as the weather. Still in no mood to go home, I started the motor, switched on the wipers and headed home anyway.

CHAPTER TWENTY

It was too early, too dark and too cold when the red-eye from Los Angeles touched down at Kennedy twenty minutes late the next morning.

I swallowed the last of my bitter coffee and rubbed my tensed neck muscles while passengers shuffled off the air bus and down the narrow walkway into the overheated terminal. Where was Tony Weston?

A tired-eyed blonde, mink-coated to her ankles, cell phone to her ear, passed me. Two earnest men, in close conference, straggled off. The pilots, wheeling carry on bags behind them were the last two off the plane.

Finally, there was Tony, in a camel's hair polo coat, dawdling at the plane's exit with a stewardess.

He was tanned. Two days in L.A. and he had a tan. And a doting stewardess hanging on his arm.

She touched Weston's cheek in an intimate way, and said something that made him laugh. He hugged her, tossed his two-suiter over one shoulder and strolled my way, taking his time.

His eyes skimmed past me, traveled to the nearly deserted arrivals terminal and returned to focus on me in a shock of recognition. He froze, tensed like an animal poised for flight, panicked eyes darting.

"Detective Harmony," I said, standing square in front of him.

"I remember you." Weston's face tried to right itself but he couldn't pull it off. "Is something wrong, uh, officer? Is Annie ...is my wife all right?"

"Yes, as far as I know. How about I give you a ride home? We can talk."

He stiffened and swallowed air, pulled a pair of sunglasses from his coat pocket, gained confidence as he masked his eyes and said with a toothy white smile, "Lucky me."

I headed for the down escalator. Weston hung back a split second, then squared his shoulders and matched his step to mine. He topped me by about five inches.

"I'm a little out of it," he said. "I didn't sleep on the plane."

I bet he didn't. Too busy swinging with the stewardess. "Got any luggage?"

"This is it."

"Then let's go."

Downstairs, the automatic doors opened onto a stinging rush of frigid air. I tugged my cap over my ears, pulled my scarf up to my chin and braved the cold.

All around us, passengers dashed in and out of taxicabs, irritable voices shouted, and skycaps slung luggage on crammed hand trucks. I steered Weston through the hubbub to my 'Vette parked in the no-waiting zone, unlocked the trunk and stowed his bag.

"Get in," I said. Maybe my tone was a little hostile. So what.

He climbed into the passenger side car and gave an exaggerated shiver. "I bet it's below freezing. It was ninety in L.A."

I ignored his chit-chat, ignored the yield sign, ignored the red light, and swung into the eastbound traffic.

Weston said, "I can see that you're an excellent driver," and fastened his seat belt a shade ostentatiously.

Faced with my tight lipped profile, he lapsed into a nervous silence, his left knee jiggling. He leaned his dark head against the head-rest and stared out the window. The parkway lights, still burning, cast yellow shadows on the snow.

I exited the airport onto the Van Wyck Expressway and barreled into the fast lane to pass a semi that rumbled up, hemming us in. Weston removed his sunglasses, closed his eyes and wiped a film of sweat from a face gone the color of putty.

"Sorry, I get car sick."

"You mean now?" I said.

He nodded. "Could you pull over? I'm sorry. My stomach is … I - I've got to …."

I cut across three lanes, pulled onto the frozen grass and watched him climb out, hang on to the car door for a moment, and then stagger through the snow and disappear behind a stand of pine trees.

When he finally came out from behind the trees, white-lipped, he leaned his forehead against the car roof.

"You feeling better?" I said.

"I - I...panic attack."

Good. My hostility had unnerved him. Or was his guilty conscience surfacing?

Weston's shoulders heaved, his hands made futile chopping motions. "I can't breathe!" He sucked air. "Oh my God, that was my last...hu...hu...I can't....

He clutched at his heart.

I jumped out of the car. If this was an act, it was some act. Weston swayed toward me, mouth hanging open, tongue extended, eyes popping. I could actually see his heart pound as his face alternately flushed scarlet and paled to ashen.

"Coat, hu, p-pocket," he stammered.

I patted him down and found a Walkman and earphones in one pocket, a silver pillbox in the other. I shook out one of the pills and tried to give it to him, but his flailing hands were curled into claws. The pill dropped into the frozen grass at our feet.

"My heart...s-stopped. Not b-beating."

"Don't conk out on me. Here," I shook another pill out of the silver pillbox and forced it between his lips. I felt for a pulse. It was racing but strong.

"Oh my God! Air. I need air. H-have you...got a p-paper...bag?"

"What? No. Listen, lean on me. I'll help you. That's it. Easy does it." I opened the car door. "Get in. I'll take you to a hospital."

Seated in the car, Weston's color began to return to normal and his breathing became less labored. I breathed easier too.

"Don't need h-hospital." He pointed to the Walkman in my hand. "M-med-d-itation t-t-tapes."

I forced his contorted hands open and clasped them around the Walkman. As I adjusted the headphones, my fingers brushed his hair. Springy. And thick.

He tuned in to his tapes, eyes closed.

I watched him for a few seconds. He seemed calmer so I climbed behind the wheel, skidded into the parkway traffic and drove the gas pedal to the floor. Traffic had thinned to a few trucks and an occasional car.

I looked sidelong at him, slumped in his seat, eyes closed, and wondered if his wife had discovered there was no one home behind that rugged front. He looked like gangbusters, but it was all window dressing.

We passed a fork lift truck as if it was standing still. I glanced at the speedometer and braked, slowing to eighty. Beside me, Weston began to take deep breaths, filling his lungs and blowing the air out in whistling gusts.

He pulled off the headphones. "Sorry about that. I'm okay now. The Xanax you gave me, and the meditation tapes worked. If I'd had a paper bag to breathe into, I'd have recovered faster."

"Next time."

"I get these anxiety attacks. They just come on. It's like I'm sucked out of myself."

"Was it just anxiety?"

"Just anxiety?" He was insulted. "You've obviously never had an anxiety attack or you wouldn't say that. Try to imagine all your automatic responses shutting down, being terrified you're dying."

He was working himself up again. "Have you ever felt your heart stop? Had to concentrate on each breath to make it happen?"

"As a matter of fact my allergy attacks...."

Weston didn't want to hear about me. He was too full of himself. "Has your throat ever closed, choking you, while wave after wave of adrenalin floods your body till you're completely overwhelmed?"

"O.K. Shut up about it, already. That's not what I want to talk to you about."

Weston shoved the Walkman into his coat pocket and looked sullen.

I said, "I don't know about anxiety but I do know what a terrible thing guilt is to live with."

"What do you mean, guilt?"

"Listen, it's just the two of us here. Let your hair down. Where did you sneak out to after your New Year's Eve party? Get it off your chest."

Beads of sweat pearled his even tan. "Get what off my chest?"

Would he relapse into another attack if I leaned on him? How far could I push him? I decided to take a shot.

"Come off it, Weston, I know you were with Mona Raeburn."

He tried to laugh, but it strangled in his throat. "You've got it all wrong. I was ...."

"Doing the dishes? I have witnesses say different."

Behind that polished façade he was plenty scared.

I said, "We'll ride over to headquarters now and sit down together and talk a little."

He faced me, nervous mouth twitching. "Are you arresting me?"

"No," I said. "But we should talk."

I turned onto the Belt Parkway. Ahead of us, in the east, black clouds veiled the sky. A few drops of rain hit the windshield. I switched on the wipers.

Weston shifted in his seat. "Why should I talk to you?"

I signaled, changed lanes and swung onto the Southern State Parkway, eastbound. "I think you can clear up a few things in this case."

He licked at his lips and chewed on a fingernail. His skin was streaky with sweat but he still looked like a Calvin Klein ad.

I changed the subject. "I hear you've got a big part in *"Scottish Mists."*

"I've had bigger ones. But it's an important role. It's pivotal. "

"What would I have seen you in?"

"*The Invasion of the Iguanas*."

I kept my eyes on the road. "Never heard of it."

"It's a cult movie."

"That so?"

"It plays the midnight show all over Manhattan. But it's been two years since I made it. Mona was my chance at a life changing break." Weston shook his head. "My wife doesn't understand me. She's content to live her life in Seaview. I'm not, damn it!" He pounded the car door with a clenched fist.

"Hey! What are you doing?" My arm shot out and the back of my hand smacked him in the nose. "That's my car!"

Weston's mouth made gasping movements and he brought his hand to his face. "I'm bleeding!" His fingers came away tinged with red. "I'm bleeding! This is police brutality."

I'd hit him because I'd felt like hitting him. Because I thought he'd murdered Mona Raeburn and because he was married to Anne Weston - who probably understood him too well. Now I had to apologize.

"Sorry I did that. But this is a classic 'Vette. All original parts. Body never redone. You practically broke the door."

He touched his nose. "I'm bleeding."

"Kleenex in the glove compartment."

He groped for the Kleenex and tilted his head back. "I can't believe you hit me." He sounded half-strangled. "My nose better not be broken."

"Your nose is fine. Don't make a mess. Put those tissues in the ashtray."

I had a blood sample now. Send it to the DNA lab – they'd compare it with the DNA in the semen samples found on the victim's body. And it'd match up.

I turned off the Southern State onto the Meadowbrook exiting onto Old Country Road. Blustery winds hurled a silver sheet of rain at the windshield and I nosed forward cautiously. A traffic light, swinging overhead, changed to a watery green. Most of the cars had their headlights on. I flipped on my fogs.

Weston's fingers drummed on his knee, keeping time with the drumming rain. "My stomach hurts," he said.

I headed west past the Court House, and another two blocks to Franklin, turned left, accelerated through the whirlpools overflowing the storm sewers and tested the brakes. A little wet.

He doubled over. "I need Maalox."

Two blocks later I pulled into the lot behind headquarters. "Come inside and I'll get you fixed up."

I drove to the empty far end, and parked diagonally across two spaces, taking my usual precautions.

"Get out," I said. I stuffed the bloodied tissues into a plastic baggie and sealed it.

He tumbled out into the lashing rain and shuffled along beside me. "You sure you've got Maalox in there?"

"I'll get you some."

CHAPTER TWENTY ONE

I took him in through the precinct's back entrance. The dim lighting masked the narrow hallway's flaking green paint and cast odd shadows across his face. Clutching his side with one hand, Weston shivered like a wet dog.

"Where's the john?" he said and limped off in the direction of my thumb, with me close behind him. I wasn't letting him out of my sight.

Under the men's room's bright lights, I came to face to face with the cruel contrast of our mirrored reflections. There was I, short, fat, moon-faced–balding. Beside me, Weston was tall and elegant with his square cleft chin, thin nose, high cheekbones and deep-set hazel eyes.

He concentrated on the mirror, exploring his nose with tentative fingers. Vain? He took vain to a new dimension.

Suppose I collared him for the Raeburn murder. Barbara Walters would interview him. He'd write his memoirs and make a fortune on the TV dramatization. Maybe even play himself. A first time offender, if he was found guilty, he'd get the minimum.

But maybe his wife would leave him.

I leaned against a wall and unwound my scarf, balled it up, smoothed it out, watching him splash cold water on his face.

"Look at my nose," he whined.

"I thought it was your stomach hurt."

He winced, playing up his suffering. "It does."

"You finished here?"

I grabbed his elbow and propelled him out the door and up a flight of stairs. On the second floor, I shoved the metal door open and a uniform jumped to attention.

"Officer...?"

"Graham."

I showed my badge. "Harmony, Homicide. I'll be using Lieutenant Faber's office, Graham, to interview this suspect."

The Lou's office was a little bigger than my walk-in closet at home. Two of the green-painted walls were lined with metal files, and across the third wall a crack meandered like a demented web. Behind the battered metal desk, rain pelted steadily against a window half-covered by a Venetian blind with a broken cord.

I parked on the edge of the desk, motioned Weston into one of the two straight-back chairs and paged Sergeant Wolfe. When she called back, I told her to get to headquarters on the double.

While I spoke to her, I spread the blood-stained tissues on the desk to air dry.

"Maalox," Weston reminded me.

"Stop off on the way and pick up a bottle of Maalox," I said into the phone.

I hung up and eyed Weston. His abject attitude begged mutely for sympathy.

Not from me.

I said, "We get guys in here all the time, doubled up in pain like you. It goes away like magic, once they admit to what's really eating them."

"What do you mean?"

"I guarantee you'll feel better once you stop lying to me and tell the truth."

His handsome face was frightened. "What do you mean? I've told you the truth."

"The thing is, you haven't. You were with Mona Raeburn when she died. Maybe you helped her die."

His mouth hung open. "Wha?...I...No!...I didn't... Are you crazy? I wasn't...."

"I have proof you were there, so do yourself a favor, get it off your chest."

He licked his lips. "Proof?"

"You were seen entering Mona Raeburn's house at twelve-thirty five. And at twelve-fifty you were seen leaving. Did you kill her, Tony?"

Lines furrowed his beautiful forehead. "This is unreal. Why would I kill Mona? I'd have been out of my mind to kill her. She believed in me. She encouraged me. She understood that I need more than a suburban life with a suburban housewife."

I said, "Tony, there are two witnesses who place you at the murder scene. Not one who might be mistaken, but two. So level with me. It was an accident, right?"

"What do you mean?"

"See, if it was an accident, I can help you."

"I don't like the way you're trying to put words in my mouth. There was no accident."

"You killed her in a rage then?"

Weston dredged up weak defiance. "What do you mean? I didn't kill her!"

"You were in her bed."

"No!"

"Yah, you were, Tony."

"I wasn't. What makes you think... No, I...." He stared at me and worked his mouth.

"You left traceable evidence behind."

His defiance oozed away. A tear slid down his high cheekbones, and he rubbed at his long lashed hazel eyes. Bloodshot now.

I pointed to the tissues on the desk top. "These blood samples will go to the lab. When it turns out that your blood matches the semen found on the victim's body, figure it out. You're in deep shit, Tony."

He half rose from his chair and sat down again. "If I tell you...oh, God!" He shifted uneasily. "Does Annie have to know about this?"

"I can't make any promises until I hear what you have to say, but maybe I can help you. The best thing you can do for yourself is to tell the simple truth. This is just between the two of us. No one's taking notes."

Weston looked at my sincere, helpful face; wavered and crumbled.

"I was with her."

"That's more like it."

"But I didn't kill her. She'd asked me to come by. When Mona asked for something, it was a command. I didn't dare refuse her. I didn't go there to make love to her but...."

He stroked his hair a couple of times and went on, "When I came in she was lying on the couch, naked. She started playing with herself. Watching me watch her in the candlelight."

His voice broke. "Please, I...don't want to tell you this."

I sat quietly, waiting to hear the rest.

"She...she said, 'I've got a hell of an itch and I need you to scratch it for me.'

Sleazebag. Cheating on his wife with a woman who apparently spread her legs for every man who walked through her door.

"So you jumped her."

Weston reddened and scrunched down in his chair. "We began to...but she passed out. I...when I realized she wasn't conscious, I... started to pull out...still coming."

He wiped his forehead. "I–all over the cushions. I swear that's what happened. I swear it. I wasn't there for more than fifteen minutes altogether. She only passed out. She wasn't dead! She was snoring a little. I covered her with her fur coat and went home."

He sighed and looked into my face anxiously. "That's what happened. That's all that happened. I didn't kill her."

Had I fished the truth out of him? When suspects begin to crack, there's always more story they haven't spilled.

"Sure you didn't cover her body with your kilt?"

"My quilt?"

"Your kilt."

"What kilt?"

"The kilt you wear in *Scottish Mists*."

Weston's face was a mixture of fear and puzzlement. "What about it?"

"You planted it, hoping we'd think it was Taylor's."

He covered his face with his beautiful thin fingers. A very graceful movement. "I don't believe this," he moaned.

"You wanted to make it look as if Taylor killed Mona."

"Why would I want to do that to Taylor?"

"You tell me. Forensics can prove it was your kilt."

Weston looked at me with hate in his long-lashed eyes. "Forensics can't prove anything because you don't have my kilt. Mona was alive when I left her. How often do I have to say it?"

I hopped off the desk, walked to the door and tried another angle. "Did you let the dog loose?"

"Poochie? No. I heard him barking, but...I didn't pay any attention to him."

I opened the door.

Weston turned to me in alarm. "Where are you...."

"I'll be back."

I went into the corridor to wait for Wolfie. Leave him alone to let his nerves work on him. But was I still so sure he was the murderer?

CHAPTER TWENTY TWO

Wolfie puffed up the stairs, her face reddened by the cold.

"What are you up to?" she said when she saw me standing in the hallway.

I pointed behind me. "I left Weston alone to sweat it out. Maybe he'll work himself up to a confession."

We went back into the office together. Weston had pulled his chair up to the desk and fallen asleep, his head cradled on his arms. So much for terrorizing him.

"Wake up Tony, Sergeant Wolfe brought Maalox."

He batted his long lashes at Wolfie with a wan smile. "I guess I fell asleep. I came in on the redeye this morning, from L.A," he said to her, the charm turned on automatic.

Dazzled, Wolfie handed over the Maalox.

"Thank you." He gazed into her eyes. "God, I feel awful."

She was all sympathy. "I'm so sorry. Can I get you a cup of tea?"

"Gosh, thanks." He'd turned the charm up a few notches and she was bowled over.

Smiling all over herself, she ran off. He took a swig of the Maalox, and wiped the chalky residue from the corner of his lips. "I want to make a phone call."

I nudged the phone on Lt. Faber's desk toward him. "Be my guest."

He dialed, waited and spoke into it with a worried face. "It's me, Babe, I'm in trouble."

Babe? Not his wife. Not his lawyer.

"A detective picked me up at the airport and I'm in a police station now." Gesturing at the phone, he said to me, "I'm leaving a message. Where are we?"

"You're at 1490 Franklin Avenue, Mineola. Homicide division."

He croaked the address into the phone and added lamely, "Talk to you later." He held on to the receiver in a futile effort to prolong the contact.

I said, "You called Babe Freeman. Why not your wife?"

"I don't have to answer that." He returned the telephone to its cradle and sagged against the straight chair.

How much time did I have to try to get him to talk before Babe arrived and shut him up?

I leaned my back against the window and fiddled with the broken blind's cord. "Isn't this what happened?" I said, "You sneaked out to meet Mona thinking you'd snatch a little private time. You thought she would open doors for you. But instead she told you she'd changed her mind about doing the play. She was going to Hollywood. Dumping you. When she brushed you off, you went crazy. You hardly knew what you were doing."

"It was nothing like that!"

"If that's how it was, if you lost your head, her murder wasn't premeditated. It's manslaughter. First time offender, you could even get off. Why don't you come clean with me. Make it easy on yourself."

"I didn't kill her! She never said anything about going to Hollywood." Weston looked at me with desperation. "I didn't kill her! I told you what happened. Why won't you believe me?"

"Maybe I do believe you."

He eyed me with suspicion, expecting a trick.

Wolfie came back, carrying a tray loaded with one mug of tea, two cups of coffee and a bag of donuts.

She had combed her hair, slicked her mouth with pink gloss. Her face no longer red with cold had a pretty glow. And she was gawking at Weston like a besotted groupie.

Weston pulled the other chair over for her to sit on, thanked her for his tea and stirred it. When his mouth wasn't smiling at a woman, it was dissatisfied.

I offered him a donut and he shook his head.

I said, "Mona Raeburn is dead. I want to know who killed her. I'm, sure you do too."

He nodded.

I sipped the coffee. Wolfie gaped openly at Weston. He posed for her; a lock of hair falling across his forehead, his head turned three quarters to display his profile.

I bit into a glazed whole wheat.

Officer Graham knocked on the door, opening it wide enough to stick his head through. "There's a pissed off woman and a pissed off lawyer looking for you downstairs," he said.

"Babe," Weston said. "Thank God."

"Bring them up," I said. "Wait a minute." I found labels and a paper bag in the desk drawer, bagged the air-dried tissues, sealed the bag and marked it: Raeburn case – Urgent, dated and signed it and gave it to Graham to run down to the lab. The faster it got to Serology, the better.

The door slammed open and Babe Freeman burst in. A squat, big-eared man with a thick neck and almost no shoulders, followed behind her.

Thick-neck's round hazel eyes were indeed, pissed off at me.

"I'm Mr. Weston's attorney," he said. "Alfred Middens." He patted the pockets of a very nice gray suit and withdrew a pair of black-framed reading glasses. Tapping them in his palm, he said, "Is Mr. Weston under arrest, Officer?"

"Detective Harmony. No."

"Then why is he here?"

"We were chatting about a murder case I'm investigating."

"Babe?" Weston reached out a hand.

"Tony." She knelt beside him, covering his hand with hers. "Don't worry. I'm here."

Weston kissed her hand with a hangdog expression. I couldn't figure their relationship. Was Weston servicing her too?

Clutching Babe's hand, Weston said, "You can't believe what I've been through." He pointed to his nose and whispered into her ear.

Her face stiff with fury, Babe said, "Tell Mr. Middens what you just told me, Tony."

With his hand locked into hers, Weston was brave. "I was struck, unprovoked. Look at my nose. Is it broken?"

Babe stroked his face gently. "Gross police brutality."

"Not at all," I said, fighting the temptation to take a swing at her. It didn't seem a viable alternative under the circumstances. "My car skidded and I threw my arm out; like this."

My arm whipped backward, stopping short of Weston's nose. He ducked, shielding his face.

"It was a courteous, reflexive gesture on my behalf to insure his safety. I came into contact with his nose entirely by accident."

Babe turned on me with a wintry smile, "Little men need to exaggerate their little authority. But you'll rue the day you bludgeoned Tony."

"Bludgeoned?"

Her furious eyes met mine. "This incident will be reported to your superiors."

The only thing that would make me happier than proving Weston a murderer, would be to prove Babe one.

Middens said, "If you're not booking my client, Detective Harmony, he's free to go."

I didn't have enough to detain Weston.

The three of them walked out.

Wolfie took one donut and gave me the rest of the bag. I ate all four of them on my way to the hospital to see Charlie.

CHAPTER TWENTY THREE

Babe Freeman was the quintessence of all I do not like in a woman. Abrasive condescending bigmouthed interfering....

The wind had blown the rain away and a weak sun was trying to brighten the clearing sky. There was very little traffic. Ten minutes later I pulled into Mid-Island Hospital to report to Charlie. I cruised the parking lot twice before I backed into an empty slot reserved for MDs and jogged to the hospital entrance, stomping through puddles.

In Room 219, one bed was stripped to its plastic-covered mattress. Charlie, very large in flamingo printed pajamas, was in the other, munching on a pink Hostess Sno Ball.

Her bandages were gone, exposing seamed, shiny skin that looked parboiled. Not a pretty sight.

"How y'doin'?" I said, averting my eyes.

"Fit as a fiddle with busted strings. Nah, I'm okay. Getting out of here tomorrow morning. I waited for your call all day. What's up?"

I brought her up to date, beginning with Evelyn Blackmon and ending with Weston leaving headquarters with his lawyer and Babe.

"I got Weston to admit he dropped by to see Mona after the party. Says they had a quickie, but she passed out in the middle. Says he left her snoring. It's a viable story."

Charlie said. "You believe it?"

"Not sure. Babe Freeman said her car's headlights picked Weston up running across the lawn at twelve fifty. If Mona was still alive when Raeburn got there at one twenty, Weston didn't kill her. And if she answered Taylor's phone call at one a.m. Weston didn't kill her. But something's not right."

I stretched out on the stripped bed and stuck a pillow behind my back. "You should have seen him, Charlie. He all but wet his pants when I started to lean on him. But Babe trotted the lawyer over and I had to let him go."

Charlie said, "For my money, Taylor's the killer. He's got spook's eyes. I never knew a man with eyes like that who wasn't a villain."

"He may be a villain, but he didn't kill Mona," I said. "Taylor made two phone calls to her a few minutes before one. The first time she hung up. The second time he spoke to her. The calls came from his apartment. I checked with the phone company records."

"If she answered the phone, then she was alive after Weston left," Charlie said.

"But what if it wasn't Mona who answered the phone? What if she was already dead and the killer answered the phone? See, what bothers me, is the dog."

Charlie poured a glass of ice water, drank it and squashed the paper cup between her red swollen hands.

"I'm thick, I know. Explain that to me."

"Gresham says the dog was barking when Mona locked him up. Weston says he heard the barking but didn't see the dog. But someone let him out before Raeburn showed up fifteen minutes later. He bit Raeburn."

Charlie tossed the cup at a wastepaper basket, missing it. "Either Weston let the dog out and lied about it.... Why would the fuck would he do that?"

"Or someone else was there during those fifteen minutes between the time Weston left and Raeburn arrived," I said.

She swallowed the last of her Sno Ball and brushed coconut crumbs from her pajama top onto the white thermal blanket.

I said, "Whoever let the dog out is our murderer."

She licked her index finger, picked up two coconut crumbs and licked her finger again. "The first guy, Gresham, says he went out the back door when he saw Weston letting himself in. So she was alive when Gresham left."

"That's right. Alive and ready to bed down with Weston."

Charlie's swollen finger stabbed the air. "Taylor heard Gresham and left. Gresham saw Weston and left. Babe saw Weston and left. Raeburn saw Berger and left. You think Mona handed out numbered tickets? It's after midnight in a fucking blizzard, there's no electricity, still everyone in this fucking case manages to see everyone else either go in or come out of the fucking Raeburn house.

"And Mrs. Weston, with a headache that sent her upstairs to bed, watched the whole parade. But she didn't see her husband?"

"She didn't see Gresham either, Charlie."

"Yeah and maybe she saw dipshit, sweet peaches. What if Mrs. Weston let the dog out?"

She reached for a package of Bubblicious gum on the table next to the bed and unwrapped a piece of Gonzo Grape. "Shit! I said it before, it'd be the easiest thing in the world for her to slip out, hold the pillow over Mona's face and plant the kilt."

I said, "Wouldn't she be afraid we'd think the kilt was Weston's?"

"Why? Taylor was wearing a kilt. Not Weston."

"Weston says she was upstairs in bed," I said.

"Now we're believing Weston? He wasn't up there with her, was he? She had the opportunity, the means and a motive."

The room reeked with the fake odor of grapes.

"What motive did she have? Mona ruined her party?"

Charlie blew a purple bubble and inhaled it. "Maybe you should get into another line of business, sweetheart. Her husband was having an affair with Mona, for Chrissake."

"She didn't know that."

"Of course she knew. What are you, Dumbo all of a sudden? The whole fucking town knew."

She shook the blanket, scattering crumbs to the floor.

"All right, Charlie, Anne Weston's a possible suspect. I've got a flash for you: so is Babe Freeman. She's out there, sitting in her car. What if after she sees Weston leave, she goes inside and smothers Mona. After all, she'd just threatened to do it. Her exact words were, `I'm going to kill you, you heartless bitch'."

"Yeah," Charlie said.

"Then she lets the dog out to stop it barking, and drives back to the diner."

"No. Babe was gone when Raeburn arrived. And she had to have been at the diner for a while before Berger came in. You think she had time to drive there, do all that work she said she did and have an urn of coffee ready ? I don't think so."

"I'm just saying it's possible."

Charlie's lashless, red-streaked eyes blinked. "Who else 've we got? Raeburn?"

I shook my head.

"What are you shaking your head for? He doesn't have a motive? Ex-husband burgles the place–cool as cool. Maybe Mrs. Raeburn woke up, surprised him and he killed her."

"With his daughter waiting for him outside? Audrey wouldn't be protecting him if he'd murdered her mother."

"He killed the poor mutt, didn't he? Or maybe they teamed up together to do it. Audrey and him."

"Possible," I said. "Not very probable."

"They see the kilt in the hallway after they kill Mona and they plant it on the body. Raeburn needed money, right? Audrey was inheriting."

Charlie yawned. "Get me my robe, kid, need to stretch my legs."

I opened the clothes locker and tossed her a frayed rayon tent.

"Of course," she said, shrugging into it, "Alan Berger could have killed her before he reported finding the body."

She squatted down to root under the bed, stood up with a pair of flip-flops, slid her blue-veined feet into them and said, "Let's take a walk."

The sounds of daytime television, game shows, talk shows, cartoons and soaps leaked from each room we passed. I kept my eyes on the freshly waxed floor, avoiding a possible glimpse of somebody stuck full of tubes and monitoring machines.

The corridor ended in a circular room furnished with red vinyl couches and a table stacked with tattered magazines. A dirt-streaked window next to the elevators looked out on an air shaft.

Charlie plunked down on one of the couches. With her eyebrows and lashes singed off and her furrowed forehead, she looked like a sunburned Klingon. "This damn thing's made of cement."

She spread boiled-looking hands on her knees. "Let's consider Berger."

I said, "Berger got to the Raeburn house at one-twenty-five according to Audrey. And Anne Weston said he ran out of the house a minute or two after he arrived. He didn't have enough time."

Charlie shifted her wide thighs, trying to get comfortable. "All right. So Berger's not our best suspect. If Mona was dead by one o'clock, he's clean. But we gotta consider him. He found the body."

She stood up. I stood up too. Her belt had come undone and she double-knotted it. "I'm going back to my room now, Jake. Dinner'll be coming soon. I ordered chicken a la king. And rice pudding."

"O.K. I'll go." I pressed the down elevator button. "See you on the job tomorrow," I called to her broad back, and got a wave in return.

CHAPTER TWENTY FOUR

At half-past eight the next morning when I arrived at the bottom of Wellington Road, Charlie was behind the desk in the mobile crime unit as if she'd never been away. A pair of tortoise framed drugstore sunglasses camouflaged her missing eyebrows and lashes, but her seamed face was shiny pink and blotched with crusty patches. Her hands, holding the Raeburn file, were twice their normal size.

She glanced up and saw my expression. "Will I scare little kids?" she said.

"I've seen you look better."

I tossed my hat up on the coat rack, unbuttoned my jacket and was about to say, 'Coffee?' when Officer O'Neill burst in the door, all his freckles vivid on his pale, excited face.

"APB just came in. They've got a dead body at the Seaview library."

Charlie lumbered to her feet, scattering papers.

O'Neill knelt to retrieve them.

"Leave it! Let's go."

* * *

The siren's staccato coughed into silence as we pulled up to the library. The three of us jumped from the car slamming the doors, drowning its death throes.

Light snow, red-tinted in the car's flashing lights, floated in the damp-smelling air and a brown mongrel dog circled, snapping at our legs. We marched behind O'Neill's uniformed arm, through the small snow-dusted crowd of jostling women in plastic rain hoods.

I shoved open the plate glass door to the library.

"Keep those people down here," I flung at O'Neill as Charlie and I clattered up the stairs.

A uniformed officer guarded the staircase to Taylor's apartment against a whispering knot of women gathered at the book checkout.

"Homicide's here," I said.

The uniform opened the staircase door. "Upstairs."

The door to Taylor's apartment was half-open and I pushed it wider. Two elderly women huddled together on the sofa. Opposite them, another uniform sat at the scarred library table, eyeing a plate of meringue tarts.

He stood up hastily when he saw us. "Officer Tuffy," he said. "William Jarvis Tuffy."

Charlie pulled out her notebook. "You were the first officer?"

"Yes. Officer Dunn and me, we were cruising in the vicinity. The dispatcher sent us. On entering the premises, we found the victim in the kitchen. Unconscious. I immediately called for help and then attempted resuscitation."

Moisture beaded Tuffy's upper lip. "The body was identified as Ashley Taylor, head librarian, by these two ladies–witnesses– who I detained."

Charlie looked up from her notebook to scowl at the nearest woman on the sofa. "Who are you?"

"I am Grace Chartwell, research librarian," she said, her intelligent face, bare of makeup regarded Charlie with distaste.

"You discovered the body?"

"Yes. We both...." Her eyes flickered to the kitchen door, "found him. My assistant, Mrs. Mott and I found him...found Taylor. We were together."

Mrs. Mott half-rose from the sofa with a wavering smile, then sank down again. She was small and plump, with papaya-colored hair that rippled to the shoulders of a fluttering pink blouse. I'd seen her type before. Too much rouge settling into wrinkles on a sixty year old face.

"Good morning," she said, nervously gathering her ruffles closer to her sagging chin. Her eyes darted to Charlie's seamed face and slid away.

"Christ!" Charlie said, scribbling away, "Is it a good morning when you find a dead body?"

Mrs. Chartwell tucked a strand of gray hair behind her ear. "This situation is difficult enough. Must you be so rude?"

While Charlie looked at her with choked fury, I said, "How did you happen to find the body?"

Mrs. Mott stared at her white Nike Air Trainers, crossed them and recrossed them.

Mrs. Chartwell rose from their sofa with tall dignity. "Taylor is usually downstairs in the morning when we arrive, at eight."

Her voice quavered. She stopped, tensed with the effort to control it and went on. "But this morning he wasn't. I unlocked the door, went to my desk and arranged today's work. When he still was not down, I called him on the intercom. There was no answer. I thought...."

Mrs. Mott made a strangled noise.

Mrs. Chartwell ignored her. "We feared something might be amiss, and went upstairs. The New York Times was still on the mat in front of his door. I knocked. When there was no answer, I tried the door. It was unlocked."

Under violet-shadowed lids, Mrs. Mott's faded eyes blinked and dared to look directly at Charlie. She said, "We went inside. He was lying on the kitchen floor, face down. A chair had fallen over him."

"I picked the chair up," Mrs. Chartwell said.

I said, "What else did you do? Did you touch him?"

Ramrod-straight, Mrs. Chartwell fixed her gray eyes on my face. "I put my hand on his shoulder and tried to rouse him. To no avail."

Her manner was formidable but I noticed that her hands, clasped at her brown tweed waist, trembled.

"Taylor has had a problem with alcohol," Mrs. Mott said. She had chewed most of the lipstick from her mouth but the dry edges of her upper lip were still faintly scarlet.

"They thought he was drunk," Charlie said, making a note.

Mrs. Chartwell said, "No, young woman, we did not!" Her left hand went to her neck and twisted a strand of pearls. "That is, perhaps we did at first. Then…"

She couldn't keep the horror from her face or voice. "We realized... something... was very wrong."

She sat down abruptly on the edge of the sofa. "I called 911 and we came out here to wait."

"Tuffy, move these witnesses out of the crime scene. Put them across the hall," I said. "Let's have a look at him, Charlie."

* * *

The odor of stale death permeated the kitchen. Taylor lay face down on the floor, a yellow plaid kilt thrown across his legs. One hand clutched his throat, the other rested on a broken cup.

We knelt beside the lifeless body.

Charlie said, "He's been dead for hours, poor bastard.
Another fucking kilt! Is this the perp's fucking signature?"

"The other one was red, this is yellow, Charlie."

"I'm not saying it's the same kilt, sweet peaches, I'm saying it's another fucking kilt."

I sniffed the broken cup without touching it. We couldn't touch anything until the Crime Scene arrived.

Strolling into the kitchen, Tuffy said, "I found this box." He held out a small cardboard container.

"What are you doing, you moron? Put that down. It's goddam evidence," Charlie yelled. "Don't you know enough to keep your hands in your fucking pockets when you're at a crime scene?"

Tuffy dropped the box on the kitchen counter next to the electric coffee pot. Charlie said, "I know crime is not a way of life in Seaview, William Jarvis Tuffy, but for your information, you don't pick up evidence with your sweaty ham-fists because there might be recognizable fingerprints on it."

Tuffy shifted his feet.

"Let's try to pretend you're a professional and stop ham-footing around destroying more evidence. Our job is hard enough; it's harder when you're stupid and incompetent. Aah! Get your ass out of my sight."

Tuffy backed out of the kitchen.

"Cytotox," I said, reading the label. "Look at the list of ingredients on this box, Charlie. Almost pure cyanide."

She shook her head. "I didn't smell it on him." Meaning cyanide's bitter almond odor.

"No, I didn't either. We wouldn't if he's been dead for more than three hours. But look at his skin."

She squinted at Taylor's body and wrote, 'cyanide powder found at scene, although cyanide odor absent, victim's pink skin suggests cyanide as possible cause of death'

Tuffy rapped on the door- jamb.

"The M.E. is here."

Dr. Byrd, nodded at us, pulled on a pair of gloves and got down to business. When he turned the body over, Taylor's dilated pupils stared blankly. I thought of him as he had been and a chill skittered across my nerves.

"I said, "Cyanide?"

Dr. Byrd peeled the thin gloves from his hands. "I can't tell anything yet, except he's been dead for about twelve hours, give or take.

He's just coming out of first state rigor. You'll hear from me after I get a look at the contents of his stomach."

He shrugged into his coat and left.

The Crime Scene Unit arrived then and we got out of the kitchen while they did their job: photographing, measuring, sketching, bagging, scraping....

In Taylor's bedroom, a young woman with short tawny hair, looked up from her flashing camera. "I'm Wanda Koutoupiazis."

"Spell that," Charlie said.

She did.

I said, "That's not a name, it's an eye chart."

She ignored me and went into the rectangular alcove between the bedroom and the bathroom. We heard her camera clicking rapidly.

Taylor's bed had not been slept in. Piles of books were stacked on the olive-drab blanket. A lamp still glowed beside the bed. I followed Wanda into the alcove.

While she brushed powder onto the built-in desk, leaving behind a film of black dust, she said, "Nothing definite on the computer keys. Smudges. No prints on the pen."

"Printer on or off?" I said.

"Printer's off, computer's on. Now for this printout here, the best thing is take it to the lab and process it with Ninhydrin, we'll have results tomorrow."

"Charlie, come here!"

I pulled on a pair of disposable gloves and lifted the computer printout by its edges with the tips of my fingers. We read the message together:

I have been profoundly depressed since I caused the death fo Mona Raeburn. I can't live with the terrible pressure of my guilt. I am paying for my crime by taking my life with my own hand.

A.T.

Taylor's initials –A.T.– were scrawled in green ink beneath the printed note. And green ink, I recalled, underlined the lines in Anne Weston's Bible.

"So, I was right, all along." Charlie said. "I knew he did it."

"For the love of Mike, Charlie, anyone could have come in here and written that. It's not even signed."

"It's initialed. I find a suicide note, a dead body, and a confession, I say–case closed. Especially when I thought he was our man in the first place." She pointed to the fine-point green Scripto pen. "Here's the pen he used to write his initials."

I said, "Wanda just told us the pen was clean. Why would Taylor wipe the pen, Charlie, before he killed himself? And we know he didn't kill Mona Raeburn."

"What's this `we know' shit? I don't know that."

"He telephoned her from here minutes before she died."

She turned an exasperated face to me. "Those phone calls are bullshit. He made them up." She jabbed at the printout without touching it. "Why would Taylor commit suicide because he killed Mona Raeburn, if he didn't kill her?"

"I hear you, Charlie, but I don't believe my ears." I shook my head. "The telephone company corroborated his calls."

"They make mistakes all the time."

"Oh, sure. I suppose Taylor slogged for miles in the snow storm to kill Mona and planted the kilt by her body so we'd be sure to suspect he was the killer."

Still grasping the printout by the edges in my gloved fingers, I went to the Adult Education classroom across the hall where the two librarians waited, and placed it on the desk.

"Would you look at this please, without touching it?" I said. "Could this have come from Taylor's printer?"

Both women bent over the note. Mrs. Mott gave a mouse-like squeak, but Mrs. Chartwell maintained her cold dignity as she looked up from the printout.

"It's a laser printout and Taylor has the only laser printer. The ones downstairs are dot matrix. But I can tell you with certitude that Taylor did not write those initials."

"Now you're a handwriting authority?" Charlie snapped.

Mrs. Chartwell said, "Taylor never wrote with anything but his own Parker fountain pen. He always carried it with him. It has a wide nib. And he eschewed colored inks."

Mrs. Mott bobbed her head, in agreement.

Charlie took off her sunglasses and wiped them. Her blood-shot eyes, sunk in their swollen pouches, drilled Mrs. Chartwell.

"He was under stress," Charlie said.

"Taylor did not initial this," she said.

I said, "Who could have come in here and used this computer?"

"Nobody."

Charlie masked her eyes with the sunglasses again but not the belligerence on her corrugated face. "Nobody could have used this computer but Taylor. And Taylor didn't write this note."

"To be quite precise, I said he didn't initial the note. There are other computers downstairs for common use, but Taylor had his own password to activate his private files."

I suddenly remembered Anne, saying, `It's his name in Latin.'

"Do you know the password?" I asked Mrs. Chartwell.

"I do not."

"Could I get a Latin dictionary up here?"

"Of course." Her gray eyes quizzed me. "But perhaps I can help you."

"You can, if you know the Latin word for tailor."

"Taylor, I don't believe there is..."

"Tailor, with an i."

"Oh. Yes," she said, "That would be textor, of course."

"Of course, how did that slip my mind?"

I went back to the alcove, gave the printout to Wanda for further testing and clicked the mouse to get into the directory.

A box appeared on the screen: PLEASE ENTER PASSWORD.

I entered: TAYLOR.

Invalid Password, appeared on the screen.

I typed TEXTOR. Invalid Password.

Over my shoulder, Charlie who'd followed me in, said, "Try, Open Sesame."

"Are you kidding?"

"Humor me. Try it."

I shook my head, but I typed: OPEN SESAME.

Invalid Password.

"Enter Sesame, just Sesame by itself."

I did. Invalid Password.

"Well, that's that," she said. "We're locked out."

I leaned against the wall feeling irritable. I didn't like the way things were going. "If Taylor was the only one who could get into his computer, he was the only one who could type that note."

"Check."

I said, "Did you notice? The word 'of' is misspelled in the note."

"He probably wasn't in the mood to use Spell Check."

"No. Somebody else wrote it. Somebody writing in a hurry, who overlooked the mistake. Somebody wearing gloves. There aren't any prints on the pen."

Charlie shrugged. "There are plenty of explanations. The point is nobody but Taylor had access to his computer. What did the old lady say? She knew with certitude?"

"Taylor's password wasn't all that secret. He told it to Anne Weston."

Charlie said, "Mrs. Weston is the only other one who knew Taylor's password? How interesting."

"I didn't say she was the only one. I'm sure she's not the only one. And anyway she told me she didn't remember it."

"Then, naturally, we don't have to question her."

I felt my neck get warm. "Of course, we'll question her. It's possible she mentioned it to Weston and he knows it. And I bet you Babe Freeman knows it. She and Taylor were engaged weren't they?" I snapped my fingers. "Remember Babe told us to come looking for her, if anything happened to Taylor."

"Yeah. She said that."

"She fits what I call the ABA Syndrome."

"What's that?"

"Accumulated bad associations," I said. "*One:* Her last boy- friend before Taylor was found dead. Maybe suicide, maybe not. *Two:* She threatened to kill Mona Raeburn. Mona Raeburn's dead. *Three:* She threatened to kill Taylor. Taylor's dead. How come the people she threatens end up dead?"

"You're way off track. Babe was at the hospital with me last night. Brought me a steak sandwich. And was I glad to see her! I was starving. Supper was a dish of glue they call chicken a la king followed by a bowl of glue supposed to be rice pudding."

"Nice of her."

"Bet your ass. It was a Cajun steak sandwich with green chilies, and mustard sauce. I coulda ate two of 'em."

"What time did she arrive with all this?"

"Eight-thirty. And she stayed after visiting hours were over. She didn't leave until the nurse came in to take my temperature."

"What did you talk about all that time?"

"Didn' talk. We watched TV."

I shut down the computer. "I don't think Taylor would have worded a suicide note like that. A librarian would be meticulous about his use of words."

"Now you're a literary critic? The guy was about to off himself. He wasn't thinking about how his composition would sound to Jake Harmony. Just like he grabbed the first pen in sight."

"And wiped it clean of fingerprints."

Charlie shrugged.

I said, "He tried suicide once before. I wonder, did he leave a note that time? If he did, I want to see it."

Babe Freeman would be able to tell us about that. I'd ask her. And ask her about Taylor's password. And ask her if she'd been in his apartment last night.

"Did Babe bring you dessert with that dinner?"

"Lemon meringue tart."

I led her back to the library table and pointed to the plate of lemon meringue tarts. I moved one aside exposing the thin blue logo on the dish: *Seaview Diner*.

CHAPTER TWENTY FIVE

"So what?" Charlie said. "Doesn't mean Babe was here. "Maybe Taylor had dinner at the Seaview Diner last night and brought dessert home."

Maybe but I didn't think so.

The two librarians sat on wooden chairs in the Adult Education room. As we walked in, Mrs. Mott wiped tears and lavender shadow from her eyes with a lace-edged handkerchief.

Charlie went to the window and stood with her back to it, focused on her notebook.

"Life is so strange," Mrs. Mott said. "Just last night we had such a pleasant evening with Taylor. And now...this."

"We?" I said.

Mrs. Mott's rouged cheeks reddened. "Our embroidery class."

"Adult Education," Mrs. Chartwell said. "Anne Weston teaches it Wednesday evenings. From seven to nine."

"Not last night, Sarah," Mrs. Mott corrected her. "Last night we broke up at eight-thirty."

She caught my eye and immediately looked away. Her eyelids fluttered. "Because Anne was ill. I think the poor child has that stomach flu."

"It's going around," Mrs. Chartwell said. "Everyone has it."

"Yes, it's going around." Mrs. Mott sighed.

"It is," I agreed. "Are you in the class too, Mrs. Chartwell?"

"No, young man. I am not. I was in my office working late and I joined them for coffee."

Mrs. Mott's eyes darted to Charlie and then to me. "I'm making a set of needle point covers," she said. "For my daughter's dining room chairs."

"That's a big job," I said.

"Oh yes."

Charlie made a circular movement with her left hand, meaning move it.

"How many ladies are in your class, Mrs. Mott?"

Her lips moved silently as she counted on plump pink tipped fingers. "Six. But last night we were only four. There were ten of us at first but there are always drop- outs. The class was almost canceled."

I crooked a finger at Tuffy. "I want names and addresses for everyone who was here last night. In fact, get them for the original ten. "

Tuffy looked up from his notebook. "Ten. Names and addresses."

Mrs. Mott waited until my attention turned to her again, and continued in a quavering voice, "We usually have coffee with Taylor after class, in his apartment. Anne baked chocolate chip cookies."

Tears filled her eyes.

"This is very difficult for you, I know," I said and waited a tactful moment before I asked, "All of you had coffee?"

"Yes. Decaffeinated, of course. I get terrible palpitations from caffeine."

Mrs. Chartwell said, "Amanda. Don't you remember, Anne asked for tea."

"Yes, that's right. Anne had tea."

"The rest of you had coffee."

"And cookies," Mrs. Mott said. "They were excellent. Quite a nice treat. We finished them. Every crumb."

"Who made the coffee?"

The two librarians looked at each other.

"Enid? Did Enid make the coffee?" Mrs. Mott said.

"I thought it was Frances," Mrs. Chartwell said," but perhaps Frances set the table."

"No, Janice and I set the table. So either Enid or Frances made the coffee."

"Frances brought the pot in and poured for everyone."

"Yes. So she must have made the coffee." Mrs. Mott nodded and smiled. She had cleared that up.

Charlie left the window. "Who gives a pea turkey damn who made the coffee? Where was Taylor?"

"At the table with us."

"And you all had coffee and ate the cookies?"

"Well, Anne went inside to lie down for a while."

"But the rest of you ate and drank the same stuff and Taylor was O.K.", I said.

"Oh, yes. He was quite cheerful."

I looked over at Charlie to make sure she'd noted that 'cheerful'.

"Who went into the kitchen after you finished eating?" I said.

"I stacked the dishes in the dishwasher," Mrs. Chartwell said.

"Did you wash the coffee pot?

"No. It was still almost half full. I left it plugged in, in case Taylor wanted some later."

"Somebody washed it. It's on the counter now and it's clean. Did you see any meringue tarts?"

"There were no tarts here last night," Mrs. Chartwell said. "I would have seen them when I put away the milk."

"But this morning," Mrs. Mott said, "we found them on the platter on the dining table."

"How did they get there, I wonder?" I said. "And when?"

"How many tarts were there?" Charlie said.

Mrs. Mott got very red in the face and I realized that she'd eaten some, and was ashamed to admit she'd been able to eat with Taylor lying dead in the next room.

"How many?" Charlie insisted.

Mrs. Chartwell took over. “Well, there are two here now. Amanda and I shared one and we gave one to the officer downstairs and one to this officer.”

“I think he had two, Sarah.”

“This officer ate the fu… ate the evidence?” Charlie said.

Tuffy looked at his feet.

“We all ate them,” Mrs. Chartwell said.

“Were they room temperature or refrigerated?” I said.

“They were room temperature,” Mrs. Mott said and turning to Charlie: “There were six.”

“Everyone who ate them seems to be in good health,” Charlie said, glaring at Tuffy.

“Who else went into the kitchen?” I asked Mrs. Chartwell.

“Well, we all tidied up out here but I think Anne did. And Taylor.”

“That so?” Charlie said. “While you ladies `tidied' up, Mrs. Weston was in the kitchen with Taylor?”

“Yes, she had asked Taylor for some aspirin and he brought it to the kitchen where she could get a glass of water.”

“Just the two of them were in the kitchen.”

Mrs. Mott blinked. “Yes. I heard them talking while I stored the wools and the patterns in the cupboards.”

She turned mild blue eyes on me. “The door was ajar, I wasn't eavesdropping. Their voices carried....”

“Poor man,” Mrs. Chartwell said. “God rest his soul.”

“What did they say, Mrs. Mott?”

“I didn't actually hear words. I wasn't listening, you know.” She leaned forward. “Anne came out, looking so pale that Enid insisted on driving her home. Fortunately, Frances didn't have her car. She'd come with Enid. So Frances was able to drive Anne's car home for her. We turned out the lights and called goodnight to Taylor.”

Charlie said, “Did Taylor answer you, when you called goodnight to him?”

They looked at each other. “I believe he did,” Mrs. Chartwell said.

"He must have," Mrs. Mott said. "Yes. I remember Anne remarked how tired he sounded."

"Yes. She did."

"You all left together? Nobody stayed behind?" I said.

"No. I locked up behind us," Mrs. Chartwell said.

"Thank you, very much for your help," I said. "We won't detain you any longer. This floor will have to be sealed off for the time being. Officer O'Neill will remain here to make sure that nobody unauthorized disturbs these premises. I hope it won't inconvenience you too much."

I waited until Tuffy had escorted them out and they'd disappeared into the crowd below, to tackle Charlie.

"You said Babe left the hospital last night after visiting hours."

"About ten."

"If the sewing class ended at 8:30, these women would have left by then, even if they hung around to have coffee. With Anne sick, they must have cut that short. Taylor called goodnight to them. So he was alive when they left."

"Whoa! Don't jump to conclusions like that." Charlie took off her sunglasses and pointed them at me. "Did they hear Taylor say goodbye? Or did Mrs. Weston suggest to those suggestible ladies that he did...sounding tired."

She pocketed the glasses and scratched the side of her nose. "Let's grab some lunch."

"The Seaview Diner?"

"Best food in town."

Driving the squad car to the diner, I went over the morning's events. I didn't believe Taylor had killed Mona Raeburn. I didn't believe Taylor had killed himself. I didn't believe he'd written that suicide note. I didn't believe Charlie believed it either.

We settled into the same booth we'd taken before and a young waitress came by with two carafes of coffee. "Decaf or regular?" she said as she polished the tabletop.

"Two regular," Charlie said, "Where's Josie?"

"She comes in later."

"Babe?"

"She's not coming in today."

"Do you know a man named Ashley Taylor?"

Two vertical lines appeared between her eyebrows. "I don't think so."

"How long have you worked here?" I asked.

"It's my first week. Can you tell I'm new?"

"No, you're doing fine. Ashley Taylor is the town librarian."

"Oh, I think I know who you mean."

"Was he in here last night?"

"I didn't work the late shift. But I'll ask for you. Are you ready to order?"

"We sure are, pussycat. I'll have two fried eggs with melted Swiss, and a small steak. Bloody on the steak. Sour dough toast and cottage fries well done."

I ordered Special K with skim milk.

Charlie pushed aside the sugar bowl. "Bottom line is we've got a suicide-confession note. Unless Dodo Byrd tells us different, I say Taylor wrote the note, spiked his coffee with cyanide and signed out."

"What motive did he have to kill Mona Raeburn?"

"We don't need to look for a motive. We've got his confession."

I shook my head. "It 's a clumsy attempt to look like he wrote a confession. He didn't even sign his name. Why would he bother to shut off the printer? Why would he wipe his prints off the pen? And those women said he was cheerful last night. Doesn't sound to me like he was thinking of ending it all. Come on, Charlie, he was murdered."

"Maybe Mrs. Weston poisoned him. You told me she knows Taylor's secret password."

"She said she forgot it."

"Maybe she remembered it all of a sudden, while she was lying down."

"Charlie, did she have time to open up the computer, type the suicide note, print it out, put the computer on stand by and shut down the printer?"

"How long would it take? She was the last one to be with Taylor. They were together in the kitchen. He's drinking coffee. She gets him to turn his back...asks him for something. And dumps the Cytotox in his cup."

I felt cold prickles on the back of my neck. "If she did that, he would have been dead before the women left. You know how quick cyanide is. The librarians heard him say goodbye."

"They think they heard him. I could get them to think not, like that." She snapped her fingers. "Mrs. Mott doesn't remember hearing Taylor, she remembers Mrs. Weston saying how tired Taylor sounded."

I had to admit she was right. Witnesses color their impressions less by what actually happened than by what is suggested to them.

"They called good night to Taylor and locked up," I said. "Suppose he was alive when they left and Babe arrived after they'd gone. The same scenario you played with Anne. She goes into the kitchen with Taylor. Nice and cozy, they have coffee. The autopsy report will tell us if he ate the tarts she brought. Babe dumps the Cytotox in his cup and leaves him to die while she sets up the note on the computer. She has plenty of time, he's dead."

Charlie pursed her mouth and stared at me under her swollen lids.

"Hot plate," the waitress said.

Charlie smiled at her. "Thanks, sweetheart."

"That man you were asking about wasn't in here last night," she said.

"Thanks, doll." Charlie poured ketchup over her plate, loaded her fork with fried egg, steak and potatoes, shoveled it in, and said, "It crosses my mind that Mrs. Weston's health has a way of deteriorating very conveniently."

I fiddled with a spoon. "I don't think she's a logical suspect here, Charlie."

She snorted, spraying some of her lunch down her chin. "That's a good one. I say we question her after we finish lunch."

"It's Babe Freeman I want to question. Where did she go last night after she left you? How did those tarts get into Taylor's apartment? The two old ladies and Tuffy ate them this morning and nobody fell over dead."

"The cyanide, if that's what killed him, was probably in the coffee."

"But the point is, was Babe there?"

Charlie drank a little water and chewed on an ice cube. "We'll question her. But Mrs. Weston first. Just remember, kid, all of them had coffee last night, but she had tea."

"What's that supposed to mean? None of the women died from the coffee."

Charlie dumped more ketchup on her potatoes, polishing them off with fast snapping bites. "Speaking of coffee, I want some. Where is that girl? Oh, there she is. Another cuppa, doll, and the damages."

When she finished the coffee, she let out her belt a notch, paid the bill, heaved herself up and said, "Well, let's go listen to Mrs. Weston's version of the evening."

CHAPTER TWENTYSIX

At the Weston's front door, I rapped the brass knocker. Under my hand the brass lips touched.

Charlie cleared her throat and spit a disgusting glob onto the frozen grass. "Sappy door knocker."

I knocked again.

"People who lay it on thick and lovey-dovey, always turn out to hate each other's guts."

My hands dropped to my side. "Nobody home," I said and half-turned to leave, when the door opened.

Anne Weston looked terrible. Purpled shadows swelled beneath her silvery yes and her fine- boned face had gone puffy.

"Oh, it's you, Jake," she said.

Seeing Charlie, she gathered her wooly blue robe closer to her body.

I said, "This is Detective Alberts."

Anne drew back with a shake of her head. "Please, would you gentlemen call again later? I'm afraid I'm not feelin' myself at the moment."

"You're ill," I said, shocked at her appearance.

Again that shake of her head as her lips formed a soundless, "No."

Charlie said, "Maybe we could talk to your husband, Mrs. Weston."

"He's not here."

Charlie shouldered past me. "We'll come in and wait for him."

Intimidated by her insistent bulk, Anne flinched away, trembling.

"You seem pretty frazzled, Mrs. Weston," Charlie said. "Let me give you a hand."

I watched, amazed, as she led Anne gently to an armchair, fussing and clucking like a god-damned Girl Scout.

"Maybe you'd like a glass of water. Jake, bring Mrs. Weston a glass of water."

These were new tactics for Charlie. What was she up to, oozing compassion in that oily tone of voice? And why was Anne in such a funk? She'd been crying.

In the kitchen, a crate of narcissus blooming on the scrubbed butcher block table nodded their white heads. By the time I found a glass and filled it with tap water their cloying perfume had got to me and I sneezed about two dozen times before I made it out of there and into the shadowed living room. The curtains were drawn, blocking out the winter light.

Charlie scrunched on a footstool at Anne's feet, her heavy body off balance. She reached up for the water glass and twisted around to place it in Anne's shaking hands, spilling some.

Anne stared at the spreading wetness on her robe.

Charlie leaned towards her. "Are you sick, Mrs. Weston? Would you like us to call a doctor?"

"No. I don't need a doctor."

"I understand you were sick last night."

"Yes, I was."

"Yet you were at the library."

"I teach a class there on Wednesday," she said, running her fingers over the dampness.

I said, "There was an accident after you left the library."

Her hand clutched the robe. "Accident? What kind of accident?"

"We don't know, yet," I said.

Charlie said, "Ashley Taylor is dead."

Anne's head snapped back and her laughter filled the room. Laughing and weeping, she fell back into the chair.

I took what was left of the glass of water from her hand.

"What a spectacle I'm makin' of myself," she said, reaching for the glass again. "My nerves are so ragged, I declare I'm weak as this water."

Charlie said, "Were you a good friend of his?"

She reached into a pocket for a tissue. "Of Taylor's? He was no friend of mine." She wiped at her eyes.

"But his death seems to have upset you very much, Mrs. Weston," Charlie said.

Anne smiled. "I'm not upset about Taylor! Who cares about Taylor? If you want to know, I'm relieved that I won't have to invite him to my home any more."

"Then, why are you so upset?"

She closed her eyes for a second and then she looked into Charlie's face. "Please, won't you go away? I'm in no fit state to talk to anyone."

"I don't think you should be left alone," I said.

"Alone. Yes, I'm alone."

She rocked back and forth in the chair in the partial darkness, almost talking to herself. "I'm alone."

"Where is Tony?" I said. "I'll call him for you. Someone should be here with you."

"He left me." She began to cry again. "Tony left me. I told him to go and he left me. He's gone."

I said, "Where did he go?"

"To Hell, I hope! He...he humiliated me in front of.... He spilled out all our private secrets in front of Babe. An' she was listenin' with both ears. I'd like to have died."

Her hands crossed on her shoulders, holding herself together.

"He said...he'd been havin' an affair...with Mona. I'm such a fool, I never suspected...Not with Mona. But it seems you knew, Detective Harmony. You knew all about it. Tony was afraid you'd tell me."

Yes, I thought, she was a fool about Weston if she didn't know him for the stud he was.

"As long as I live, I'll never forget he brought that woman here to witness my shame."

Somewhere outside, a car alarm went off and Anne turned her head toward the noise. It stopped abruptly.

She said, "He cut my heart out. And then he cried like a little child and begged me to forgive him. In front of Babe! I told him to get out and never come back. I respect the oath we took before God. But he...."

Charlie lumbered to her feet. "I sympathize with your distress, Mrs. Weston."

"I am purely shamed to have you all witnessin' my troubles like this." Anne put her hand over her mouth and closed her eyes.

Charlie crossed to the window and parted the heavy drapery. A thin line of sunlight striped the parquet floor.

Anne opened her eyes. "Please."

She let the curtain fall back into place.

"Oh, blessed God! What is happening? Mona's dead and now Taylor's dead. Nobody's safe any more and I'm all alone."

"Isn't there someone you can call to come and stay with you?" I said.

She shook her head. "My momma and sister are in 'lanta. I couldn't face anyone else. Never you mind. I can't possibly cry any more. I'll be all right."

Charlie said, "We came here this afternoon because we're investigating a suspected poisoning. It may involve a pesticide called Cytotox. Have you ever heard of it?"

"What? I don't know. I can't think. Did I ever hear of what?"

"Cytotox."

"Can't you ask me these questions another time? How can you expect me to sit here and answer you?"

"We need your help," I said. "It's important."

"Important."

"Yes."

"Of course. I'll try to help. Cytotox you said?'"

"Yes."

"We use something in the summertime to get rid of the yellow jackets."

"You still have it?"

"My goodness, I don't know."

"It's a small white box with red lettering."

"If we have it, it'd be in the garden shed."

Charlie lifted a corner of the drape. "That the shed?"

"Next to the garage, yes."

"Would you mind if we had a look in there?"

"Goodness, no. We keep it padlocked, but the key's on a hook 'longside. "

I said, "Let's go Charlie."

* * *

A collection of sharp instruments: axes, shovels, loppers, clippers, saws - a stockpile to gladden a murderous heart - hung from grimy pegboard. I choked on the acrid dust as the door closed behind us.

Charlie said, "Multiply this by all the garden sheds in Nassau county and it's a wonder people are still walking around in these peaceful suburbs."

She ran her hand over the disorder of opened bags and rusty cans, raising more dust. "There's enough poison in this shed to murder all of Seaview."

I fumbled in my jeans for my inhaler, shook it up, puffed medication down my throat, inhaled deeply, held my breath for as long as I could, and exhaled slowly.

Charlie began a search of the shelves that ran the length of the shed.

"I don't see it," he said. "Jake? Are you all right?""

"Look again." I forced the words out, and staggered into the air, leaning against the weathered boards until I could breathe.

She came out a minute or so later, slapping at the dust on her clothes. "Are you O.K., kid? "

I nodded, not able to speak yet.

"It's not there."

She snapped the padlock closed and we went back to the house. Anne was standing in front of the drinks table at the end of the room.

"We couldn't find the box," Charlie said.

"Maybe Tony threw it away. Or loaned it to someone. Neighbors are always borrowin' things. Maybe we never had it."

Charlie stumped toward her, going in for the kill. "Maybe you brought the Cytotox with you last night." Looming over Anne, she whipped out the accusation: "Maybe you sprinkled it in Taylor's coffee while you were alone with him."

Anne's hands grasped the edge of the table for support. "Oh,my!... oh...oh. Taylor was poisoned? And you think I...oh, no.... Well, I could have done that, Detective Alberts. But I didn't."

She backed away from Charlie. "You don't know me but if you did, you would know that I am always truthful. I never lie."

"Taylor is dead," I said. "Tell us what happened last night."

She settled down into the armchair, legs tucked under her. "I wasn't feeling well, you know, and the class broke up early. We always have coffee with Taylor after class and I'd brought chocolate chip cookies."

"Mrs. Mott said they were delicious. Home made." I said.

"Yes."

"How did you manage to bake them if you were feeling so unwell?" Charlie said.

"I didn't. I took them out of the freezer."

"Who made the coffee?" I said.

"Goodness, I didn't notice. I asked for tea and I think... yes... Enid brought me a cup of tea. I was feelin' like somethin' the cat dragged in and I asked Taylor if I could lie down for a bit while the rest of them had their coffee."

"How long did you lie down?"

"I don't know. Taylor came and asked me if I wanted some aspirin and I got up and went to the kitchen with him. For a glass of water. When I came out, Enid offered to drive me home. I was mighty grateful and I left with her."

"Where was Taylor?"

Her silvery eyes with their black-rimmed irises were transparent as glass. "He came with us to the door, with Enid and Frances and me."

"Mrs. Mott said you all left together and Taylor was still in the kitchen."

Anne shook her head. "She may have said that, but I recollect that we left first, the three of us."

She tightened the robe around her, the movement outlining her breasts. I looked away quickly and met Charlie's knowing stare. Caught ogling her like a damned pervert. Damn it.

Charlie said, "Did you use Taylor's printer last night?"

"My goodness, no."

"What is the password to access his computer?"

"I don't rightly remember. It's somethin' in Latin. I know that."

"What time did you come home last night?"

"I...I was feelin' too poorly to notice. Enid can tell you, I'm sure...."

"What time did your husband come home?"

Her eyes filled with tears again. "I don't rightly know. It was very late." She rose unsteadily from the chair. "I'm sorry, you must excuse me now. I'm purely worn out."

I said, "We've disturbed you long enough. We'll be going now. C'mon Charlie."

Coming out of the dim house into sunlight, Charlie shielded her eyes from the glare with one hand, searching for her sunglasses with the other.

We got into the squad car. I was driving.

She said, "That woman lies like a rug and she plays you like a violin."

I backed up with a squeal of tires.

"Shit," Charlie said. "I almost swallowed my gum."

I felt the muscle in my jaw twitching, and hit the brakes. The car brakes and my own brakes.

"Where does Babe Freeman live?" I said. "Weston may still be with her. Which way?"

"Make a right and head south to the Harbor. I have the directions here somewhere." She fumbled inside her coat pocket. "Main Street to County Drive, to the Nautical Mile...."

I stopped listening, my mind on Anne. Who'd been telling the truth? The two librarians? What would Enid and Frances say?

CHAPTER TWENTY SEVEN

"...and right at East Cove Road."

We were the only car on the Nautical Mile. The salt-smelling bay, lively with fishing boats in the summertime was deserted now except for a lone sea gull that hovered over us.

Charlie said, "Mrs. Weston talks a lot about God."

"When? I didn't hear that."

"You were getting the glass of water."

"Oh."

"I don't trust people on speaking terms with God."

"She's Southern. Southerners talk religion. That's their thing."

"I don't know." She snapped her gum. "Maybe Mrs. Weston's one of those 'God-made-me-do-it' nuts. "Where was she when Mona Raeburn was murdered?"

"You saw her statement."

"Yeah. That's what I mean."

She craned her neck to look at a street sign. "This is Fisherman's Wharf. Turn here."

We drove along a stretch of idle boat yards and then cut through a small park; a frozen still life of skeletal trees. The road curved toward the bay past old Victorian homes with curlicued widow's walks and deep front lawns.

"East Cove," she said. "Take a right here. Mrs. Weston's a good looker, I'll give you that. Just keep your dick zipped."

"What are you talking about?"

"You know what I'm talking about. Whoa! There it is. Number five."

Babe Freeman's house was at the end of the lane with a small strip of beach between it and the bay. Tire tracks had gouged dirty streaks into the snow blanketing the driveway. I coasted in, avoiding the ruts, and parked next to a black Lincoln Navigator.

We walked up a narrow path to a wooden porch hung with empty flower pots. When I rang the bell, Tony Weston opened the door. His spooked face reminded me of a rabbit caught in a car's headlights.

"You, again!" he said and tried to shut the door, but I'd planted my boot too solidly for that.

Through the narrow opening, he said, "What do you want?"

"Auditioning for butler, Weston?" I said. "That's not the way I'd play it."

Charlie stepped up from behind me and hit the door. Weston hared off, and we heard a woman's distant questioning voice.

We were in a sun-porch, glazed in green tinted glass and crowded with peeling wicker furniture. Charlie made herself at home in a rocking chair, rifling through her bubble gums.

"What a view, Charlie," I said, looking out at the water. Covered with a thin skin of ice, it glittered white in the sunlight, turning silver as it stretched to the horizon. Here and there patches of black water lapped at the ice.

Babe Freeman appeared in the doorway. "You're looking a little better, Charlie. How do you feel?"

"What doesn't kill you, hurts," she said.

"I see you have your sidekick with you. Detective Harmony?" She was enveloped to the ankles in a white cotton apron.

"That's me." Every time I came across this woman I felt like pushing her face in. I could never hit a woman. Nevertheless....

"The sunsets must be spectacular here," I said.

She thawed a millimeter. "Yes."

"This is a wonderful old house. Fabulous."

"You can dispense with the hyperbole. Most of the other houses here were built even earlier than this one."

I turned back to the view. In the east, black clouds were gathering.

I said, "Been here long?"

"Six years. Six years, and two months."

Outside, a door slammed. A car motor whined and caught. I raced out in time to see Weston pull the Navigator out of the driveway and burn rubber down the street.

I came back to the porch, slamming the door closed. "Weston took off," I said "Damn it! Where did he run to now?"

"What are you so angry about?" Babe said. "I sent him on an errand. He'll be back. I assure you he hasn't run away."

Maybe, but she looked as if she thought she'd put one over on us.

"I have to talk to him."

"He'll be back in about twenty minutes. I asked him to pick up my cat at the animal hospital. Surely nothing you want to say to him is so urgent that it can't wait twenty minutes."

Maybe Weston was picking up the cat and maybe he was getting rid of something.

"He went to pick up your cat?" I said. "You have a cat?"

"Is that a problem?"

"Yes.... I'm allergic to cats."

She untied her apron and tossed it on a wicker chair, her narrow legged jeans and ribbed sweater emphasizing her slenderness.

"Then perhaps you might want to leave-before Tony brings Kubla back. I don't want your hostile presence upsetting him, his first day home from the hospital."

Charlie rocking comfortably in the wicker chair, said, "Sit down, Babe."

Babe sat on a lumpy looking davenport.

"You light somewhere too, Jake."

I pulled up a chair that looked as if it was on its last rickety legs. I sat. It didn't collapse under my weight.

"Do you remember telling me, `If anything happens to Taylor, you can come looking for me'? "I asked Babe.

"No, I do not."

Charlie said, "Where did you go last night after you left me?"

"I met Tony."

"Where did you meet him?"

"Here. Why all the questions? Charlie?"

He said, "You and Taylor broke off your engagement, right?"

"Yes, why...."

"Has he been moody or depressed lately?"

"He's always moody. Charlie, what's this all about?"

"Why would Taylor commit suicide?"

"What?" Alarm widened her eyes. "Why are you asking? Did he...he didn't...."

Charlie nodded, her swollen eyes unreadable.

"Oh, my God."

Babe buried her face in her hands.

"You were engaged to marry him," I said. "And you broke it off."

She raised her head. Her lashes were wet. "If he killed himself, it was not because I broke our engagement. Trust me."

My ex-wife, Paula, taught me not to trust anybody who says, `trust me.' I said, "Did you visit Taylor last night?"

"No."

"You didn't go to his apartment."

"I've already told you, no."

"A plate of lemon meringue tarts from the Seaview Diner was found on his table."

"What if it was?"

"We know Taylor wasn't in the diner last night. How did it get there?"

"I haven't the faintest idea. Why does it matter? Taylor is dead and you're asking me about tarts?"

"Do you keep them refrigerated?"

"What? What is this?"

"Do you?" Charlie said.

She shook her head. "They can be refrigerated but they should be eaten at room temperature."

"Would they go bad if they were left out on a table overnight?"

"No, I add calcium phosphate powder to the meringue. What is the point of this culinary discussion?"

"Taylor may not have been a suicide," I said. "He may have been murdered. You told me once that if anything ever happened to him I should come looking for you."

"I don't remember saying that, but if I was planning to kill Taylor, I know I certainly wouldn't announce it to you!"

"We found a note."

"For me?"

"No," I said and looked at Charlie, throwing her the ball.

She picked it up. "When Taylor attempted suicide before, did he leave a note for you?"

"Yes." Babe stood up.

It was only noon, but the clouds had gathered to blot out the sun. She flicked on the porch light and a yellow glow warmed the room. She sat down again.

"What did it say?" I asked.

She hesitated, and then recited: "'*For many a time I have been half in love....*"

Her voice broke.

The only sound was Charlie's squeaking rocker until Babe spoke again: "'*with easeful Death.*' It's a quotation from Keats."

"The note was in his handwriting?" I said.

"Of course. Oh, if only I...."

I said, "The most despairing words in the language: if only."

She pulled a handkerchief from the back pocket of her jeans and blew her nose.

Charlie, rocking placidly, unwrapped some gum. I teetered on the unsteady chair, planting my boots to anchor it.

"Taylor had a secret password to access his files," I said.

"Yes. Sartor Resartus. It's a literary pun on his name: The Tailor Reclothed.

"Who else knew the password?" I said.

She shoved the handkerchief back in her pocket and stood up, pacing back and forth on the flaking painted floorboards. "I don't know. How would I know?"

"I thought you might." I glanced at my watch. "It's been more than thirty minutes. Where's Weston?"

"Maybe the waiting room was crowded. He'll be here."

Car lights flooded the porch. Babe's face, momentarily spot-lighted, went tense.

"There he is. That's Tony," she cried, and flung out the door before we could stop her.

CHAPTER TWENTY EIGHT

I dashed after her and reached Weston on the outside porch before Babe could speak to him.

With me there, she couldn't warn him but she tried. She lifted her chin and shook her head signaling to him but Weston didn't get it.

Indignant growls came from inside the black cardboard case he carried. He knelt down and freed an angry Siamese.

"You can clear something up for me, Weston," I said, backing away from the cat. "What time did the two of you leave Taylor's apartment last night?"

"About eleven, wasn't it, Babe...." Weston began, struck dumb in mid-sentence by her grim face.

"Taylor's dead, Tony." She turned on her heel and went back to the sun-porch.

The cat rubbed against my pants leg, depositing cat hairs. When I nudged it away, it waved its kinked tail and disappeared into the house through a trap door.

"Taylor's dead?" Weston said. "Gee...I–I'd better go to Babe."

"In a minute. Right now, you'll tell me what went on in Taylor's apartment without any coaching from the lady."

"Nothing went on. He wasn't home. Babe asked me to go with her because she didn't want to be alone with him. But when we pulled up, his place was dark and he didn't answer the doorbell."

Weston kept looking over my shoulder anxiously as if he expected Babe to come out and rescue him.

"Then what?" I said.

"Well, he wasn't home. Babe said she'd run up for a minute and leave some cake for him. To let him know she'd been there."

"You went there with her so she wouldn't be alone with Taylor, but you waited in the car."

Weston blinked at me. "He wasn't home. She didn't need me."

I pointed to the porch door. He went inside and took the spindly chair I'd been teetering on.

The cat ran over to me rubbing against my legs again, purring. My eyes began to itch.

Babe looked a question at Weston but he avoided her eyes.

I said, "Tony, here, got you into a little hot water. He says you did go to Taylor's apartment last night. Do you want to change your story?"

She bit her lip, frowning. Then she said," Oh, all right. I was there. When you told me Taylor was dead, I didn't want to admit it. That's understandable isn't it?"

"But you were there."

"Yes."

"What time?"

"You seem to think I look at my watch obsessively. I'd guess about 11."

"Why did you go?"

"That's hardly a question I have to answer."

Charlie's flat gaze changed her mind.

She scratched the cat's ear, not looking at me and said, "I went because Taylor phoned me. He said he knew who had killed Mona. I didn't believe him. I thought he was just trying to get me to his apartment."

The cat brushed its head against her cheek, purring.

"He was insistent and I gave in. Then I picked up Tony and we drove to the library. Taylor didn't seem to be home but we went upstairs anyway."

Weston, looking unhappy, cleared his throat.

"What?" I said.

"Um…nothing. I didn't say anything."

Babe went on. "The door was locked. I still had a key. I'd meant to return it, but...I guess it slipped my mind. We went inside and Tony called out to him. When Taylor didn't answer I assumed that he'd gone out somewhere. He was like that."

Weston's face had grown unhappier and unhappier as he listened.

I said to him, "Your version's a whole different story isn't it? Because I didn't give you two the chance to concoct one together."

"No," he said. "Babe's right. That's what we did. That's how it was. We went upstairs together. Both of us."

He went to Babe's side and put his arm around her shoulder. She reached for his hand and squeezed it. The cat stalked away.

I said, "You stayed in the car. Babe went upstairs alone."

"That's not true," Weston said, anxiety and guilt chasing each other across his face. "I...I just forgot for a minute. I was nervous. Mixed up. You make me nervous."

"I'll talk to you later," I said, and faced Babe. "You went upstairs by yourself, you poisoned Taylor, wrote a phony suicide note and ran back down where Tony was waiting for you in the car."

"Charlie!" she said.

Charlie was recording the conversation in her notebook. Without looking up, she said, "You better start telling the truth, now, Babe, or I'll be forced to agree with Jake."

"I see…" She was still holding onto Weston's hand. "It's true. Tony wasn't with me. But I didn't see Taylor. I just left the tarts and came back down. That's the truth. Was he dead by then?"

"We don't know that."

The sacs beneath my eyes were swelling up fast. I yanked out my inhaler, hoping that the medication would counteract my allergy.

I said, "Would you put your cat in another room?"

Babe picked him up. "My sweet puss-puss don't be afraid because the bad man doesn't like you," she said. "No. I won't put him in another room."

I retreated to the door, opened it and took some deep breaths.

Charlie said, "You ever use pesticides in the garden?"

"I can't use poisons because of Kubla. He's allowed outside."

I leaned against the open door. "Ever use Cytotox? Here, or in the diner?" I said.

She made a good show of thinking it over before she said to Weston, "That pesticide you gave me, in August, Tony. What was it called?"

"I don't know. Why would I remember?" He sounded put-upon.

"Do you still have it?" I said to her. "The name would be on the box."

"I gave it back to Tony."

A fit of sneezing shook me. I tried to fight it off but once an attack like this started, I was virtually helpless. Bent over nearly double, wracked with wheezes, my eyes reduced to slits, I was conscious of Babe's eyes on me.

I fumbled with the inhaler and dropped it. Picking it up, Charlie helped me out of the house.

After a minute or two in the cold air, I stopped choking and shoved her aside.

"I'll be okay."

"If you go back inside, your allergy 'll kick in all over again. Take the car and go. I'll get their statement."

"And stay for dinner?" I needled her.

"Something tells me I won't be invited." She walked me to the squad car.

I said, "First Weston says he didn't go upstairs. Then he says he did. Goddam puppet!"

"I'll straighten him out."

"He has to look at Babe for instructions before he opens his mouth. She feeds him all his cues."

Charlie leaned her chin on her hand. "You think Taylor did know who murdered Mona Raeburn?"

"I've always thought so. And Babe's afraid we'll find out what he knew."

CHAPTER TWENTY NINE

I turned in the squad car at the Seaview police station, noted the mileage, retrieved my 'Vette, and drove to McDonald's. I put away two Quarter Pounders with cheese, a double order of fries, a hot baked apple pie and a vanilla milk shake, then started for home. I'd just eaten a week's worth of calories in ten minutes.

I stuck my hand in my coat pocket, searching for a tissue to wipe my hands and my fingers found something else: A folded note, engraved Anne S. Weston in blue script.

I unfolded it. *'Please!'*

The winter sky loosed a shower of frozen rain and a mean wind rose and whistled around the car windows.

What did it mean? I was glad she wanted to see me. But I didn't trust her motivation. What did she want? Am I suspicious because I'm a cop or am I a cop because I'm naturally suspicious? I turned up the heater and headed back to Wellington Road.

* * *

My heart knocked against my ribs in tempo with the pounding door knocker. Anne opened the door, shivering as a gust of cold wind whipped at her loose blue robe.

"It's you," she said. "I'm so glad."

She had braided her hair tightly back from her face. The hairdo, and her pale down-turned mouth gave her a look of prim melancholy.

She peered beyond me. "Are you alone this time?"

"Yes." I held up a rain-spattered hand. "And I'm being rained on."

She gathered the folds of the wooly robe closer to her body and, with a backward inviting glance, turned and glided away.

I let the door close behind me, dumped my wet hat and coat on a bench in the hallway and followed her into the shadowy living room, the heels of my boots staccato on the parquet boards.

She faced away from me, peering into the mirror over the fireplace. Her eyes met mine in the glass.

"Don't look at me. My eyes are washed out of my head from cryin'."

"Anne," I said, coming closer.

She turned then. "You found my note?"

"Yes, in my coat." Over her head I could see my reflection. I brushed at my flattened hair with my fingers, realized it was a nervous gesture and stopped.

I said, "What did it mean: `Please!'"

"I'm plumb distraught." Two delicate fingers pressed against her lips. Her silvery eyes swimming with tears, she stammered, "And so unhappy....I hoped...I thought... you were a friend and yet you came here thinkin'...you and that other detective... askin' did I sprinkle Cytotox in Taylor's c-coffee? Huntin' in my shed for the very box. Accusin' me of poisonin' Taylor."

"Anne," I said, "I'd like to be, but I'm not your friend. I'm a cop."

She took a hesitant step towards me and whispered my name. "I just can't bear it if you turn against me."

I flatter myself I'm not easily seduced but my pleasure at her words was intense and involuntary. I tried to stifle it but she must have seen it in my face. She smiled.

"You haven't," she breathed. "I knew it."

"Look, Anne," I said, moving a deliberate pace away from her, "I'm investigating a homicide and your statement contradicts Mrs. Mott's."

She bowed her head like a reprimanded child.

"I want to believe you," I said. "But the facts don't fit."

"I...after you told me Taylor was dead I... " She raised her lashes and searched my face. "I was just so confused. I might be wrong but I did think Taylor came to the door with us. But maybe he was in the entry to the kitchen."

"Which was it?"

She touched her upper lip with her tongue. "I don't rightly know."

"The night Mona Raeburn was murdered," I let a trace of doubt color my voice. "You watched the comings and goings at the Raeburn house, even though you had a bad headache. Did you really see all that or was it imagination too?"

She stretched out her hand, palm up. "I'll show you. Come upstairs and look out the window for yourself."

She gathered up the hem of her robe and brushed past me. Three steps up the staircase, she stopped, leaned over the oak banister and called, "Come on, I'll show you where I was sitting."

At the foot of the staircase, I hesitated a heart beat, heart beat, heart beat. She was already halfway up the stairs.

I followed.

When I got to the top step, she took my hand, twining her fingers around mine and led me down the hallway.

"This is Tony's room, and the one between's a little sittin' room. This one's my room."

They had separate bedrooms. As I'd suspected from the first, something was wrong with their marriage long before she'd asked Weston to get out.

Her bedroom, carpeted and draped in white, smelled of jasmine. A bunch of white pillows were stacked like a snowdrift on the white queen-size bed.

Anne glanced at me flirtatiously. "Wouldn't I be a scandal back home in 'lanta? Receivin' a man alone in my boudoir, even at this hour." She spoke lightly, but her flush betrayed her.

Her hand traveled the length of her body, flattening her robe, her long thighs and legs. Like a hypnotized cobra, my eyes followed her hand. She was tantalizingly close.

"Not if the man was a police official on business," I said. She'd planted that note in my pocket and had been calculatedly seductive since I showed up.

I walked over to the window seat, parted the heavy curtains and could see the Raeburns' front walk below. Christmas lights were still strung through the leafless tree branches. The porch and front door were visible, and so was the street where Babe had parked.

"Just as you said." I let the curtains fall into place again, and heard a muffled sob behind me.

"Oh, Jake. I can't bear for you to disbelieve me," she said, tears shining in her eyes.

She took a hesitant step towards me and then she was in my arms, parted lips raised to mine. For a long second, thought and feeling battled it out. When I kissed her, I tasted the salt in her tears.

The belt of her robe fell away, and the naked length of her clung to me. With her yielding softness in my arms, the urgency of my body almost overwhelmed caution. Almost.

Delicious and desirable she might be but she was a prime suspect and I was way off base. Even though I had a feeling that we could fall off the earth together into Paradise.

Her breath was warm on my cheek, her fragrance teased me....

I tied her belt firmly in place. "I have to ask you some questions," I said, "and I need more official surroundings than this."

I took to my heels, out of her bedroom and down the stairs, her light tread following behind me.

In the living room, she switched on all the lights and nestled into the big club chair.

"I'm a cop, Anne. I have to ask questions."

"Five minutes ago I was in your arms and now you want to cross-examine me?"

"Sorry," I said. And I was.

"Who was she?" Anne said softly. "Did you love her? The woman who hurt you so much?"

I laughed. She sounded like a 40's B movie.

Behind the fringe of black lashes her eyes went gun metal hard. She sat straighter in the chair. "I won't throw myself at you again." Her voice was splintered crystal, not a trace of honey. "What do you want to ask me?"

I steepled my fingers and regarded them intently. "A note found beside Taylor was signed with a green pen like the one you used to underline passages in your Bible."

"Was it my pen? Is that your question? No it was not. I didn't leave a note for Taylor!"

"You were with him just before he died. You may have been the last person to see him alive. Or the first to see him dead."

Her hand went to her heart. "My gracious, how can you say such a vile thing to me?"

"That's not an answer."

"I've already told you I didn't poison Taylor."

Her back stiff with resentment, she marched to the hallway and gathered my coat up, thrusting it in my arms as I crossed the threshold.

"Taylor's murderer will burn in the fires of Hell through all eternity."

I left.

I drove home watching the rain wash away the snow.

When I pulled into the garage I got out a big sponge and a chamois and concentrated on wiping the "Vette down, detailing the body, polishing the chromed wire wheels. I worked up a sweat, tuning out murder.

Then I jogged over to my place, drank a diet Dr. Pepper, opened a box of Cheez-It, and finished the whole box while I wrote up my notes on the lap top. I have a photographic memory but Lt. Faber and the D.A. insist on seeing things in writing.

That out of the way, I did twenty- five sit ups, ten push ups, turned on the TV, clicked through all the channels, shut off the TV and went to bed.

Sometime during the night, I woke, erect with desire, a trace of jasmine lingering on my skin.

CHAPTER THIRTY

I spent Friday morning talking to Frances Nicols who it turned out had made the coffee and also driven Anne home; to Enid Braun who had driven Anne's car, and to Janice Hartman who hadn't done anything much. They were very nice cooperative ladies, shocked by Taylor's death and eager to help me.

Frances Nicols didn't remember if Taylor answered her when she called out goodnight to him. She thought he had. Why wouldn't he? She was quite sure everyone left the library together. She remembered Mrs. Chartwell locking up.

Enid Braun thought that she and Anne had preceded Mrs. Chartwell down the stairs and that Taylor had said goodnight and thanked them for a pleasant evening.

Janice Hartman, who hadn't been wearing her hearing aid, had heard nothing but thought that she had been the first one to leave.

The only thing they agreed on was that Anne hadn't been feeling well.

When I arrived at the mobile unit, Wolfie was at her computer and Charlie in the back of the bus, was waiting for coffee to drip through the pot.

I detected from the evidence of two Dunkin' Donuts cartons open on the desk that she hadn't breakfasted at the Seaview Diner. So Babe was on her suspect list at last.

"Morning, Charlie," I said. Her lids were still swollen and glistening hideously with medication.

"Hey, peaches, we got the lab report. Traces of cyanide in the broken cup. But not in the coffeepot. It was clean. And zilch prints on the suicide note. Nada. See for yourself."

She picked at a scab at the corner of her mouth. "Sgt. McFarland sent out a press release stating that new evidence uncovered by Ashley Taylor's apparent suicide points to him as Mona Raeburn's killer."

"Taylor was no suicide."

"Keep your hair-piece on. That's just the official line, to get the press off our necks. If Taylor was murdered– remember that `if'–the killer will think he misled us."

"Maybe." I pulled a chair up to our desk and checked out the donuts.

A red light flashed at the bottom of the pot, a little cloud of steam hissed and coffee fragrance wafted toward us. Charlie poured two cups, handing me one.

"As far as the public is concerned, the Raeburn case is closed," she said. "But we're still on it. We'll move out of here to the Seaview station for the time being and work from there."

"It'll take all day to break down the bus," I said.

"Tuffy's assigned to help us."

She poured condensed milk into her cup, chose a glazed donut and sat down next to me, spreading a paper napkin across her knees.

"Tomorrow. O.K.?"

"Sure." My donut looked better than it tasted but the coffee was good.

Officer Tuffy came aboard in a blast of cold air, and strolled toward us, clapping his hands together to warm them.

"I smell coffee."

"Help yourself," Charlie said.

Tuffy grinned all over his amiable face. He poured coffee and poked through the donut boxes.

Perched on the desk with a steaming cup and a Boston cream, he reached into his car-coat for his spiral notebook. "I have the names and addresses you asked for." He bit into the donut, spurting custard onto his chin.

"What names?" Charlie said.

"The names of the ten women originally registered in Mrs. Weston's class." He wiped the custard from his chin.

"You want a prize for that?" Charlie said.

Wolfie came down the aisle. She said, "I think Taylor overwrote the OS." She poured a cup of coffee.

"No shit." Charlie clambered out of her chair, dropping the paper napkin to the floor. "Explain that."

"He modified the operating system to accept two different entries. He entered one word, then another. The first time the 'enter your password' screen came up he typed 'Sartor', then, enter. When the 'enter your password' came up again, he typed in 'Resartus', and pressed enter again. Anyone typing Sartor or Resartus and pressing enter would get an 'enter your password' screen and figure they had the wrong password."

"Of course," Charlie said. "Why didn't we see that?" She skewered another donut and sat down again

"You're a genius," I said. "How did you figure it out, Wolfie?"

"I noticed an unusual system document at boot up and managed to pry it open."

I wasn't going to go into that with her. Some things I don't have to understand. "So anyone who knew that rigmarole could have entered Taylor's computer and written the suicide note," I said.

"So far that's Mrs. Weston and Babe," Charlie said.

"They may not be the only ones. Taylor was murdered. There are just too many questions for it to be suicide and he was murdered because he knew who killed Mona."

Charlie belched. "The note links both murders. So we have one perp."

"Unless two of them are working together."

Charlie muttered, "Like Anne and Tony Weston or Fred and Audrey Raeburn. Where were they Wednesday night?"

"Or Babe Freeman and Tony Weston," I said. "Remember my ABA theory?"

Wolfie said, "ABA theory?"

"Accumulated Bad Associations," Charlie said.

"Six years ago, Babe's boy friend died mysteriously. The death was listed as accidental. Now, Taylor dies, also under questionable circumstances."

"That's ABA?" Wolfie shook her head. "It's coincidence."

"I don't think so. I think she and Weston poisoned Taylor. They've both done some fancy lying."

Wolfie said, "How did her boy friend die?"

"Asphyxiated."

Charlie said, "I don't buy it, Peaches. There's no consistent M.O."

"These killers kill on impulse with whatever is at hand."

"So tell me, smartass, if Babe and Weston are accomplices, why did she tell us she saw Weston coming out of the Raeburn house after Mona's death? I've got a better theory."

We looked at her, waiting, and she grinned.

"I call it my "Oh, Shit!" syndrome. Mrs. Weston looks out her window, and in the headlight's of Babe's car, she sees her hubby running out of the Raeburn house. 'Oh, shit!' He's been screwing Mona. She slips over there and puts a stop to that.

Then Taylor accuses her, and `Oh, shit!'–now she has to get rid of him too."

I couldn't picture Anne turning her back, unconcerned, as Taylor choked his life out. Not after what she'd said about hellfire.

On the other hand, I could easily visualize Babe Freeman lacing Taylor's coffee with cyanide and planting that phony confession. With Weston looking on.

I said, "No."

Charlie raised what would have been an eyebrow if it hadn't been singed off.

"Weston fits the classic sociopath profile," I said. "We know he comes from a dysfunctional family, was raised by a single parent and was abused as a child. He's self-centered, manipulative, plastic...."

"You do like to badmouth that guy," Charlie interrupted. "The only thing we can be sure of is that the killer will feel pleased with himself when he reads McFarland's news release in tonight's *Newsday*."

"*Newsday*!" Wolfie said. "Did you see yesterday's feature on the Seaview Players? They're going ahead with the production of *Scottish Mists*."

"Without the leading lady?" Charlie said. "I didn't see it. Did you Jake?"

"No."

"Here, I have yesterday's entertainment section," Tuffy said.

Charlie held out her hand.

She found the story and read it moving her lips silently; then she looked up and said, "Audrey Raeburn is taking over her mother's part. Opening night is Friday. A week from today."

"I bought three tickets for us," Wolfie said.

CHAPTER THIRTY ONE

Rain streamed steadily down all day Saturday while Tuffy and I worked to close down the mobile bus and transfer the Raeburn files to the Seaview Police Station.

Charlie had to be at a special hearing in Judge's chambers. She came by to lend us a hand at 6:00 with two pepperoni pizzas.

It was after eleven o'clock, and still raining, when we knocked off. Going down Main Street, I made every light but one.

I was looking forward to my day off tomorrow. I'd buy two bagels with everything, read the Sunday *Times* in the morning and settle in to watch the Giant-Philadelphia game. After that, I'd put together a couple of ham and cheese sandwiches and catch the Raiders and the Broncos.

The light turned green. I took off past Main Street's shuttered storefronts and cruised the Seaview Diner, checking to see if Babe's Navigator was in the parking lot.

The Diner's interior was dark and as I slowed down, the neon sign overhead blinked off, plunging the parking lot into darkness. A woman came out of the diner struggling to open an umbrella. Only one feeble street lamp silvered the slashing rain- not enough light to penetrate the black shadows.

I parked and lowered the car window. Breaking down the bus had been dirty work and I was wearing an old college sweat shirt over a flannel shirt, blue jeans and a baseball cap.

A gust of wind blew in and sopped me with freezing rain. I rolled the window up again watching the woman pick her way across the parking lot.

Behind her, a motor started up and a car raced toward her. No headlights.

There was a crack of shattering glass and a shriek. I jumped out of the 'Vette sprinting for the parking lot, running flat-out.

My brain kicked in, and I turned and streaked back to radio:

Officer needs help. Seaview Diner. Main Street. Send ambulance.

I started the 'Vette, plowed into the driveway at full throttle, skidded onto the lot, brakes whinnying in protest, and rolled up on the left side of a black Lincoln Navigator.

My headlights sliced through the curtain of rain, picking out a mangled red umbrella under the left front tire. The car door on the driver's side hung open.

I left the 'Vette and circled the Navigator, playing a pocket flashlight on its interior. The key wasn't in the ignition and the driver had fled, swallowed up in the shadows.

I scanned the parking lot. Deserted. Except for the woman's twisted body lying motionless on the wet blacktop, a foot or so from the dead umbrella. She was Babe Freeman.

Her pulse beat steadily under my probing fingers. I gathered the damp folds of her coat around her, took off my hat and covered her head.

She stirred and groaned.

"Babe." It was the first time I'd called her by her name.

"Yes. Who....?"

"Shh. It's all right. It's Detective Harmony."

Dazed eyes tried to focus. She wiped at her rain drenched face. "What happened? You...what are you....?"

"I called an ambulance. Lie still, I'll be right back."

I doubled back to the 'Vette and rummaged through the emergency equipment in my duffle bag; grabbed a silver thermal survival blanket for Babe and a yellow emergency poncho for me. I pulled my sweat shirt hood up, even though it was wetter than I was by now, slit open the wrapper and threw the poncho over my head.

As I approached her again, Babe struggled to sit up but fell back, wincing in pain.

"Lie still," I said, draping the blanket over her shoulders.

"Lie still? I'm in a river here."

She huddled into the blanket. "Did you say you called an ambulance?"

"Hold on. It'll be here any minute."

"I don't need an ambulance." She struggled to her feet, resisting my efforts to keep her quiet.

"Oh, my God! That's my car," she said, and swayed.

I steadied her.

She slapped my arms away and I saw her flinch–saw the raw scrapes on her hands before she hid them behind her back.

"I'm all right," she said. "I'm fine. I just need to rest a minute. What possessed you to call an ambulance?"

"I thought you were run over."

A strand of hair whipped across her cheek. "Well, I'm not. I tripped...getting out of the way."

"Did you see who was driving?"

"No." She started to limp toward the Navigator, clutching the blanket.

I stepped in front of her. "You can't touch anything 'til the car's been processed."

"Get out of my way."

A squall of rain buffeted my face. I said, "Your car's a piece of evidence at a crime scene."

"Get out of my way." She faced me, scowling. "What crime scene?"

"Somebody tried to kill you."

"Don't be ridiculous."

"Whoever it was, tried to run you down. Look at that umbrella. It could be you."

She stared at the mangled wreckage.

I watched her mouth open and close, at a loss for words, for once.

The blood drained from her face and her knees buckled. I caught her in my arms as she pitched forward. Her long legs curled against me, and her surprisingly sweet perfume mingled with the smell of rain.

She pulled away, but we were still very close.

I said, "Let's get out of this rain," and led her to the 'Vette supporting her against my shoulder. I opened the car door with my free hand. Shucking off the poncho, I draped it over the door hoping it would keep the rain from dripping onto my leather upholstery.

Before Babe sat down, I spread the dry side of the blanket under her to protect the seat, closed the door and ran around to the driver's side.

I said, "Slide some of that blanket over here for me to sit on. I'm wet and water is murder to get out of these leather seats."

"If you'd let me drive home instead of shoving me around like this, you wouldn't have to worry about it. I don't need your help and I don't want it."

She swiped at her wet face with the back of her hand, glaring at me. "I don't understand. How did you happen to be here just now?"

"Luck. Sometimes you're just in the right place at the right time."

I was wetter and crankier than she was. She had my hat, a raincoat and a blanket while I'd raced around in the downpour with a sopping hood leaking cold drops down my neck.

I said, "You can't drive home. I told you - your car has to be processed. Are you sure you didn't see the driver? Even if you only got a fleeting impression...."

"I didn't see anything. It was dark. I...."

In the distance, sirens wailed, came ear-shatteringly near, and then tapered off in a blaze of flashing, rotating lights. The blacktop shimmered with watery red and white reflections.

Cars rumbled up. Doors slammed.

"Over here," I yelled.

Voices barked orders in a pandemonium of yellow slickers. A flashlight cut through the darkness as a burly paramedic splashed toward us, his buddy following with a stretcher. Babe tried to block the flashlight's beam, raising her scraped hand to her eyes.

I opened the car window. "Over here," I yelled again.

"Yo."

I left her to them and sprinted into the rain again. I was drenched anyway. A pair of uniforms stood beside the Navigator watching the crime scene go to work. They would diagram the scene, gather the glass fragments, fine-comb the interior–hunting for the something always left behind at a crime.

I gave them my name and went back to Babe.

She was out of the 'Vette, fighting the paramedics.

"Take your hands off me, you goons!"

"Chill out, lady."

"You chill out. This lot is private property. Mine. You're trespassing."

The second paramedic, a black giant in a yellow rain slicker, ducked her sharp heels and flailing arms. "Down, Tiger. We come out on a call. Now we're here, we gotta take you back for observation."

"I didn't call you." Babe pointed a finger at me. "That idiot made a precipitate assumption."

"What a mouth on her," the paramedic said.

I nodded agreement. They were only doing their jobs. What was she so mad about? She was always mad about something.

"Detective Harmony. Homicide. I put in the call. Release her to me. I'll take the responsibility."

"You can have her, man. What a ball- buster!"

"She don't appear like she's got anything broke," the first paramedic said.

Babe slumped against the 'Vette, rain trickling from the baseball cap into her coat collar. I grasped her elbow and pushed her back inside.

I got in on my side, mopping at my face with a wet sleeve. Water was pooling onto the floor mats.

"I'm not going to a hospital," she said.

I started the motor. "I'll drive you home."

CHAPTER THIRTY TWO

Shivering, Babe pulled the edges of the blanket around her, the shock hitting now.

"She took a deep breath. "Why...Who would try to run me down?"

"You tell me."

She shook her head.

"Where are your car keys?"

Her hand went to her pocket and came out with a silver key chain hung with charms: a white enamel "B" and a red heart. Women like stuff. Men try to carry as little as possible.

"Who else has a key to your car?"

"Tony."

"Who else?"

"Only Tony."

"Do you know where he is?"

"Why?" she said, voice high with annoyance.

The rain-slicked road was deserted and I drove faster than I normally would on a wet dark night, leaning forward to keep my soaked shirt away from the back of the seat. I was thinking furiously and what I was thinking was that if Weston had been behind that Navigator, I had to find him before he covered his tracks.

Babe propped a hand on the dashboard. "I'm not in a big hurry to get home, you know. You can slow down."

I tapped the brakes.

If he'd been behind the wheel his prints would be all over the Navigator. I bring him in for attempted vehicular homicide, he panics and confesses to the other crimes. Admits Babe was his accomplice? But why try to run her down? Why did he want to be rid of her?

"You don't know where Weston is."

"I didn't say that. I don't know why you're interested in Tony. But he'll be home in a few minutes. He called from the dress rehearsal of *Scottish Mists* and said he'd probably be home before I would."

"Home? We're not going to the Weston's."

"He's staying at my house."

"Moved in has he?"

"No. He's staying for a few days."

Her face glimmered, pale in the dim light. I didn't like her. Even discounting that I suspected her of murdering her ex-boyfriend and Mona Raeburn and Taylor, I didn't like her. And she certainly didn't like me. And neither of us was doing anything to mask our hostility toward each other.

Babe yawned. "Do you live with anyone?"

"No."

No pantyhose dripped from my towel bar, no long hairs clogged my bathtub, no high heels crowded my boots. My closets didn't share.

The rain drilled loud on the car roof. I stopped for a light and looked at her. A sodden mess stiff with resentment.

She clutched the blanket. "I'm cold and wet and I hurt. I need a drink."

"No alcohol. You might have a concussion."

"Don't be ridiculous. How would I have a concussion?"

"There's a lump the size of an egg swelling up on your head."

She touched her forehead, winced, and went very quiet.

"I want to be sure I have this straight," I said. "There are only two keys to your car. You have one and Weston has the other."

"You just went through a red light."

"It was still yellow."

"I didn't realize you could be color blind and still qualify as a detective."

Shrew.

I said, "If Weston has the only other key to your car, then it was Weston who tried to run you down."

"Sophist reasoning, Detective Harmony. Tony wasn't driving my car. I know that."

I gritted my teeth. Mustn't confuse her with the facts. "You `know,' even though you didn't see the driver."

"Tony was at the rehearsal."

"You know that too?"

"Yes. He told me."

"I see. He told you."

"Yes. Even you should be able to deduce that they can't rehearse without him."

She gasped, somewhere between an `eek' and an `ow!'

"What?"

"Of course! It must have been Anne!"

"Anne Weston?"

"Yes." She shuddered. "You didn't see how she looked at me when Tony said he was leaving her."

"Wasn't it the other way around? Anne made him leave."

"Ah, is that what she told you? That insinuating snake. Did she tell you that she attacked Tony? And how he begged her to stop with tears in his eyes. He was afraid.... We were both afraid for his life."

"Aren't you being a little overdramatic?" I said.

"You weren't there! It was a nightmare. I only went with him because Tony persuaded me that if I were with him Anne would be less emotional. He was quite, quite wrong."

I considered the possibility that Anne Weston had been the hit-and-run driver.

"How'd she get your car key?"

"From Tony, of course."

Yes. I could picture the scene: Anne, stealthily pocketing the key, the way Ingrid Bergman stole Claude Rains' key to the wine cellar in *Notorious*. Planning to murder her rival.

Maybe. I'd ask Mrs. Weston a few hard questions in the morning. Or send Charlie.

* * *

The rain was tapering off when we pulled into her driveway.

"Here we are. You're home."

"But Tony's Jeep isn't here. He must have...."

"Must have what?"

"Sometimes," she avoided my eyes, "he stops off at the Huddle Inn."

"Oh?"

"It's a bar."

The Huddle Inn would be my next stop.

"Give me your house keys." I said.

"Here. One key opens all the doors."

"Stay here. I'll go in and check things out."

Her eyes flashed alarm. "I won't stay here alone."

"Lock the car doors."

"No. I'm coming with you."

Leaning on my shoulder, one hand gripping my arm, she hobbled up the porch steps.

Hard to imagine anyone smelling better than she did. Miserable murdering witch.

I opened the door and we stepped into the darkened house. She switched on the light and crumpled into a wicker chair. "My legs are shaking."

"The normal reaction to shock," I said. "You've got to get out of that wet coat and take off your shoes and stockings.

"I–I– "She licked at her lips.

"That swelling on your head has to be iced."

Her fingers probed, and fluttered away. "There's a gel pack in the freezer."

I made my way to the kitchen, turning on lights as I went. The rooms on this floor were undisturbed. At one of the kitchen sinks, I splashed warm water on my face and dried off on a blue-checked dishtowel. I brushed my hair back with my hands and squeezed some of the water from my shirt collar.

To the left of the kitchen, a door led to the basement. I ran down and did a quick check to make sure no killer lurked below, came back upstairs and called the precinct to request a uniform to stand watch after I left.

I opened the freezer and found bags of Starbucks whole bean Colombian, ice cubes and two gel packs.

Babe had slipped out of her wet coat, but she was still sitting where I'd left her, staring into space.

"Do you still have the shakes?"

"A little." Beneath the tight skirt, her stockings were in shreds. I bent to take them off.

"What are you doing?" She slapped at my hand, turned her back and stripped off the ruined pantyhose.

I said, "You need cleaning up."

She got to her feet painfully. "There's antiseptic soap and peroxide in the bathroom."

Still feeling the cold rain in my bones, I said, "I'll make us some tea."

"Liquor is quicker."

"No, I said, "we'll have tea."

I got a kettle of water boiling while she washed up. "Where do you keep it?" I yelled.

Suddenly she was beside me, cleaned and neatened, opening a cupboard. Like we were playing house.

"Go inside," I said, thrusting away the cozy feeling. Counting her ex-boyfriend, three people were dead, very possibly at her capable hands. "I'll bring in the tea."

Antagonism flared in her dark blue eyes and I braced for an argument, but she went. Meekly for her.

When I came in with the steaming cups, she was stretched out on the velvet sofa, blue gel mask on her forehead, feet propped up on two tasseled pillows; narrow, high-arched feet with scarlet toenails.

"I put in two sugars."

"I don't take sugar."

"Tonight you will. It'll be good for you."

A familiar dryness behind my eyes, precursor to itch and swelling, made me wary. "Where's your cat?" I said.

"At the vet. He's got chronic otacariasis."

"Sorry to hear that."

Her lips curved. "Ear mites."

She liked to make me feel like a fool. I stood up. "I'll check upstairs," I said. "Make sure no one's under your bed."

"If you want to change out of your wet clothes, Tony has a few things in the upstairs guest closet."

When I returned, dressed in Tony's too tight, too long trousers and a cashmere pullover, Babe had finished her tea.

I sat down in a wing chair opposite the sofa.

"Big house."

"Yes." She took the ice pack from her head and balanced it on the empty teacup. "I didn't always live alone. Have you ever heard of Georges Jaques Brulard?"

"No."

"He was a prestigious chef. He's written four books and Gourmet magazine ran a two-page feature on his chocolate mousse cake. This was his house. He used to come to Seaview for the fishing and one morning he walked into my diner. I was doing omelets."

Her smile, not directed at me, was gentle.

'That's not how you make omelets,' he said.

'It's how I make 'em.'

'*Permit me.*'

"He came around behind the counter and began beating eggs, tossing them in a pan, flipping them; showing off. Like Charlie did with her egg cream, remember? That was seven years ago. We were inseparable for five and a half of those years."

I kept my tone careless. "Where's he now?"

She swung her feet around and sat up, moving a pillow higher behind her back. "He's dead."

"I'm sorry. Want to talk about it?"

Her dark blue eyes glanced at me, slid past me. "Oddly enough, I do."

Her voice was so low I had to lean closer to hear it, made aware again of her special fragrance.

"One night, Georges came home, drove into the garage and...." Her speech was disconnected, the memories painfully dredged up. "He must have somehow miscalculated...crashed into the wall. His head hit the windshield. When I came home from work, I saw... the garage door... closed. The car motor still running...."

Her voice broke and she stopped, fighting for control.

"I found him...he.... He must have been already dead. Carbon monoxide.... But I couldn't believe it. I pulled him out. I tried to... revive...the kiss of life.... But...I don't know how long I...he just never.... I couldn't....

"I was frantic. I ran inside.... I called Tony." She stared into space.

"You called Weston?"

"Yes."

"Most people would call nine-one-one. Or the fire department."

"But I've always.... Tony and I have always.... When he got here, he called the police. They said... accident. But the insurance company suspected suicide."

She closed her eyes. "I was willed this house. At first I thought I could never stay on by myself. But then, it was a comfort. He's near me still."

I sat in the wing chair watching her tired face. It could've happened the way she told it. But he rammed his own garage wall hard enough to knock himself out? What was he doing? Eighty? Even I brake for the garage. And how did the door get closed? Maybe she'd knocked him unconscious and closed the garage door herself. Not accident. Not suicide. Murder, not investigated too thoroughly.

She'd been in front of the Raeburn house at twelve forty-five. The crucial time period when Mona was killed. I had only her unsubstantiated word that she'd seen Weston leave and then driven to the diner.

But, what if she was telling the truth? I stretched my legs. Tonight in this pleasant setting it was easy to believe her. Even possible to believe that Taylor was dead when she went to his apartment.

Several framed photographs were grouped together on the low table beside my chair. One, of Tony, was in an ornate silver frame. I had seen an empty frame exactly like it, fallen to the carpet at Mona Raeburn's crime scene.

"Good picture of Weston," I said.

"He gave it to me for Christmas."

Of course, Weston's idea of a Christmas present was a picture of himself. Probably he'd given one to Mona too, in the same frame and removed his picture after he'd killed her.

The doorbell rang and I went to answer it. Officer O'Neill's open freckled face grinned down at me from his six feet whatever.

"I've secured the inside of the house," I told him. "Look around outside. Then make sure nobody bothers the lady. I'm leaving in a minute."

O'Neill nodded and went off, his flashlight beam a yellow ribbon in the darkness.

I stood at the threshold of the living room. "An officer is stationed outside. Name's O'Neill. He'll make sure you're not disturbed tonight."

She nodded. "If you think it's necessary."

I said, "This accident was two years ago? Before Taylor came to Seaview?"

"Yes." Babe punched at a pillow. "Taylor moved to Seaview a little over a year ago. From a detox center."

She looked into my face, obviously puzzled when I didn't react. "But I suppose you know that. You're learning everything about all of us, aren't you?"

"I'm going now," I said. "O'Neill's a good man. If you hear or see anything out of the ordinary, yell for him."

Her eyes darted around the room, but her voice was cool. "All right." She made a huge effort, "Thank you."

"Where is The Huddle Inn?"

"A block east of the Seaview Police Station. On the corner." She glanced at her watch. "It will be closed."

"You said Weston's there."

"The regulars have keys. They let themselves in after hours."

"Like in *The Apartment*. Do you know that movie?"

"Shirley MacLaine. Jack Lemmon."

She was full of surprises.

"Detective Harmony….-"

"Yeah."

"Tony would not try to run me over."

I was on my way to find that out for myself.

CHAPTER THIRTY THREE

Red, white and blue bunting muffled most of The Huddle Inn's front window, but wayward slivers of light leaked out in a white zigzag across the wet sidewalk.

A gilt eagle brooded above the doorway, painted eyes glaring down, fierce beak screaming soundlessly. Raindrops molted from its wooden wing feathers. I pulled the poncho's hood over my head and turned the brass door knob. Locked.

While I fumbled with the latch a cigarette-hoarse voice said, "O.K. I got the door. Come in out of the rain."

A dense fog of gray cigarette smoke floating to the tin ceiling intensified the odors of beer and rank sweat. A dozen boozing middle-aged men, mostly uniforms, stood at the mahogany bar goggling at the flickering TV. It was tuned to the Blue channel. A naked blonde fondled her thrusting breasts while she whispered, "Come...."

Her glistening lips moved, but whatever they said was drowned out by back-slapping snickers and whistles.

I wasn't surprised to find so many uniforms here. At least half of the old-guard cops are stoned alcoholics. Most of the younger ones, like me, are more apt to ease the tensions of a bad case with a workout in the gym and some sports water.

I spotted Tuffy, walked over to the bar and said hello.

He nodded recognition, eyes glued to the television. "Still raining?" he said.

"Letting up," I said. "See Tony Weston here?"

"In the back." He waved at the wooden booths in the rear. "Poured into a pew, the last I looked."

"When'd he get here?"

He tapped the broad nose that meandered across his good-natured face. "I got here eleven-thirty. He came in about a half hour later. Cheez! Will you lookit those knockers! Think they're real, or fake?"

"Tuffy?"

"Yeah?"

"What difference does it make to you?"

"If they're implants, I hear she don't feel nothin'."

"Why don't you call her up and ask?"

"Not at $8.50 a minute."

I scooped up a handful of free peanuts. Stale. I dumped them back into their brass dish, wiped the sticky salt from my fingers with a paper coaster and waggled them at the bartender.

"Any non-alcoholic beer?"

"Sharp or Buckler."

"Buckler."

The blonde slithered a boa across her buttocks and bent over, peering at us between her legs. The roomful of watchers cheered and pounded their beer bottles on the bar.

"And a plate of nachos," I said.

Cigarette clamped between pursed lips, the bartender dumped some Fritos on a platter, poured out Cheez Wiz, sprinkled chopped jalapeno peppers over all, and popped the dish into the microwave.

Ninety seconds later, I carried my Buckler and nachos to a rear booth, and sat down opposite Tony Weston.

He was slumped across the table in a clutter of empty beer bottles, face buried in the shelter of his arms.

I shoved the beer bottles aside. "Mind if I join you?"

He lifted his head, eyed me blankly and then, with slow recognition, smiled a truly beautiful smile, dimpled at the corners.

He really was like a movie star. He had charisma. And instinctively or deliberately, used it.

Weston said, "I am very drunk, Detective Harmony. Very, very drunk. Don't sit down unless you're willing to listen to me cry into my beer."

I tried a nacho. Not so bad.

"Know why I'm drunk?" he said. "You don't give a damn, but I'll tell you anyway."

I had another nacho.

"Did your whole life ever spin out of control? Everything you try only makes it worse?"

He didn't wait for an answer. The words spilled out of him. "My life's fallen apart. And I can't get the pieces back together again."

"Humpty Dumpty."

"I don't need you to make my life into a nursery rhyme."

"Sorry. Tell me about it."

He tilted a bottle of Bud to his lips, swallowed and said, "I went to see Alan Berger yesterday."

I popped another nacho. They were addictive. "Mona Raeburn's agent?"

"Well, I'm shopping for an agent. He came flying out of his office when he saw me with his fists up, swinging at me. I said to him, `What's eating you, Berger? Are you crazy?' "

Weston rubbed his hazel eyes. "I couldn't believe it. He said: `Get out before I kill you with my bare hands. Maybe you can fool the cops, but I didn't just fall off the A train. You son of a bitch - you murdered Mona when she told you she was dumping you.' "

He stared at me. "Dumping me? What was he talking about?" His tangle-lashed puzzlement was pure ham. And he was very articulate for a man who professed to be drunk.

"Berger says Mrs. Raeburn withdrew her support of your... career before she died."

"No she didn't! I don't know where Berger got that idea."

I leaned over, thrusting the litter of beer bottles out of my way. "I guess it would of made you pretty sore, if she did dump you."

His handsome eyes turned flinty. For an instant he was appealing as a shark that smelled blood. Then he slipped on the mask of charm again.

"Well she didn't. She wouldn't."

I shifted gears. "How'd the rehearsals go tonight?"

"Audrey's O.K. But without Mona we'll give a couple of performances in Seaview, and then it's history. Mona would have... I could have been a star."

His eyes brimmed with tears. "I was so close. So close."

I wondered what it was like to be that self- centered.

As if he'd read my thoughts, he said, "You don't think very much of me."

"That's right."

He stood up, weaved, and balanced himself with one hand on the tabletop. "This is my booth. I don't remember inviting you to join me."

"I thought you wanted someone to listen to your troubles."

"A friendly ear." He looked around. "I don't see one."

"Sit down," I said. "I'm not friendly, I'm not unfriendly. I came in to ask you a question."

"Ask it then, and go."

"Is your car outside?"

"In the parking lot. I'm not too drunk to drive, if that's what you're getting at."

"Which one's yours?"

"The Cherokee. You giving out tickets now? My inspection sticker's up to date."

"Sometimes you drive a Navigator."

Weston connected wet circles on the table with the bottom of an empty beer bottle.

"Babe Freeman's Navigator," I said.

"Well...."

I polished off the last nacho and downed some of the Buckler.

"You have your keys on you?"

"Of course!"

"What about the key to Babe's Navigator?"

The glass slid from his shaky grasp and crashed to the floor. He looked down at the splintered shards and made a halfhearted effort to kick them under the table. "Yes and I have a key to her house too. What about it?"

"Let's have a look at them."

He started to reach into his pocket and stopped.

"No."

The beer in his belly may have stiffened his spine, but there was a glint of fear in his eyes.

"Cut the crap," I said and leaned across the cluttered table, so close to him my nose protested his beery breath. "You tried to run Babe over with her own car tonight."

Weston's face went white, the skin pinched around his mouth. "What?"

"You heard me."

He stumbled to his feet. "You're crazy. Did someone tried to run her over? Is she O.K.?"

"She's swell. Sit down."

He sat.

"Since there are only two keys, yours and Babe's, I figure you for the hit and run."

"Wait a minute. Wait a minute." His face was glazed with sweat and a tic dragged at his left eyelid. "You think I would hurt Babe? Why..."

"That's what I want to know, why?"

"You'll accuse me of trying to kill Annie next."

"You said it, I didn't. But I advise against it."

He leaned on the table, using his arms to heave to his feet. He straightened, hanging on to the back of the booth for support and stood bristling at me. "I'm going to piss, now. Don't be here when I come back."

What a lousy exit line. I watched him stagger to the men's room. His show of indignation almost came off as genuine. He'd dazzle a jury unless I came up with an airtight case against him. I didn't have one. Yet.

I made my way past the empty booths to the bar, into the fog of cigarette smoke. Every eye there was glued to the TV screen where the blonde darted her pink tongue over a banana. "Like a taste?" she crooned.

Tuffy moved aside to make room for me. "How about that?" he said. "I've got a hard-on. Can you believe it?"

Weston came lurching up to us. "Listen Harmony, Annie has the Navigator key you're looking for."

He reeked of beer.

"I leave it on my bureau tray." He leaned on the bar for support. "Annie must've taken it."

In his panic to save his skin, he was ratting on his wife with a story lifted from Hitchcock no less. I was fed up with him, and suddenly very tired.

"Goodnight," I said. "See you, Tuffy."

As I left the bar, I heard Weston say, "Did you notice his sweater? I've got one just like that."

CHAPTER THIRTY FOUR

I drove home with the window wide open to clear the stench of smoke and stale beer from my nostrils. Forensics would come up with something inside the Navigator. Prints, a footprint, a hair, a thread, something, anything, and I would use it to nail Weston.

I was tired. Of the Westons. Of the Raeburns. Of Babe Freeman. It was after two.

I hung the yellow poncho in the hall closet, bundled Tony's borrowed clothes into a shopping bag, brushed my teeth and fell into bed, asleep as soon as my head hit the pillow.

I woke at nine to brilliant sunshine. The rain had washed the last of the snow away, and outside my window two cardinals chased each other across the stiff winter grass.

It was Sunday. I rolled over and went back to sleep.

Three hours later I got up, took a long shower, decided not to shave, dressed in blue jeans and a sweatshirt and went out for the paper and bagel and coffee.

At one-thirty settled down in front of the television with the Giants winning and a pint of low fat frozen yogurt and a diet Dr. Pepper, I was a happy man.

The telephone rang at two. It was 10-7 Eagles. I picked up on the fourth ring.

"Harmony," I said.

"Hello, Detective Harmony. Tony Weston here. Can I...."

"The Giants are inside the twenty and you're calling me?"

"I'm sorry if this is a bad time, but I wondered...."

"What do you want, Weston?"

"I know it's Sunday," he floundered.

The commercials started. I muted the volume. "All day."

"Could I talk to you?"

"Why?"

"I wasn't exactly straight with you last night."

Big surprise. "Where are you? I'll call you back."

I recognized he number he gave me as his home phone. So he was back with Anne. Had he got her to claim she was the hit and run driver?

The Giants won. I called him back, and told him how to find my cottage. Six o'clock, I said and turned on the Raiders-Broncos game.

I always root for the Raiders to lose, but by half-time it was clear they were going to win big. I went outside to polish the 'Vette.

He arrived at six-thirty-three. And Anne was with him.

"What a charmin' home you have," she said, the treacle thick in her drawl.

They sat down together on my sofa, Weston sagging into the cushions.

"We won't stay but a minute," she said.

He squeezed her hand. "Let me talk to him, honey."

His chalky face looked exhausted, the cheekbones stretching the parchment skin. "I did a lot of stupid things last night," he said. "I don't know what got into me."

"For instance," I said.

Weston tugged at his shirt collar. "It was me driving Babe's Navigator. Like you thought."

"You're confessing to attempted vehicular homicide?" I said.

"What? No." Beads of sweat mustached his chiseled lip. "I didn't try to run her over. See, I thought if I could make it look like a killer was after Babe, it would take suspicion away from her. I guess it was pretty dumb but it seemed like a good idea at the time. It was all my idea. She didn't have anything to do with it. I know she didn't kill Mona. Or Taylor. But it looked bad for her the way she lied about my going up to his place."

"You didn't go upstairs to Taylor's apartment with her that night," I said.

He looked sheepish. "No."

Anne covered his hand with hers.

Only hours earlier Weston'd wanted me to believe Anne was driving the Navigator. Now he'd decided to confess he was. A new invention. His version of events changed every time he opened his mouth.

"You tried to run Babe down."

"No, no. Don't you understand? I just wanted it to look like someone wanted to kill her." His thick hair curled damply around his handsome face. "I waited in her car until she came out of the diner. And then I started it up. I planned to miss her. But the pavement was wet. I skidded. And I...I was afraid I'd run her over."

"So you ran."

He tugged at his collar. "I saw another car coming towards me. I got spooked. I drove to the Huddle and started drinking, to blank it out. I was afraid she...."

"You thought you killed her."

Weston nodded, morose.

"Bungled it all around. Why did you tell me that you thought Mrs. Weston was the hit-and-run driver?"

Anne edged away from him. "What is he talkin' about, Tony? Did you say that, Tony?" She drew in her breath sharply. "Whatever possessed you to say that?"

"Umm...."Weston struggled to find his voice. "Honey," he said.

"You wanted the police to think I tried to kill Babe!" Anne said.

"You know that's not so, honey." He made a clumsy reach for her and she winced away, her teeth clenched on her bottom lip.

"Annie! I only said it because you couldn't have done it."

"But land's sake, Tony, you...."

Weston said, "See, Detective Harmony. "Babe's car has a five-speed manual drive. Annie doesn't know how to drive a shift car."

"No," she said. "I never did learn how to manage a stick shift."

Weston buried his head in his hands. "I was drunk. Clutching at straws. I didn't think. That's the only reason I.... I was clutching at straws. Annie, I love you!"

Turning to me, Anne said, "I reckon we'll let you be now that Tony's said his piece."

Weston stood up. "That's the whole truth," he said.

Sure.

And I believe in the tooth fairy too.

CHAPTER THIRTY FIVE

Monday morning I washed and polished my 'Vette, drove to Mamma David's for cappuccino and a pan-chocolat, gassed up at Rube's Service Station, and pulled into the Seaview Police Department's rear parking lot. Half a dozen medium-priced, inconspicuous cars were lined up beside a half-dozen patrol cars. I parked my wheels at the far end of the lot. Upstairs, I tapped on the pebbled glass partition that separated the computer bank from my and Charlie's desks. Wolfie waved hello.

Charlie was hunched over her tan metal desk, one hand resting on a stack of printouts. Babe Freeman sat on a matching straight-backed chair opposite, her hand very close to Charlie's.

She smiled at me. Not friendly exactly, but the most pleasant one I'd received yet.

"How's your head?" I asked.

She touched it gingerly. "Better, thanks."

Charlie motioned to me, and I drew my desk chair up to hers.

"O.K. Babe, tell it one more time so Jake can hear too."

Her eyes flashed annoyance. "I've already told Detective Harmony that Anne Weston tried to run me down."

I said, "The bottom line on that scorecard reads: Assumptive Evidence: one hundred per cent. Proof: nil. Mrs. Weston is off the hook for this one. I have new information that clears her."

"I'm listening," Charlie said.

"Yesterday Weston confessed that he was the hit and run driver."

Charlie stayed cool but it was obvious I'd handed Babe a shock. The purse on her lap slid to the floor and she bent to pick it up, attempting to hide surprise she couldn't conceal.

"I don't believe you."

"Nevertheless it's true. He said if he could get us to think the killer was attacking you, you'd be clear of suspicion."

Charlie sighed. With her sagging cheeks framed by two vertical lines, she could have been a worried bloodhound. "This ball of string's getting too fucking tangled," she said.

Babe looked at Charlie for a long moment. "All right. I'll tell you what happened. Tony was afraid you'd think I killed Taylor. We decided to stage an accident and agreed to tell you that Anne had been driving. I was never supposed to be in any danger. But he lost control of the car."

"Fucking dumb idea," Charlie said, and unwrapped a piece of gum. Gonzo Grape permeated the stuffy room.

"What can I say? It was an inept attempt at obfuscation."

I said, "Weston told me that stunt was all his own idea. That you had nothing to do with it. He could have killed you."

"He was only trying to help me. He's very sweet and beautiful, my Tony, but a bit challenged."

I brought my chair a little closer to her. "Why say Anne drove the car?"

"Because we believe Anne killed Mona and Taylor."

"Maybe you believe that. Weston doesn't seem to. He went back to her."

"I wasn't aware that he had."

"They were together yesterday."

She jumped up, clutching her bag. "Talking to you is an exercise in futility."

She left, walking with her head high, but I saw her stop in the hallway and rest against the wall for a second or two before she started down the stairs, leaning on the brass banister.

Charlie came and stood beside me, watching her go. All around us telephones rang, voices muttered. We listened to the noises in silence. I went over to the dirt streaked window and looked down at the parking lot. My 'Vette sparkled in the morning sun. I went back to Charlie's desk.

"I think their relationship may be coming apart," I said.

Charlie said, "I think I ought to... Maybe I should tell you.... Oh, hell. Take a look at this. Came in this morning."

It was the ME's report. Taylor had died of cyanide poison between 9 and midnight. His stomach contents contained chicken and broccoli and chocolate chips. No lemon meringue.

Traces of lemon meringue in his stomach would have cleared Anne of suspicion. Now, it looked as if Anne was the last person to see him alive.

Charlie opened her notebook and read to me: "On Wednesday night, Gresham, went to the theater with his wife and two grandchildren. They saw The Lion King."

"And Berger?"

"At a charity auction for AIDS. At some artsy-fartsy gallery in Soho."

"Raeburn?"

"Playing guitar at a wine bar in Massapequa. Audrey Raeburn was in her apartment all night. She ordered Chinese take out and watched *The West Wing*. The Chinese food was delivered at 8:00. *The West Wing* aired from 9:00 to 10:00. Then she took a bath and went to bed."

I sat down on the edge of Charlie's desk. "The only three suspects who were at the library that night are Anne Weston, Tony Weston and Babe Freeman. One of them killed him.

"We don't know what Weston did. He says he did go with Babe. He says he didn't go with Babe. He didn't drive the Navigator. He did drive it. He planned the hit and run alone. He didn't plan it. Dust in our eyes at every point. Charlie, what if he wanted to get rid of Babe? Changed the plan. Suppose he didn't lose control of the car."

She said, "We can gnash our teeth from now 'til forever, but we haven't a shred of real evidence against him. Not a single fucking thing."

"What are you talking about? Two people place him at the Raeburn house the night Mona Raeburn was murdered, and he admits being there. Suppose he let the dog out before he left."

"Didn't you say Taylor thought a woman answered the phone when he called."

"He said it was a hoarse voice. Weston's an actor. He could have mimicked a woman's voice."

I slammed my fist into the desk. "We've got to get one of them to tell the truth."

"You'll hurt yourself, Jake. What it comes down to is Mrs. Weston was the last one to see Taylor."

"Maybe."

"And she saw everyone at the Raeburn crime scene. But no one saw her. You know I never did buy that headache of hers."

"What's Wolfie doing?"

"Working on Taylor's computer."

"Call her on the intercom and put it on speaker."

"Find anything new, Wolfie?" I asked.

"Nothing to help us. He wrote a book. Seven hundred pages, *Unsung People of Color*. There's a list of publishers and agents. Rejection letters. And an appointment calendar."

"Appointments? With any of our suspects?"

"No. And no references to Mona Raeburn that I've found yet, and I'm almost through all the files."

I turned off the intercom.

CHAPTER THIRTY SIX

The rest of the week was quiet. Day followed day and nobody killed anybody or even attempted to. We were still spinning our wheels on the Raeburn case, going the same nowhere like caged gerbils.

Thursday evening, the twelfth, was cold and rainy. Charlie called me at six o'clock.

"I'm going for pizza. How about it?"

"I don't feel like going out, Charlie."

"No prob. I'll be over with a pie before seven. See ya."

At 7:15 she yoo-hooed and flung through my front door in a cold gust of wind. Setting the pizza on my table she said, "Get it while it's hot. Any beer?"

"In the fridge."

She wiped her mouth with the back of her hand, retrieved a can, flipped the lid and faced me.

"Jake, I want to tell you something about my life. I wasn't bad looking at twenty-three. And there was a man who wanted to marry me. My mother and I were always very close and she wanted me to get married. I never was interested in men but she kept at me. She wanted me to have a child. The most wonderful experience a woman can have, she said. So I got married.

"That never should have happened, but it did. I did have a baby. A boy, born with a defective heart. For two years he was in and out of hospitals being operated on. And then he died. So I had that wonderful experience of having a child."

"Oh, Charlie, I'm so sorry."

Wiping at her eyes, she turned her back. "My husband walked away. I've never heard from him. I don't even know if I'm still married. Your father took me in hand, helped me get into the Police academy."

"My father?"

"He was one great guy, Jake."

"I know that. I wish my mother remembered it."

"Don't be so hard on her, Jake. I grew up with her. I know her. She's the kind of woman just has to have a man. All the while she was weeping for your father at his funeral, and everyone feeling so bad for her, I knew she'd be with someone soon. But listen, she was crazy about your father. If he came back today she'd leave Henry in a heartbeat."

"Maybe."

"Now I have something… I need to…."

I looked at her. Totally unprepared for what she was about to hit me with.

"Well, the only way to tell you, is to tell you. I'm in love with Babe."

I felt kicked in the stomach.

She went on, "It's just a miracle that a young beautiful woman loves me at my age. Loves me, wants me, thinks this body's beautiful. Not just at night when you can't see but in the daytime, morning, afternoon, always."

"Charlie, you can't be serious. You know better."

"I won her heart," Charlie said. "A young woman - at my age. Look at me! She says I'm beautiful."

"Charlie, this is impossible. Babe said she saw Weston running away from the Raeburn house the night of the murder. What if the two of them killed Mona Raeburn? What if she's guilty, Charlie?"

"That's a big if."

"I have no trouble with that if."

"She's not guilty."

"But what if she is? You've compromised the investigation."

"She's not! And you know what? I don't care if she is."

"You're off this case, Charlie."

"So I'm off the case." She rested both hands on the table and leaned her weight on them, exhaling onions, beer and garlic at me. "Listen to me. Never in my life have I ever.... We're in bed, I turn off the lights, she turns them on because she wants to look at me. At me!"

"Charlie, Charlie! You've lost your mind. You'll have to turn in your badge. You'll lose your pension."

"I couldn't care less. Truth is, I just can't live without her. You don't know her, Jake."

"And you do?"

"Good night, Jake. I'll see you tomorrow night at the play."

* * *

Conflict of interest in law enforcement is not to be taken lightly. We exist together through a network of expected reactions. You stop at stop signs. You wait on orderly lines. And if you're a cop you don't make love to a suspect in your murder case. Thumping my pillow, I couldn't help feeling betrayed.

I was in a completely untenable position, thrust there unforgivably. I thought, damn you, Charlie. But she's my mother's cousin. My cousin once removed. Blood is thicker than water whatever that means. With loved ones, constancy in the face of disappointment is crucial. But even allowing for lapses in loved ones, how lapsed can we allow?

Damn you, Charlie.

The next morning, Friday the thirteenth, I woke bleary eyed and headachy. Showered, shaved, weighed myself, dressed and inspected the refrigerator. Four cans of Diet Dr. Pepper. I fished a stale biscuit from behind them, crumbled it up and put it out for the birds while I breakfasted on one of the Dr. Peppers.

I drove to the Seaview police station and spent a dull morning writing up notes and laboring over files, doing my best to turn up something that would nail someone. I went over the evidence in my head again. The dead dog, the kilt, the missing necklace, the empty silver frame.

Vain peacock, Weston had given Mona his portrait in the same frame he gave to Babe. Had he given one to Anne too? In a fury at finding her husband's picture there in that expensive frame, had she destroyed it?

Or had Weston removed his picture after he killed Mona? Or had Babe, enraged at finding a duplicate that cheapened his gift to her, hurled it to the floor? Or had Weston and Babe conspired together?"

I went home and dressed for the performance of Scottish Mists. Black Levis, silver trimmed snakeskin boots and a black turtleneck. I looked dapper. Almost thin. It was showtime.

* * *

At 7:30 that evening I was at the back of the Seaview High School auditorium. Wolfie, formal in a long gray skirt and matching coat over a white silk blouse stood next to me. A hint of disinfectant wafted in by the forced air heat was unpleasantly insistent beneath the odors of perfume and sweat the audience generated. Charlie came in, nodded and stood silently beside me.

Half an hour before show-time almost all two hundred seats were filled. Mimeographed playbills, improvised into ineffectual fans, stirred the overheated air without cooling it.

Ushers in navy blazers strolled the sloping aisles counting the house. At stage right in front of the gold-fringed green velvet curtain, the Stars and Stripes fluttered beside the green and gold Seaview school flag.

Up front, on the aisle, a plump bleached-blonde sat beside the trucker, Lloyd Gresham. Mrs. Gresham, I presumed, since he was with her in public.

Fred Raeburn was hard to miss in a Hawaiian shirt and a blue tie. Anne Weston was seated two rows behind the Greshams. I searched the audience for Babe Freeman until I spotted her in the next to last row, tearing at her program with restless fingers. Behind Babe, a woman enveloped in a mink the size of a horse blanket, settled down with a maximum of commotion. She craned her neck to inspect the audience and then buried her face in the program. The man with her, a graybeard in tortoise shell glasses, kissed Babe's cheek.

"Who are they?" I muttered.

Charlie said, "That's Miss Sue, of the Miss Sue Seaview School of The Drama. The man with her, Dr. Heller, is her husband.

I wheeled around as Alan Berger, Mona Raeburn's agent, paused inside the double doors, his camel's hair topcoat slung over the shoulders of a double-breasted tux.

He flashed a fleeting nervous smile. "Good evening, Detective Harmony, Detective Alberts...." Before he could say more, an usher rushed up to hustle him off to a seat down front.

Why had he driven here all the way from the city, to a town he'd sworn never to visit again, to suffer through an amateur production of a play he'd said was from hunger? And togged out as if it was a Broadway opening.

The neon track lights switched off, the audience hushed, and the curtain went up.

All the murder suspects were present.

The curtain came up on Weston in his kilt regalia, brooding under a melancholy blue spotlight. Thick ribbed socks ended at his knees under the red and green plaid, twin to Taylor's. The kilt that had been found next to Mona Raeburn's dead body?

The spatter of applause died away and Weston paced the stage, strong and silent, projecting tension. A door opened creakily and Audrey Raeburn entered, walked slowly to front center stage, and raised her white arms.

There was no trace of the awkward girl in this actress glowing under a rosy spot. The instant she appeared, the audience loved her.

"Ian. You are returned, unscathed," she said huskily.

It went on like that, *Madame Butterfly* spliced to *Brigadoon*, until the first act finally ended to thunderous applause.

When the lights came up I checked the house to make sure all my suspects were still in place. Except for Babe Freeman. Her seat was empty.

"Wolfie," I said, "Keep an eye on the rest of them. I'm going to see what Babe's up to."

She hadn't come out past me, so I jostled my way down through the first nighters streaming up the aisle for their intermission refreshments. Bucking the assault of shoulders and arms I made my way down the side aisle, up three stairs and through the door behind the stage.

It opened onto the odors of dust and sweat and grease-paint and something that smelled like overripe fruit. Half-way down a narrow corridor, a gangly teen-ager fiddled with a CD player.

"Wadda you doin' here?" he said. "Nobody but the cast's allowed backstage."

I flashed my badge.

"Gee!"

"Do you know who Ms. Freeman is?"

"Sure, Babe. From the Seaview Diner."

"Right. She come back here a minute ago?"

"Uh-huh. I let her past. She had something for Tony."

"Where?"

He pointed, and I walked past him down a hallway punctuated with closed doors until I heard muffled voices coming from behind a thick dust-colored curtain. Without actually plastering my ear to it, I stopped to listen.

"Not now!" Weston said. "Must we have all this out now?"

"You've been avoiding me all week," Babe said. "This is the only time I knew I'd be able to talk to you."

"I can't...."

"If you'd answered even one of my calls, I wouldn't have to be here like this."

"You're breaking my concentration. I'm in the middle of a performance."

"You are so erratic, Tony. I'm beginning to be afraid of you."

I couldn't hear his response.

"I can't trust you any more, can I?" she said.

"For God's sake, where's my Maalox? I won't be able to finish the play without my Maalox. I have to go on in a few minutes. Can't we talk later?"

The sound of a door opening, and Audrey's voice said, "I can't do it. I can't. I can't go on. I can't."

Babe's mocking voice, "Drugged out. Who supplied you? Your junkie father or your pusher boy friend?"

"Tony!" Audrey wailed.

"There's my Maalox!" Weston collapsed into a director's chair breathing in labored gasps.

I parted the curtain a bit and saw him fumble with the bottle, wheezing to Babe, "Later."

He took a swig and cradled his head in his hands. "My God, how am I supposed to cope?"

Babe backed through the curtain, stumbling into me. She jumped back, startled. "You... you voyeur!" She pushed me aside and rushed off.

Audrey drew the curtain closed, but her voice carried clearly. "Oh, Tony."

"Please, sweetheart, you must stop crying. Your mother would want you to be brave."

There was silence for a moment. I lifted an edge of the curtain. Weston had a hand inside her dress.

"Oh, Tony. You do love me."

"How could any man help loving you? You're so fresh and beautiful."

"You'll leave Anne."

"I never said that."

"But you love me."

"I love Anne too."

"You said..."

"I can't leave her. She needs me."

"When she realizes we love each other, she won't want to stand in the way of your happiness."

"Aaah... She needs me."

"That's not your problem. You have to do what's best for you. Give her an opportunity to rise above herself. To become a better person."

I pushed the curtain aside.

Weston looked haggard in the harsh light in spite of his theatrical makeup. Audrey began to repair her face in a hand mirror.

The same light that drained Weston, making him look like a living corpse, flattered her powdered white skin, and her eyes, huge with tears and false lashes.

"What now?" he whined. "We're trying to put on a play!"

Audrey left.

"Oh, God," he said. "I can't handle this. What do you want? "

"You are something else, Weston. You were screwing the mother, and now the daughter."

"It's not how it looks. Audrey needs support. It's very hard for her to take over Mona's role."

He inspected himself in his makeup mirror. In the glass his eyes met mine and looked away. He plunged a brush into a box of powder, shook it off and touched it to his cheeks.

"Five minutes, Mr. Weston," The teen-age boy called.

Weston set the brush down, licked his finger and used it to flick powder from his eyebrows.

"Five minutes, Miss Raeburn," the boy called.

"Break your neck," I said.

"You mean break a leg," Weston said.

"No, I don't." I went back to the auditorium.

The lights dimmed again for Act II of *Scottish Mists*.

"If I didn't already have fallen arches, they'd fall from standing through this," Charlie said.

CHAPTER THIRTY SEVEN

When the final curtain came down and the overhead lights blazed on again, Charlie poked me in the ribs, rolled her eyes and turned two thumbs down.

I agreed.

But the Seaview audience loved *Scottish Mists*. They gave the cast four curtain calls, and gave Audrey and Weston a standing ovation before filing out in a buzz of good humor.

The curtain opened again on the backdrop of hills, heathers, Styrofoam boulders and the teen-age boy I'd seen backstage. Now he wore a car coat.

He called into the house, "Is there anything else?"

From my vantage point at the rear, I saw Babe stand up.

"No. Thank you, Jimmy."

He started to move off and turned back, shifting his weight from one sneakered foot to the other. "I stacked the glasses on the side and I left you my CD player. You'll return it?"

"Don't worry."

A high pitched voice called, "Jimmeee! Come on!"

"Well...I'm off. G'night."

I counted noses. Babe Freeman, Miss Sue and Dr. Heller had their heads together in one row. Anne Weston, Fred Raeburn and a dark-haired boy I hadn't noticed before were still seated up front.

"Who's that next to Raeburn?" I asked.

Charlie said, "Angelo Gomez. Hangs out with the Raeburn girl. Had him up on suspicion couple of times. Trying to persuade him to cooperate in the drug case I'm working. "

The double doors behind us banged open and the agent, Alan Berger, came back in, his face glowing with cold, carrying a jeroboam of wine.

"You guys like the show?" he said, grinning at us. "Was that kid terrific or what?" His eyes slid past us to Babe.

His noisy entrance had attracted Babe's attention. "You probably don't remember me," she said, approaching Berger. In her high heeled boots she towered over me but Berger topped her by about three inches. "You came into my diner on New Year's Eve."

She was decked out in a red dress that slid over her body and made you very conscious of the woman beneath it. She had pinned an enormous silk rose at her throat.

Berger wasn't exactly goggling behind his glasses. "Of course I remember you."

She smiled up at him and I remembered her declared predilection for tall men.

"I brought Chianti," she said, "to have a quick drink together before the cast party at the Yacht Club." She tucked a hand under his elbow. "But your champagne is so much more festive."

Berger beamed at her. "It's just domestic. Schramsberg, a California vintner." He managed to imply that if he'd known she'd be around, the champagne would've been the real stuff. It was certainly interesting to watch him operate.

"May I join you?" he said.

"Of course. There are plastic wine glasses up on the stage."

"I'll give you a hand." They trotted down the aisle together, smiling and chatting.

"Need any help?" the Gomez kid asked as they passed him. He seemed to have nice manners.

"No," Babe said. "But why don't we all go up?"

"O.K." The Gomez kid did a handstand spring onto the stage. Without even breathing hard.

I leaned against the back wall, trying to look inconspicuous. Charlie sat across the aisle from me. Wolfie was outside with a cigarette.

"Hey, guys," Berger called to us. "As long as you're here, join us. Have a drink."

Miss Sue stood and Dr. Heller stood with her. Enfolding her bony frame in the mink horse blanket, she said to Charlie, "Up, up, no dawdling."

She crooked a ringed finger at me. "And you too, young man."

I stuck my head out the double doors and called Wolfie. She flipped her cigarette to the floor, annihilated it with her heel and followed us onto the stage.

Gomez, sprawled on the Astroturfed stage, jumped to his feet and said, "Hello. We haven't met."

"Jake Harmony."

"Angelo Gomez."

I gave him a quick once-over. His lips were rosebud pink below clear olive-skinned cheeks. Liquid brown eyes were dreamy in a face that looked soft and indulged, but alert in an edgy way as if he knew where the exits were–in case he had to make a fast bolt.

The rest of them perched on the fake boulders. Babe slid a Streisand CD into the player and Berger next to her, tapped a foot in time to the music. He tried an arm across her shoulder, but she pulled away. Undaunted, he whispered in her ear. She shook her head, frowned, and moved off.

I wondered again why he had come.

Anne Weston walked up the steps to the stage trailing Raeburn behind her. She wore a pewter colored dress cut like a slip. Her shoulders, the color of thick cream, glowed like pale satin above the coarse lace. It was my turn to goggle.

"I'm Anne Weston, Tony's wife," she said to Berger. Scarlet lips, vivid in her white face, curved in a smile. But I noticed that while she spoke, her eyes darted to the wings.

"What's keeping them?" she said. "The play's been over for ages. Oh… here he is."

I looked where she was looking. Weston, in faded jeans and a brown pullover, emerged from backstage.

Audrey slouched beside him. She'd removed the exaggerated stage makeup, and now wore a black leotard, tights, miniskirt and work boots.

We all applauded.

Berger uncorked the champagne with a loud pop. Anne winced at the sound, touched her fingertips to her forehead, opened a small velvet bag, and inspected herself in a compact mirror. As she replaced the compact, she surreptitiously swallowed a pill, her strained face contradicting the festivity of her dress.

Champagne flowed for everyone.

"*Salud, pesetas y tiempo por gustarlos*," Berger said. "Health, wealth and time to enjoy them."

Well, it was his champagne, but why had he brought it? A last farewell to Mona?

Babe wiped a drop from the bottom of her glass with a white lace handkerchief and left it crumpled on a `rock' beside Weston's untouched glass.

From stage right, Raeburn peered at me with a vague smile, struggling to remember where he'd seen me before. I went and told him his daughter had done a fine job.

And then I heard the daughter say, "Hit me, Angel."

Gomez fished inside his jacket pocket but Audrey caught my eye and her hand closed over his. 'Not in front of him,' the shake of her head warned.

Angelo Gomez, clear-skinned and dreamy-eyed, probably had a pharmacy stashed in his jacket. As long as he kept it stashed, I wasn't arresting him.

"You're not drinking your wine, Tony," Anne said,

Weston reached for his glass, but before he could drink, Audrey, cheeks glowing almost as red as her blazing hair, tugged at his arm.

"Listen," she cried. "That's my most favorite song in the world, *Evergreen*. Dance with me, Tony."

Waving his glass in the air, shuffling along in time to the music, Weston followed her to center stage. They began a slow fox trot. Still holding his glass, Weston bent his head so that his lips brushed her bright hair. Audrey twined her white arms around his neck.

"Don't look now, Jake," Charlie said, "but Mrs. Weston's got murder in her eyes."

Anne's eyes on her husband were blazing with jealousy. Babe Freeman watched them too.

Anne started with surprise when I asked her to dance. "Why... thank you. "

She held herself stiffly in my arms, her eyes following Weston over my shoulder.

"You're still wearing Jasmine perfume," I said.

"What?" She kept her eyes on Weston. "Goodness, you are one for noticing things! Do you like it?"

"I like it."

She slipped from my arms and thrust herself between Audrey and Weston.

"Just like your mother," she hissed. "Chasing after Tony."

"Are you crazy, Annie?" Weston said. "She's a child."

Audrey said, "I'm not after your old husband." But she didn't move away from Weston.

He said, "I'll finish this dance with my wife."

"Not with a drink in your hand," Anne said.

"Take this back to the table like a good kid, will you?" Weston said, handing his glass to Audrey and waltzing off with Anne.

"Suddenly, Anne cried out, "Oh, no!" and broke away from Weston,sinking down on one of the boulders, her back to the rest of us.

Babe reached out to her. "What's the matter?"

"Leave me alone." Anne thrust her hand away. "Since when do you care about my feelin's?"

Weston ran his fingers through his hair. "Dammit, I need a drink," he said. "Where's my glass?"

"Here," Berger said, and reached for the glass Audrey had set down, but Babe picked it up. In her unsteady hands, the liquid trembled in the goblet and splashed.

"Watch it, you're spilling good champagne," Weston said.

She covered the glass with her left hand, holding it away from him. "Now I'm not."

"Stop fooling around. Give me my drink."

Anne snatched the glass from Babe. "Here." She closed Weston's hand around the stem.

A subconscious perception that something was wrong made me cry out: "Stop!"

I plunged toward him.

Weston said, "For God's sake." I closed in and smashed the glass out of his hands.

He grabbed the edge of the table, gasped, staggered and fell heavily to the floor.

"Tony!" The three women chorused.

Babe raced to his side. Berger stepped back and collided with Anne as she frantically tried to reach Weston.

"Get out of my way," she shrieked, shoving at Berger.

Charlie, who had followed right behind me, blocked her.

I motioned Babe away. "Give him air."

She backed off, her hand to her mouth, gaping, as Weston thrashed about struggling for breath, his lips twisted, face agonized.

The odor of almonds was unmistakable. I was pretty sure I'd knocked his glass away before he'd swallowed anything, but maybe he had. I couldn't assume this was just another anxiety attack. Not this time. Cyanide kills fast.

I bent over him. I wouldn't have believed anything could make me put my mouth on his, but here I was giving him the kiss of life, trying to force air into his lungs.

CHAPTER THIRTY EIGHT

"Stay right where you are. All of you," Charlie ordered. "Wolfie, call for an ambulance. Call the station. Get some Homicide people here. Then move everyone to the other side. Don't let 'em touch anything. And nobody leaves."

She knelt beside me. "Right under our goddamn noses," she said. "As if we were a couple of dumbos. That was quick thinking, Jake."

Weston's breathing was labored, but he was breathing. He couldn't have swallowed any of the Cytotox or he'd be dead by now.

"Get Dr. Heller," I said, remembering we had a doctor in the house.

Charlie escorted Heller over and he went through the motions. He sniffed Weston's lips, lifted Weston's eyelid, put his ear to Weston's chest.

"There's nothing I can do for him here."

I said, "We called for an ambulance."

"I'll stay with him until it comes," Heller said.

Behind us, Anne struggled with Wolfie. "Let me go. Let me go to Tony."

Breaking free, she flung herself on Weston kissing his clammy face. When I lifted her away, she made no resistance. She was like a stunned bird, her hands fluttering aimlessly. She couldn't stand on her feet and I helped her to one of the stage boulders.

The rest of them herded together under a moss-hung trellis. Silent. Avoiding each other's eyes. Berger puffed morosely on a cigar.

Anne's cry broke the silence. "Oh, my God." She pointed a finger at Babe. "What did you put in his glass?"

Babe said, "You'd like everyone to think that, wouldn't you? But it's you who wanted him dead. You who gave him the wine." Her accusing voice echoed in the empty theater.

Anne cringed in horror. "Don't...." She tried to stand, crumpled and dropped to the floor.

Dr. Heller left Weston and chafed her hands. "A glass of water somebody," he said.

"Nobody's giving nobody nothing," Charlie said.

"Can't you take her to the dressing room I was using?" Audrey quavered. "I'll come too." She seemed to be on the verge of going to pieces. "May I?"

I nodded.

The three of them made their way backstage with Dr. Heller supporting both women.

Wolfie called out, "I've got something!"

Charlie and I hotfooted over to her.

Wolfie drew a careful outline on the Astroturf with a grease pencil, then stood up. She held out a twist of plastic wrap. I poked it open with the pencil, exposing white powder.

"It's either coke," I said, eyeing Gomez, "or Cytotox. Criminals always try once too often."

"That's how they get got," Charlie said. Her hooded eyes swept the room and stopped at Babe.

Any one of them could have poisoned the wine, but it certainly seemed to me as if it had been Babe Freeman. She must have dropped the Cytotox into Weston's glass, her hand over its rim while we all looked on.

Every victim in this case had been threatened by her. I recalled her voice, barely audible saying, `I can't trust you any more, can I?'

The outer doors flung open. The place crowded up with uniformed and plainclothes officers barreling into the auditorium, swarming up the stage. They herded Raeburn, Gomez, Berger, and Miss Sue into the auditorium. Each suspect was assigned a row and a uniformed officer.

Miss Sue half turned and exchanged a glance with Berger. Then he sang out pitching his voice to reach me on the stage: "I resent the way you are treating us. I demand to know why we are being kept here like this."

"Sorry," I said. "We can't let you talk to each other about what has occurred until we have your statements. We will try to get them as quickly a possible. Until then, just be patient."

He sat down, arms folded across his chest. Miss Sue emitted a loud sigh. Gomez lit a cigarette, leaned across the row to offer it to Raeburn who shook his head.

I checked on Weston. Covered with Miss Sue's mink blanket, he lay still, his eyes closed. His breathing was shallow but regular. It seemed all right to leave him. I went backstage to see how Anne was doing.

Seeing me, she clutched at my arm. "How is he? How isTony?" She looked very ill. Worse than Weston.

"Cyanide kills within four to or six minutes and he's still alive. He didn't drink any of that wine."

"I–we have you to thank for that. If not for you, he might be...." Her tear-glazed eyes widened, and she shuddered.

Dr. Heller cleared his throat, took off his glasses, blew on the lenses and polished them with a scrap of flannel.

I told him, "They want you outside now, to make a statement."

He frowned, took his time folding the glasses into his vest pocket and headed back.

"You too, Audrey."

"And then can I go home? Please, I want to go home."

"Join the others," I said, harsher than I meant to be.

I saw Anne shiver and realized it was cold in the dressing room. The heat must have been turned off when the play ended.

"Wait," I stopped Audrey. "Do you know where Anne left her coat?"

"It's probably still on her seat."

"Ask one of the officers to bring it here."

When she left, I took Anne's chilly hands in mine.

Her smile was grotesque on her stretched face.

I looked at her with new attention. Images flew around in my brain. Anne, with something in her hand when Berger poured out the champagne. Watching as Weston lifted his glass. Urging him to drink. Anne, tearing the glass from Babe and forcing it into Weston's hands.

I took a step away from her, shoving my hands in my pockets. "You took a pill out of your bag earlier," I said. "What was it?"

She dabbed at her eyes, "Aspirin."

The room was small; three more paces brought me up against the opposite wall, as far away from her as I could manage. I had some hard questions for her and I wanted distance.

"When you and Weston were dancing, you stopped and broke away from him. You said, `No!' What was that about?"

Her lips trembled.

"He was going to leave you. For good this time. Is that it?"

She took a step toward me, her hands on her breast as if she were praying. "No. I...."

An officer came in with Anne's velvet coat over his arm. He held it out, stroking the fur lining. "Is this mink?"

"Nutria," I said. I know one fur from another. I'm Henry Slater's stepson, after all.

As he handed me the coat, a suede glove fell at my feet. Picking it up, I noticed a bulge inside one of the fingers. I turned it inside out and a twist of plastic wrap dropped into my palm.

"Thanks for bringing the coat," I said and motioned him out. He left and posted himself outside the dressing room.

The horrified look on Anne's face as she looked at the twist of white powder in my hand told me more than I wanted to know.

"That's not... How did that get in my glove?"

I said, "Fool me once, shame on you. Twice, shame on me."

"What do you mean?" Her rouge was garish on her ashen skin.

"It was you, wasn't it?" I said. "All the time Weston was dancing with Audrey, you watched them, waiting for him to drink the champagne you poisoned."

"Oh!" She shrank back. "You of all people–to turn on me like this. I thought you had real feelin's for me."

Sure I had feelings for her, even now when I was certain she was a killer. She sensed it. And was trying to use it.

"When Weston gave his drink to Audrey, you lost patience. You deliberately taunted her, knowing he'd lose his temper. Then you shoved that glass of cold poison in his hand. Stood there, waiting for him to drink it. To die."

"... never fixin' to harm Tony. I could never...."

I was wound up and couldn't stop. "First you tried to kill him, and then you cried over it. Or were you crying because you didn't succeed?"

"No...no...."

She stood before me, defenseless, and the words came spilling out of my mouth in a surge of fury. "You almost killed Weston. You killed Taylor. You killed Mona Raeburn."

"How can you...you're insultin' my soul. You're wrong. So wrong."

"I don't think so," I said, and led her to the waiting officer, avoiding her ghastly eyes.

I left them and went to have a few words with the Paramedics surrounding Weston. He still lay on a stretcher, covered now with a woolen blanket.

Someone had dragged a plywood table to the center of the stage. Charlie sat there with Babe.

"This is intolerable," she said as I came up. "It's an obvious ploy fraught with spurious intentions."

I scowled at her linguistic pretentiousness. “Go and sit with the others.”

I dropped Anne’s glove and the twist of plastic wrap in front of Charlie.

“This was inside Anne Weston’s glove.”

CHAPTER THIRTY NINE

Berger paced up and down the aisle, chewing on the stump of his cigar, his camel hair coat draped over his shoulders. He shouted up to me: "How many times do I have to repeat the same damn thing to you people for God's sake ? I've sworn to everything in triplicate. Let me leave already."

"Me too," Audrey wailed. "Please. I want to go home."

Berger said, "I'll take the poor kid home. You don't have to put her through the wringer like this."

We had Berger's statement.

"Audrey stays," I said. "You can leave but I may want to talk to you again."

"You think I'm coming back to this town? Someone's always getting killed here. I only came tonight as a... homage. You know, to Mona." He bit down on the cigar. "Who knew the kid would turn out to be a born actress? It's in the genes."

He pecked Audrey on both cheeks. "I'll be in touch Miss Bernhardt. But now I'm out of here before they change their minds."

We released Miss Sue and Dr. Heller. Fred Raeburn and Angelo Gomez still waited to be questioned. As I approached them, I saw a thin line of spittle trickle from one corner of Raeburn's slack mouth.

Gomez reached into his jacket for a pack of Marlboros, offering them.

"No thanks," I said.

Raeburn stirred. "I will."

Gomez lit their cigarettes. "I haven't seen you since New Year's Eve, Mr. Raeburn," he said, shaking the match. "Remember, me and Audrey were talking together until you came out of her mother's house."

Raeurn wiped his mouth. "Yeah."

He looked around for a place to stash the cigarette, pinched it out between his fingers and stuck it in his pocket.

I told Gomez to stay where he was and escorted Raeburn to the stage.

"Well," I said to Charlie, "Gomez corroborates the Raeburns' alibi."

"You never thought either of them did it."

"No, I didn't."

"Me either."

* * *

Weston lay on the stretcher, his head turned to the wall.

I told the paramedics to stand by and squatted beside him.

Anne and Babe were seated in the two front rows, with Audrey in the row behind Anne. When I approached Weston, Babe stopped playing solitaire on her Palm Pilot to watch me. Anne, flanked by two uniforms, looked from Weston to me and back again to Weston. Audrey slouched in her seat, eyes closed, but I was sure she was peeking out from behind her eyelashes.

I touched his shoulder. "Who tried to kill you, Tony?"

"Don't know."

"Help me find out."

"How?"

I lowered my voice. "I need you to do a little acting. Can you manage it?"

A corner of his mouth twitched.

"I want you to look at Anne, at Babe and at Audrey, whisper something in my ear and then act as if you're having a heart attack. Give me a death scene."

Weston shook his head. "Can't do that to them."

"You want the killer to get another crack at you?"

He thought that over. I was afraid he'd decided not to cooperate, when he half-raised himself, flailed his arms, clutched his chest, shuddered and groaned.

I lowered my head to his. His lips barely moving, he pointed to each of them, Anne, Babe and Audrey in turn.

I let them see the surprise on my face as he gasped into my ear, and collapsed.

"Medics!" I yelled.

The paramedics came on the double.

Ten minutes later, I followed behind Weston's stretcher as they wheeled him out, a sheet drawn over his face.

As we passed the three women, each of them cried out: "Tony!"

"He's gone," I said. "Massive heart attack. But before he died, he told me who tried to poison him and where to find the proof."

Babe's eyes were on me, as I spoke, venomous and calculating.

Anne broke into hysterical laughter and then went limp, unconscious of the keening sound escaping from between her lips.

Audrey stood and watched in silence as the stretcher went by, tears streaking her white horrified face.

Two officers helped Anne to their patrol car. Babe and Gomez pulled away in their own cars. Audrey left with Raeburn.

CHAPTER FORTY

I went back to the stage where Charlie was reading over the statements.

She said, "Now we've got another corpse."

"Weston's not dead, Charlie. I asked him to make a show of telling me who the killer is and then fake a death scene."

"You dope! Setting yourself up like that! Why didn't you talk to me about it first. You dumb asshole!"

"You're not on this case any more, remember? Go home. I'll stay here a while. Maybe the murderer will make an attempt to get at me."

I finished reading the statements, filed them into envelopes, labeled and dated them.

That's it, I thought, looking at my watch. Something's bound to happen tonight. The three women thought Weston was dead. They'd seen him whisper an accusation. One of them would try to silence me. I didn't know how she'd try, but I knew she would and I was ready.

I waited an hour in the empty auditorium and left.

Outside, there were only two cars in the parking lot under a yellow street light, my 'Vette and Charlie's brown Chevy. The walkway to the lot was deserted. Nobody jumped at me out of the shadows. I opened my car door, waved Charlie off and drove home.

* * *

Crossing the grass from the garage to the guest house in the sharp cold, I walked warily, every nerve alive. The sky was the color of dirty ice, the garden blanketed in purple shadow.

The porch light was out.

I moved into a shadow and froze, listening to the quiet. Then I inched my way to the dark porch and reached up to explore the light fixture. The bulb was gone.

I worked my way around to the back, to the kitchen door. Softly. Sound travels far at night. My car driving up, the garage door closing. If she was waiting for me, she knew I'd come home.

A pane in the kitchen door was broken.

I bent down to clear the shattered glass so that I wouldn't crunch it, stood up again to peer in. A shape moved in the darkness in a flashlight's low beam. The light went out.

Well, she's here. Waiting for me.

What would she try?

I let myself in, closed the door and stood with my back against it, gun drawn. A darkness moved in the darkness. I couldn't see her but she was there, waiting to spring. Was that her glued to the wall? Too dark to be sure.

My eyes began to water and itch but I stood, not moving a muscle, listening. Nothing stirred. Seconds dragged by while we stalked each other.

Cautiously, I wormed my way forward, keeping my back to the wall. I felt, rather than heard, the rustle creeping toward me and tensed, ready to strike. Something brushed my ankles.

Fear rippled along my skin. A cat. How did a cat get in here?

My chest tightened. My throat constricted. Fighting for breath, I reached for the Proventil inhaler. Had to risk the noise it would make.

I fumbled in my pockets. Couldn't find it. I'd be helpless in a few minutes. A faint fragrance reached my nostrils. She must be very close.

Not Jasmine. Not Anne.

A familiar sweet....

Babe. Babe, who had witnessed my allergic reaction to her cat the day Weston brought it home.

I backed up along the wall, to the light switch near the door. Determined not to sneeze, I opened my mouth and pinched my nostrils hard. The sneeze exploded.

Something slashed across my left arm and I felt the wet running down it. My gun blasted and slid from my nerveless hand.

Babe screamed, a high thin scream. Blood spurted, warm on my face. Mine or hers? There was a lot of it. I drove my right fist blindly into the dark, connected with soft flesh, heard a low vicious hiss and felt a slash again, across my chest. Lurching forward, I stumbled and fell, toppled by a streak of movement, a squawking furry shape. I forced myself to stand up, my left arm hanging useless. Reaching up to grab for support, my fingers gripped a wrist. With all the strength I could muster I smashed that wrist against the wall, and heard it snap.

Her fingers twisted away, fingernails tore at my face. Wheezing, tasting blood, but on my feet, I groped in slow motion until my fingers found, not the light switch; the intercom.

I pushed the buzzer. Pushed it again.

Henry's voice crackled, "Do you know what time it is?"

"Get...help. I'm hurt," I said. My hand blundered into the light switch and dragged it on.

Blinded by the glare, I shut my eyes. Opened them to see Babe standing over me, blood running down one side of her face, holding a bloody knife upraised. She crouched and lunged toward me.

A chef's knife, I noted with the automatic part of my mind. The blade flashed and arced down. I rolled and kicked out, connecting with her ankles. The knife clattered to the floor and she sagged, fell with a thud, lying with one leg twisted under her.

"You hurt me," she said with disbelief. I leaned my back weakly against the wall.

"Too bad," I said. "How did you know where I live?"

"I asked Tony."

My scheme had worked. I had my killer. But I didn't have any strength left.

The cat circled and brushed up against Babe. She touched it gently, leaving a scarlet smear on its tawny back. "Mona shouldn't have locked Poochie up," she said, scrubbing at the cat's fur. "It was cruel. I let him out."

I coughed, choking on blood. "I'm touched by your concern for the dog. Was this before or after you killed Mona?"

"She was so disgusting, lying there drunk, snoring. It was so easy. I just held the pillow over her face."

"Taylor recognized your voice...on the phone."

She lifted her arm, wincing in pain. "I wasn't sure. But I couldn't take that chance."

There seemed to be a lot of blood gushing out of me. I sneezed, spilling more blood; looked down at it puddled into a pool. I was fading. Could I stay conscious until help came? I would.

Babe's voice went on, spitting out her rage. "She was naked- the sex wetness oozing on her legs. Tony's sex. I'd kill her again."

I slid down the wall, feeling my life drain away.

"And," she said in that horrible voice, inching toward the knife, dragging her crippled leg, "now I'm going to kill you."

I saw her weaving over me, hair matted with sweat and blood, eyes crazed.

I reached my gun and fired.

And sank into blankness.

CHAPTER FORTY ONE

Voices reached me from a great distance. My eyelids were weighted down, stuck together. When I forced them open, the room went into a dizzy spin. I closed my eyes and the spinning slowed down.

One voice dominated the others. A voice used to giving orders and being obeyed. It said, "I want nurses here, around the clock. I want another bed in here for my wife."

Henry. What's Henry doing here? I tried to raise my hand but my arm wouldn't move. Horror sickened me as I understood. I was paralyzed! I yelled, but no sound came.

Concentrate.

"He's coming to."

"He's awake."

I was in a white room. In a bed with a white blanket over me. My mother was bedside me smiling bravely at me. Her crippled son.

"Jake," she said.

I tried, but it was too much of an effort to answer. Cool fingers touched my forehead. "You're going to be all right, Jake."

I drifted into blackness again.

Bright sunlight streamed through the window and when I turned my head away from the glare, there was a very fat woman in a white uniform sitting beside me.

"Welcome back to the living," she said. Two dimples dented the pillows of her cheeks. "I'm Dora. I'm your nurse."

My throat was parched. I tried to ask for something to drink. No sound came and the effort to speak made me dizzy.

Dora raised my head, offering water through a straw. "Try this," her voice soothed.

After one sip, the dizziness engulfed me. Falling back onto the pillows, I looked up into her round blue eyes. She lowered her ear to my cracked lips.

"Can't move my arms."

"Not to worry. Your right arm is strapped down so you don't dislodge the intravenous, and the other one is bandaged to your chest."

Relief was as nauseating as horror. I lay still until it stopped, drifted into half-sleep and came bolt awake.

"Babe," I said.

"Dora. My name is Dora."

I felt myself slide away again.

* * *

Indistinct voices talked over my head. Sweat rolled down my face as I struggled to sit up.

"Hey, Jake. Looking good," Charlie said.

She looked awful, her eyes pouched, her skin gray.

Dora cranked up my bed.

"Nice room," Charlie said. "Nice painting on the wall."

"Glad you like it. What happened? How did I get here?" I said.

"Babe tried to filet you, but you were too tough for her."

I couldn't move my arm. Would I be able to use it again?

"Do you know you broke her wrist and her leg before you shot her?"

I gagged, and efficient Dora produced a stainless steel bowl immediately.

"Did I kill her?"

"No," Charlie said.

That was a relief.

"You were damn lucky. Babe missed your heart by about a quarter of an inch."

"My arm. I can't move my left arm."

"It's good it's your left arm."

"No it's not. You know I'm left-handed."

Charlie looked at the picture on the wall, her neck turning red. "Sure," she mumbled. "I forgot."

"So, how'd I get here?"

"You called Henry and he called 911 and then he ran over to the guest house. He saved your life, Jake. I hear he was green around the gills, but he had a pretty good tourniquet wrapped around your arm, and his hand jammed into your chest. Trying to stem the blood."

I groaned. Now I owed my life to Henry.

"You were in pretty bad shape when the ambulance came."

What kind of shape was I in now? One arm attached to the intravenous, the other strapped to my chest. Permanently crippled?

Charlie looked out at the windows of the opposite wing, she sniffed at a vase of red roses on the window sill, and lifted the lid from a box of butter crunch.

She dug out a piece for herself and offered the box to Dora.

"Why not?" Dora said, popped a piece into her mouth and left the room.

"You didn't kill Babe, Jake, but she's dead."

I wasn't sorry to hear that. "How?"

"Massive infection." Her voice was unsteady.

"How do you feel about it, Charlie?"

Her face twisted. "I wasn't with her when she died. I should have been with her. That hurts me. That she was alone. That I wasn't there." Charlie blew her nose into a big white handkerchief.

"I wanted to die myself Jake. I came pretty near to trying."

She had a piece of chocolate crunch stuck in her front tooth. I didn't tell her.

"Charlie?" I said.

"Yeah."

"I'm glad you're still here."

Dora returned with a steaming bowl. "Let's try some of this beautiful broth."

I let her give me a spoonful. The beautiful broth turned sour in my stomach and I retched, spewing bile-green over my hospital gown and the white blanket.

She shooed Charlie. "Step outside, Detective Alberts."

"Right. See you take good care of him." Charlie lumbered to her feet. "Talk to you later. Listen, I've got the tape Babe made in the hospital. It's a full confession. Do you want to hear it?"

"What do you think?"

She rifled in her bag, brought out a tape recorder, set it on the table by my bed and left.

Dora's capable hands stripped me, replaced the soiled gown, changed the blanket for a clean one and sponged my sweaty face.

"I'm tired," I said. I was bone-weary, used up.

I dozed.

CHAPTER FORTY TWO

When I woke again, the room was dark. Dora was by my side immediately, offering a dish of red Jello that I refused and a glass of water that I sipped.

She straightened my blanket and plumped the pillows. "Do you want anything?"

"Yes. Please turn on that recorder," I said.

An officious voice intoned the details - place, time, identity; read the Miranda and then Babe's voice spoke eerily in my quiet room.

"I set it up so that Anne Weston would look like the murderer. With her out of the way, everything would have been the way it used to be between Tony and me again.

"That night, New Year's Eve, when I saw Tony sneak out of Mona's house I went crazy, I guess. I wasn't going to allow her to take him away from me. I decided to get rid of her for once and for all. "

"The key was always under the doormat. She was unconscious when I came in and I just held the pillow over her head until she stopped breathing. Then Taylor called. Twice. The first time I hung up, but when he called back I had to say something. I hoped he wouldn't recognize my voice. But I found out later, that he did. Well, I had no choice. I had to protect myself. I slipped Cytotox into his coffee. Tony had nothing to do with it. Nothing at all. I did it."

I paused the tape. Replayed it. Paused it again, thinking: The lady doth protest too much. Weston had had plenty to do with the murders but she was letting him off.

I started the tape again. Someone coughed, feet shuffled, indistinct voices murmured, then Babe continued. "I want it crystal clear. Tony did nothing to help me except to come up with his plan to clear me of suspicion. He said, 'If I make it look like a hit and run attack on you, you'll be a victim not a suspect.'

"But then he betrayed me - told Detective Harmony that Anne wasn't driving the car. That's when I realized he'd chosen. Chosen her. I couldn't allow that.... May I have a drink of water?

"I had to kill again but when I failed, I could see that Detective Harmony knew what I'd done. I'd done such a good job of implicating Anne, putting the poison in her glove. He was the only who suspected me. I had to get rid of him. So I drove to his house. I know how allergic he is to cats. I'd made Tony tell me how to get into the grounds the back way. And I just waited for him. Wearing Mona's diamond necklace under my dress."

I shut off the tape.

* * *

The setting sun gilded my eyelids when I woke. Someone was tapping lightly on the door, pushing it tentatively open.

Audrey Raeburn stood there. With her face washed, and her hair combed. Looking fourteen years old. She carried a bunch of tulips tied with long yellow ribbons and a fruit basket done up in blue cellophane. The tulips were pink.

"Come in."

"How are you?"

"I've been better."

"You look awful."

"I've never been gorgeous."

"You were so cool," she said. "Knocking the glass out of Tony's hand like that. Just like on TV."

"Thanks."

She helped herself to a piece of butter crunch. "Hey! That painting's cool. Van Gogh's *Hospital at Arles*."

"I know."

"We studied it in Art. Listen, I wanted to come and say goodbye. I'm leaving Seaview. Alan's going to help me with my career."

"Berger?"

"Alan says I have exceptional talent. And he knows everything about acting. He says I need to get into a good drama school. He can help me. He will help me but he says I must move to Manhattan."

"And he'll be your agent."

"Yes isn't that wonderful? You see, Alan's a power player in the business. He knows absolutely everyone and he's offered to look out for me. That's a lucky break for me. I can hardly believe it. See, he really did love my mother."

"And Weston?"

"Wasn't that cool? The way he pretended that heart attack. Just like a movie."

She reached for another piece of candy, studied it and put it back in the box. "Alan says I have to be serious about my craft if I want to be a successful actress. And I do, I really do. I can't allow every handsome man who's attracted to me distract me from my goal. And after all, Tony is a married man."

She leaned over and kissed me. On the lips. "But Alan didn't say anything about brave cops."

She backed off, gave me a lingering look, turned and closed the door silently behind her.

"Well," Dora said.

"She was just practicing," I said. "One day, we'll say we knew her when."

But all of a sudden I felt very good. "What's for dinner? I'm so hungry my stomach thinks my throat's cut."

CPSIA information can be obtained at www.ICGtesting.com
Printed in the USA
LVOW091640230712

291214LV00012B/52/P